Southern Comfort
An HBCU Story

by
Ron Baxter

Cork Hill Press
Carmel

CORK HILL PRESS™

Cork Hill Press
597 Industrial Drive, Suite 110
Carmel, Indiana 46032-4207
1-866-688-BOOK
www.corkhillpress.com

Copyright © 2004 by Ron Baxter

Trade Paperback Edition: 1-59408-214-6

Printed in the United States of America

1 3 5 7 9 10 8 6 4 2

This book is dedicated to the Horsemen.

BLACK MEN COMING OF AGE IN A HBCU

PROLOGUE

Completely unprepared for the future, thousands of African American high school graduates flow peacefully into the "real world" without any idea of what is expected of them. Many obtain dead-end jobs which they hate and have horribly low salaries. Some become the lost children of society: drug addicts, bums, and prostitutes. A few...a very few get the opportunity to receive a higher education in a college or university atmosphere.

For many young enthusiastic black students just graduating from high school, a university is a way to develop themselves as individuals and perfect different strategies that will help them join an active role in society. There are over one hundred Historically Black Universities in America. An average of 44% of the students who attend, manage to struggle through, and actually graduate. The temptation of living away from home is usually enough to make most students quit school the first year. Others slowly fall prey to drugs, unexpected pregnancy, and even murder.

H.B.C.U.'s (Historical Black College & University) are designed to give students more than just an education. They are also designed to allow students to evolve into the next generation of mature, responsible adults. Black universities not only allow students the opportunity to learn among their peers, but also allow students to discover their own individualism. College life allows students to mold themselves into their **true** personalities, not the adolescent images that their families were familiar with.

For students all across America, HBCU campuses have become compact universes within themselves. Black Universities will take a high school graduate fresh out from graduation and turn an adolescent into an adult. Not many people are able to make this enormous transition in life. Only through pride, knowledge, and friendship will young African Americans succeed in their struggle against the odds. This novel is based on the true stories of a set of students and their particular struggles in a black university atmosphere.

CHAPTER 1

Back to School

10:30 in the morning, sunlight had penetrated the blindless window on the 2nd floor. A student still slumbers within the room. The clanging sound of an alarm clock could be heard throughout the Monroe Hall Male Dormitory. A loud moan is heard which was followed quickly by words of profanity, "Ah, shit! It ain't time to get up yet." The voice belonged to the extremely worn-out Blanding University sophomore, Larenzo Baker. Larenzo reached his arms over his head stretching his six-foot figure, as he yawned loudly. He wiped away the sleep that had gathered around his dark brown eyes as he looked around his small dingy dorm-room. Larenzo gave a slight smile. "Well, at least it's better than livin' wit Mom," Larenzo said aloud, unashamed of his habit of talking to himself.

Even though his mother dropped him off at the university the day before, his clothes were still packed in his bags. The single iron-framed bed that occupied his room didn't possess any sheets or covers at all. Only Larenzo's yellow-stained pillow still lay on mattress of the bed. Larenzo had plastered several black swimsuit models and a few posters of Rap artist on the walls of the small room. He placed his naked feet on the uncarpeted floor wiggling his toes upon the cracked tile. A large dresser was built into the wall and an old telephone directory was leaning inside the one small open window that wouldn't stay open by itself. Since Larenzo didn't have a telephone, at least the phonebook would help to keep the window cracked open. The air conditioner didn't work, and of course, it just so happened to be the beginning of an August heat wave in South Carolina. The walls and ceiling were painted a unique sky blue tint, usually found in prisons to calm the inmates. The dorm's cardboard ceilings were riddled with fist-size holes.

Dressed only in his boxers and a pair of sandals, Larenzo staggered out of his room and down the long hallway to the public community restrooms. A giant cockroach ran across his path as he entered the bathroom. He made sure to wear sandals because it was rumored far and wide that the male dorms showers were infested with athlete's foot. Once in the bathroom, he drowsily brushed his teeth with an old toothbrush, urinated in the toilet without flushing, and then took a shower in ice-cold water. The sink was caked with rust from years of lack of maintenance. The faucets squeaked when turned on and brown water came out first before the clear water finally appeared. Feces stains were everywhere and Larenzo stepped in a puddle of someone else's urine whenever he would try to take a piss.

Monroe Hall showers were another story all together. The community showers only possessed water in two temperatures: ice-cold and scalding hot. To make the situation worst, the students never knew what temperature they were going to get. Larenzo was glad that he received the ice-cold water instead of the latter this day. The shock of the freezing water on his body was enough to wake him up, preparing him for the day ahead of him. There were no shower curtains, so anyone could just walk in and see him naked. A few homosexuals lived on that floor so at any given time a peeping tom could violate a man's privacy. Larenzo washed speedily under his arms trying to get in and out of the cold water as quickly as possible.

He was a sophomore; well, this was his second year at this prestigious state- funded black university. His first year he didn't receive enough credit hours to be officially called a sophomore, but at least he hadn't been kicked out. He grew up in the ghettos of Chicago, and he didn't want to return without a degree. His family was counting on him. No one else in his family's history had ever graduated from college and he was determined that he would be the first. He wasn't a basketball or football player and he wasn't a goofy nerd that studied all the time. He was simply lucky. Well, at least Larenzo liked to refer to it as luck. It was very odd that an African American man from the cruel neighborhoods of Chicago was lucky enough to attend college.

Larenzo wasn't disturbed by his surroundings at all. He was brought up in a two-bedroom apartment infested with roaches and rats. The outside of the male dorm was made of bricks, very similar to the ghettos in which Larenzo had been raised. His mother struggled very hard to make sure that both he and his sister Michelle were well taken care of, despite where they lived. Nevertheless, Larenzo never felt sorry for himself. His past had prepared him for the dirt and grime, which had become his present living environment. In some small sick way it actually kept him from getting homesick.

Larenzo sighed loudly as he wrapped a towel around his waist and slowly staggered back to his room. He grabbed a white t-shirt, which was dangling from his open bag of luggage and sniffed it. "Still clean," he said to himself smiling. Hastily, Larenzo threw on the same baggy jeans, which he had slept in the night before and the white t-shirt. He slipped easily into his already laced up Timberland boots, and threw his White Sox's baseball cap on his head tilting it slightly to the right covering his eyes. Finally, he attached his cell phone to the inside of his pocket. He checked the screen on the front it read twenty four messages. They were messages from different girls on the campus. He left his cell phone on silent, mostly to keep from being bothered with answering it all day.

Larenzo had a chocolate caramel complexion with shaggy black eyebrows and deep dark brown eyes. His facial hair was cut in a neatly trimmed goatee around his full lips. He liked to think of himself as handsome and irresistible to the opposite sex. "Alright," he said as he admired himself in a cracked mirror, "you a sexy nigga. Now let's get our day started."

It was the very first day back to school, and classes had already started for most of the students. Larenzo, on the other hand, wasn't even registered yet. He gave up on early registration a long time ago. He didn't like dealing with the long lines and the loud obese clerks at the front of the line. Most of the white colleges had online registration, but for some reason this black university still did it the old-fashion way. Larenzo had a busy day ahead of him and he decided that he had better start soon. He made sure he locked the door to his room before he left.

The campus was alive with the voices of students and instructors alike. Fraternities stepped lively in the street, celebrating the return of school. Blanding University's athletic department practiced at the Mackey Gymnasium on the edge of campus. And intellectuals studied the erudite arts in the library. The campus was thirty square acres, which was rather large for a black university. The grounds were decorated with scattered pine trees and the scent of anticipation from both students and teachers were in the air.

The line for "late registration" was literally flowing out of the door of the administration building. Hundreds of black students were standing in line like African slaves being marched onto a European ship. A giant sign was posted on the front of the building which read: LATE REGISTRATION $50. The school was making a fortune off of late registration alone. Larenzo looked in his empty wallet and simply shook his head. "There's always tomorrow," he said to himself as he walked past the registration building and toward the "Pitt."

The Pitt was the most frequent social meeting place on the campus grounds. It was also one of the main hangouts for Larenzo and his friends. He could smell the stench of burning meat a block away. The unique smell of the Pitt was a blend of grease and trash. This grease hole that everyone called a restaurant was built in the center of the campus, and was responsible for providing fifty percent of the food digested on the campus. Except for various points in the day where all of the employees would take breaks at the same time, the Pitt would be open from 7:00 in the morning till 11:00 at night. As a result, sooner or later everyone went there to eat. The food was nasty, the floors were always greasy, the jukebox never worked correctly, and the service was slow. Fat short middle-aged women wearing hairnets would serve the food in grease soaked paper bags. Nevertheless, the food was cheaper than the fast food joints that surrounded the campus, and as a result, all of the students ate at the Pitt.

The idea of eating in the Pitt sickened Larenzo before he even reached the door. In order to prevent him from regurgitating last night's meal, he only ordered a soda when he entered the building and sat at his favorite seat located by the window. From his position at the window he could clearly see the registration building. Even though he only had twenty two dollars to his name, he decided that he would wait for the line to die down before he would eventually attempt to join their ranks. He ignored the flirtatious stares of the young ladies as he sat at his table. Larenzo put his feet up on the table and relaxed as he sipped on his soda happily. "What's the worst that could happen? They turn me around and tell me I can't go to classes this week? Some punishment," Larenzo thought to himself in silence.

It wasn't long before Larenzo's best friend, Kelvin Jones, pranced gleefully into the Pitt with his usual broad carefree smile on his sun-reddened face. Larenzo and Kel had been best friends since junior high school. Kel was best known as a comedian. If the university gave out an award for class clown, he would have won it last year, hands down. Kel stood about five foot seven and weighed about 165 pounds. His skin was lightly tanned from long periods of sun exposure. He had allowed his hair to grow for eight months and now his dirty brown hair had grown into a large unpicked Afro. He wore a pair of raggedy jeans with holes scattered all over it that he cut himself. The sleeves of his shirt were cut off displaying his rather small muscular frame. An unlit Black & Mild cigar rested in the right side of his mouth.

"Yo, what up Renzo," Kel said as he approached Larenzo's table. "I got a bad ass chick in my math class. She got some of the thickest legs I've ever seen. Yo, for real, they look like fucking tree trunks."

Kel liked to call females "chicks," short for chicken heads. He believed it was a little bit more respectable than the word "bitch." Truthfully, he loved women of all kinds and he loved to have sex with thick women most of all. Kel was a self-described sex fanatic when it came to thick-legged woman and the idea of another semester of enticing and taking advantage of young women thrilled him. Kel grinned a childish grin as his mind danced with figments of naked women falling victim to his boyish charm. His sense of humor had allowed him to sleep with an extraordinarily large number of women. Women seemed to be naturally attracted to his sense of humor and youthful appearance.

"My nigga, Renzo," Kel said as he slid into the seat across from Larenzo greeting him with dap. "The new freshman class is filled wit these beautiful thick-ass woman. Yo, I'm telling you these chicks is bad as hell. What type of girls you got in your classes so far?"

A look of disgust erupted on Larenzo's face when he heard the question, "Nigga, please. You know we don't go to class first day of school. You the only one breaking tradition." Kel's question surprised Larenzo a little. Larenzo and Kel had made it a point never to attend class on the first day of school. Their "tradition" was created years ago in high school. For Kel and Larenzo, the first week of school was usually a buffer period for the freshmen and transfer students, a meeting period, if you will, which allowed the students to become acquainted and accustomed to their new instructors. It was common knowledge that teachers never gave work the first couple of days. As a result, it seemed kind of pointless to attend class.

"Yeah, I know," Kel replied as he lit the cigar in his mouth. "Yo, but I couldn't help myself. These chicks is bad as hell. I followed one of them right into one of my classes. Just sitting in my class chilling, you believe that? I was like, 'yo, you got to give me the digits.' And she said, 'Do I?' And I was like 'hell yeah, you do!' Outcome: you know I got the phone number. Anyway. I know you ready for tonight."

A look of surprise emerged on Larenzo's face.

"What's up for tonight?" Larenzo asked, not truly thinking about what the date was.

"How'd you forget about the back-to-school-jam?" Kel replied. "You know the spot is at Red's crib. Yo, I invited everyone. Ain't nobody not gonna be there." Kel yanked out a long list of female phone numbers and began to read off some of the names aloud. "Lydia, Tammy, Treese, Stephanie...." Kel would have read off the entire list if one of the rotund lunch ladies working behind the counter in the Pitt didn't interrupt him. "Sir? Sir, can you please put that thing out." She waved a spatula at the Black & Mild cigar, which was clearly visible still dangling in his mouth.

Kel took the still lit miniature cigar out of his mouth and held it in the air with his middle finger protruding up. "What cigar? I don't know what you're talking about. Honest," Kel replied jokingly at the lunch lady. "I ain't got to do nothing." He replied blowing a puff of smoke in the air. "This is my school! I'll smoke when and where I want. If she knows what's good for her, she'll stay out of my business and go on a diet. She looks like she's been eating more food than she's been serving."

A glance of anger was visible on the lunch lady's face when she saw the middle finger. She cleared her throat and gave Kel a harsh look that would intimidate the average student. Kel simply giggled at her pathetic attempt at discipline and sat back down in his seat continuing to smoke. Larenzo gave a loud yawn of boredom and leaned back in his chair even more. He was no stranger to scenes such as this. Kel enjoyed pushing people to their limits emotionally; in some sick, demented way it actually gave him pleasure. Kel would harass people just to see how far he could push them before they simply couldn't take it anymore.

"C'mon," Larenzo said quietly. "Leave that bitch alone, man. I don't know why niggas want to always fuck wit people who fix their food. What's the sense in something like that? You know she gonna spit in your food or drop it on the floor or something when you're not looking." Kel shrugged his shoulders in reply to Larenzo's statement as if to say he didn't care.

"Man, that chicken-head will be alright," Kel smiled from ear to ear. "Shit, she just needs to be able to take a joke. That's all it is to it." For Kel, life was better viewed as a big joke rather than a series of serious decisions. He never took anything too seriously, and as a result he seemed to be happier than the average student that attended Blanding University.

The lunch lady walked away into the kitchen portion of the restaurant. Under her breath she mumbled the statement, "I ain't gonna be too many more bitches around here. Kids don't have any manners nowadays." Extreme aggravation was present in here voice as she walked away. Kel had won the little struggle between himself and the lunch lady and a victorious smile spread quickly across his face. "Fuck this place. Let's go check out Malik," Kel said. "I wasn't hungry anyhow. And she's probably pissing on my french fries, right now."

"Kel, why do you smoke those things in public places anyhow? I mean, I ain't never seen a fuckin' physical education major smoke so much," Larenzo said jokingly as they walked out the front door.

"Yeah, well I ain't never seen an English major curse so much," Kel quickly rebutted laughing hysterically to himself. "C'mon, let's see if we can drag Malik away from his girlfriend for the night."

The two friends laughed out loud merrily as they left the Pitt. In moments they had walked to the female dormitory Clark Hall, near the far end of campus. Slouching on the front steps of the dorm was Malik Brown. Malik Brown was the black militant of the university with the heart of a poet. He was well known for rebelling against society and preventing "the man" from standing in the path of young brothers and sisters. Malik was a very tall, thin, light-skin brother. His reddish-brown hair was neatly braided back and had little shells at the ends. His eyes were a hazel tint and he possessed very little facial hair at all except for a neatly trimmed moustache. He was dressed in a pair of black army fatigues, tied up at the bottom and a black and red Marcus Garvey T-shirt. Around his neck was an official African tribal necklace; not the cheap stuff that vendors sell on sidewalks. He wore a pair of black FUBU boots on his feet. He reeked of incense and marijuana. Malik, like usual, was holding a sagebrush green duffel bag filled with candy bars and a lollypop was in between his teeth. As normal, Malik was surrounded by a swarm of students bickering loudly amongst themselves.

"See, it's a proven fact, Man was granted power over everything on the planet, including women. Don't get mad at me, that's just the way it is." At once the crowd of women booed angrily at his statement literally jumping up and down in defiance. Malik Brown was no stranger at dealing with situations like this. When he was younger he studied the Muslim teachings against the objections of his Christian mother. At first he would have yelling contest with her about religion and other controversial issues. As a result, he barely speaks with his mother nowadays. He realized a long time ago that it was best to allow women to express their views fully before attempting to change their minds. As the women yelled loudly among each other at his statement, Malik simply sat back confidently and allowed them to express their opinions of his seemingly openly sexist statement.

The women surrounding him, munching quite contently on pieces of candy, were a few of the ladies that lived in that dorm. They were dressed in short shorts, T-shirts and tight miniskirts. Their hair was done, either braided up or naturally loose. Even though they argued with Malik, it was obvious that many of them were attracted to the young man chewing on a lollypop. Their eyes danced with delight as the black militant began to justify his case.

"It's a woman's responsibility to obey and serve her man. It's right there in the wedding vows. They're naturally emotional creatures, simply not designed to lead," he paused to allow the large group of women to once again disagree loudly. "See, every culture on the planet believes that a female is honor-bound to listen, cherish, respect, and follow her man. The facts speak for themselves. There are no women in charge of any major countries. Even in the past, societies were looked down on when they elected a female ruler. They're way too emotional to be put in charge of that much responsibility.

Especially now with the creation of nuclear weapons, a woman might be on her period and blow up the entire planet. Simply put, they can't do the job." Even with his black militant background, it was obvious that Malik was a very good speaker.

"Well, what about Cleopatra?" one of the women questioned in an upset tone. "She was queen of Egypt and the most beautiful woman on the planet." The women who spoke up sounded meaner than she looked. She had a small figure and large light brown eyes. Her buttocks and thighs were very thick compared to her smaller upper body. She was no doubt a freshman, and Malik knew that from the captivated look in her eyes, he was the very first upper classman that she had met at Blanding University. She bit down on her lower lip as she waited for Malik to answer her question.

A part of Malik actually enjoyed tormenting others with controversial issues and then proving his point. Moreover, he enjoyed being right, and in some way the sensation of winning arguments, crushing the very themes that people based their lives on actually helped to relieve the stress of everyday life. Malik was a junior psychology major and in some manner it thrilled him to get reactions from different people. He considered the public a testing ground for emotional experiments. He liked to refer to the student body of Blanding University as the intelligent sheep of society.

"Cleopatra was a whore. Despite what the history books force-feed you as a child. She was a African queen who fell in love with two high ranking devils at the same time," Malik retorted smiling. "As a result of this love, Egypt, the most powerful civilization on the planet fell to the Caucasian Roman Empire. She was responsible for crumbling one of the most powerful empires on the planet simply because she allowed her emotions to get involved. Other countries like England only use a queen as a figurehead. Queen Elizabeth has no real power. She can't go to war or even raise taxes if she wants. It's all there in black and white. Go ahead and look it up."

"Well, what about God?" the small woman continued. "God loves everyone, and the Bible says that we're all equals." Even under several layers of makeup Malik could tell her face was visibly young. She smelled of coco butter and the shine of innocence still glimmered in her eyes. This was her first year away from home and she was trying to make herself appear older. *"Freshmen,"* Malik thought to himself. *"how easily they were to manipulate."*

"The Bible?" Malik repeated with a slight scoff on his face. "You got to be kidding me."

"Yes. You have heard of it, right?" the small woman replied sarcastically.

"What's your name, sister?" Malik asked casually. He still referred to black women as "sisters."

"Shawna," she answered. Malik knew that he had her hook, line, and sinker. Malik had piqued her interest, and he knew it.

"Are you a religious person?" Malik asked good-naturedly.

"Third Gospel Baptist Church," she answered very proudly with her head up.

"Well Shawna, the Bible never speaks of males and females as being equal. In fact, it actually proves the opposite. In the Holy Book, man was formed first and woman was created from a single rib of man. She didn't even get an important bone; she got a rib. None of the prophets were females and none of the disciples were females," Malik paused for a moment purposely to show his pearly white teeth. "Furthermore, the majority of the women written about in the Bible were viewed as evil or ungodly. Eve tempted Adam to bite from the fruit. A woman asked for the head of Peter. A woman cut the hair of Samson. A Babylonian whore is even present in Revelations to insure Armageddon and the end of the world. So for goodness sake, don't talk to me about the Bible saying we're even. You should read that book again with your eyes open this time and tell me what you think."

Startled at his knowledge of the Bible, Shawna blushed slightly as she continued to stare at Malik in awe. Malik smiled slyly as he realized that he had effectively broken down her natural defenses. He secretively lived for that exact moment where everything someone believed was suddenly and irrevocably changed. It gave him pleasure that his knowledge was instrumental in the teaching of the public. He knew that after his small speech that he had forever changed the way she viewed her own religion. Unable to think of any other points to defend her position, Shawna became silent.

The crowd of young ladies surrounding Malik had also became silent. They had begun the conversation so very sure of themselves and their beliefs. Malik had stripped them of their certainty, placing the seeds of doubt in their minds. What had begun as a possibly hostile group of girls had been reverted to a flock of docile, moldable young ladies. "*How easily the minds of women were to change,*" Malik thought to himself. Malik wasn't a sexist in the normal sense of the word. He honestly believed that everyone played a role in the grand scheme of the universe. To Malik, a woman's role was simply that of following. It was the man's job to make the money for the family. He liked his women to be barefoot and pregnant.

From behind the head of Shawna, Malik caught sight of his approaching friends, Kel and Larenzo. Kel walked with a youthful exuberance, providing natural bop in his every step. He rubbed his hands together when he spotted the group from a distance. Just the sight of youthful women cluttered together in a small building brought happiness to his heart. Kel's whole body seemed to be energized as he approached the large group of women with Malik.

Alongside Kel, Larenzo walked slowly with what was referred to by many as a "pimp walk." He strolled casually with one hand in his pocket and one dangling to his side. He slouched as he sauntered yet kept his head high in the air at all times. Larenzo had gained quite a reputation as a lady's man over the last couple of years. His walk was a mixture of being raised with street knowledge and a cocky pride for his reputation. He believed that no woman on the campus was beyond his reach, and he carried himself accordingly. He had a relaxed demeanor, which usually put others at ease.

"My brothers, what's good?" Malik asked in a well-mannered tone as he caught the eyes of Kel and Larenzo. "I'm just sitting here educating my young Nubian sisters on the role that nature has granted them." Malik had known Kel and Larenzo since the year before and had formed a strong friendship with the two men from Chicago. Malik tossed a free piece of candy to Kel and Larenzo as they approached him and the group of women.

Kel placed the small piece of candy in his pocket; his hand then grabbed one of the light-skinned thick women by the waist. "Yeah, she's ripe. I'm gonna take this one off your hands Malik. You got too many anyhow and this one just earned the VIP list at the party tonight." A slight giggle broke free from the young girl's lips when Kel's fingertips gripped her massive hips from behind. This man she had never seen before was grabbing her freely wherever he wanted and his presence alone had totally fascinated her. Kel smiled as he spoke, "I'm calling dibs on this one." Dibs was a expression used by Kel and his friends which meant the female was off limits to any one else until he had slept with her first.

Larenzo popped the small piece of candy in his mouth and then shook his head. He was used to Kel randomly grabbing girls and making sexual plans for them. He mostly ignored Kel when he gripped girls like that. "One day one of those girls is going to slap the shit out of you," Larenzo smiled as he spoke turning his attention to Malik still chewing on a lollipop stick. Larenzo began to laugh, and with that laugh his next few words weren't felt as viciously. "Yo, Malik when are you finally gonna stop selling candy and start hustling some real products? All this candy stuff is cool but if you gonna be an entrepreneur, at least start selling ecstasy. I ain't telling you to become Escobar or anything; I'm just saying, let's make some real money. You already got the clientele." Larenzo nodded toward the women still sitting on the stoop of the stairs as he mentioned the word "clientele."

To Malik the idea of selling drugs was self-destruction. Malik smoked marijuana, as did many young black men that attended college but that was as far as his drug use went. "Naw man, I'm not trying to go to jail. That's what the white man wants of us young brothers and sisters, killing each other with their little pills. Besides, I'm trying to uplift my fellow black sisters and brothers. Society needs strong black men to keep the race surviving." Malik had already considered Larenzo's career option of selling ecstasy or some other sort of illegal drug instead of candy bars and lollipops. It's true, he did need the extra money, but to sacrifice the lives of African American men and women was too much of a loss. Unlike other black spokesmen at the time, Malik actually believed in everything he preached. He didn't want anything to do with degrading the black race and he was adamant in separating his people from the pitfalls of society.

"Alright, don't preach to me Minister Martin Farrakhan X. I know all about it. You know and I know that the majority of your sisters and brothers aren't going to make it out the hood anyway. I'm just saying, you might as well make some money now while the opportunity still presents itself," Larenzo replied to Malik's adamant rejection.

Larenzo knew that Malik was going to turn him down his suggestion. Drugs were a dirty business venture for anyone, especially a
student with a promising career in psychology. Larenzo didn't know
any rich drug dealers from his neighborhood. If they did get rich, it
was never for too long. Usually, most of them ended up in jail or
dead.

It was noon and the large bell tower located in the center of campus rang for lunch. The group of girls, except Shawna, began to
rush off for the cafeteria. Malik watched as the group of ladies began
to leave for lunch, "They remind me of sheep, you know what I
mean? Following each other because someone told them that it was
feeding time." The trio of men didn't go to lunch at the arranged
time like the rest of the student body. They believed that allowing
the school to dictate when and where to eat was one step away from
slavery. Kel whispered some words into the ear of the light-skinned
girl still in his arms, and she slipped him her phone number before
she ran off with the rest of the group. When the bell rang Shawna
broke abruptly from her dreamy-eyed hypnotic stare at Malik Brown.
Shawna followed behind the group of girls, but before she departed
she tentatively kissed Malik goodbye on the cheek. The group of
women moved with a switch in their hips as they rushed off to lunch.

Kel skipped happily towards Malik and Larenzo sitting on the steps
of Clark Hall. "Yo, Malik let's roll on down to Red's house to make
sure he's straight for the party tonight." Malik was originally from
the area that the school was in and he usually drove his mother's car
Cadillac back and forth to campus. "I'm telling you that party is
going to be crazy!" Kel said in an upbeat tone.

Malik checked his watch confirming that he didn't have any more
classes for the day. "You know I'm ready for the party," Malik said
confidently. "C'mon, let me run in here and tell my queen that I'm
leaving," Malik said as all three men still stared at the large buttocks
of the women leaving for lunch. "I got to tell Ebony that I'll get up
with her later on tonight after the party." Malik didn't have to get
permission from his girlfriend to let him leave; he simply believed
that it was his responsibility to let his girlfriend know what he was
doing for the night. Malik and his girlfriend had been officially ex-
clusive for two years, but unofficially they had been in love with each
other ever since they were high school freshmen. It wasn't a secret to

many of his friends that Malik meant to marry her when he graduated.

First, Malik rubbed his cheek to be sure that Shawna didn't leave
any lipstick on him. Then, he led the other two men up the stairs
into Clark Hall. Behind the front counter in the lobby Malik's girlfriend, Ebony Richards sat comfortably in a brown cushioned chair
talking pleasantly on the phone. She was the R.A. of Clark Hall.
Every dorm on the campus had a Resident Assistant. An R.A's responsibilities included answering phone calls and making sure that
the freshmen girls didn't sneak any men up to their rooms. It was
easy work and Ebony truly enjoyed the respect that she got from the
other women who lived in the dorm.

Clark Hall was much smaller than Monroe Hall, the male dormitory where Larenzo and Kel lived. The smell of marijuana wasn't in
the air, or the unsightly appearance of graffiti on the walls. Other
than that, the female dorm was only slightly better looking then its
male counterpart. The lobby contained a wall-to-wall gray carpet on
the floor, which was spotted with juice and gum stains. The walls
were off-white far different then the prison color walls in the male
dormitory. A few plants were scattered around the lobby and the
office area that Ebony worked in. The aroma of coconut incense
draped in the air thanks to a stick Ebony had lit.

Ebony Richards was a dark chocolate complexioned woman. Her
skin was smooth, and she was never seen wearing makeup or nail
polish. Her hair was neatly twisted into small dreadlocks, which hung
shoulder length. She wore a tight fitting black t-shirt cut low in the
front showing off her well-shaped, large breast. The words "All Natural" was written in large pink letters on her shirt. Her hips were large
and voluptuous, perfectly shaped for her well-built buttocks. She
smiled a full set of beautiful white teeth when Malik entered the
building. When she smiled her eyes grew bright with the happiness
that can only be achieved when a woman is in love.

"I'll talk to you later Cynthia," Ebony said into the phone while still
smiling happily at her boyfriend. "My man just walked in. Bye girl."
Ebony hung up the phone when her eyes met with Malik's. There
was instant electricity in the air when they were close to each other. It
was almost like music was being played that only they were allowed
to dance to. At first sight they appeared to be created for one an-

other, true soul mates. They complimented each other in every way. Malik was a self-described "black militant" and Ebony was an "all natural," young, black woman in tune with her spiritual side.

When Malik walked up to her office he reached into his candy bag and he pulled out a single red rose. Ebony's face lit up with delight when she saw the flower in Malik's hand. "I'm sorry baby. I can't go out with you tonight. I gotta go to Red's party tonight and help the fellas out. I know that you don't like the party atmosphere so I'll make it up to you later on, alright." Malik reasoned with his girlfriend using the little boy voice that he used with women to get what he wanted. Malik knew that Ebony loved roses, and he knew she couldn't resist him when he used his little boyish voice. Malik had come well prepared for the conversation with his girlfriend. In order to prevent a future argument he brought a flower as backup. The flower would keep her satisfied until he called her later on tonight.

"Oh, a flower!" Ebony yelped with genuine surprise in her voice. She took the rose from his hand carefully not to prick herself with the thorns and quickly placed it in a vase of water. "I understand sweetie," Ebony responded managing to a slight smile still a little disappointed that Malik was standing her up. "You go have fun with your friends. I don't mind. Besides I'm going to be busy working around here." Ebony wasn't dumb. She knew that it was the night of the "Back-to-School Jam," and she knew that she wasn't going to see her boyfriend later on. Red's parties never ended until late, and she realized Malik would be covered with tramps trying to sleep with him. She accepted these facts and not once did she ever complain. Ebony knew that deep down she had an African-American king, and there was nothing that he wouldn't do for her. Decent men were hard too find, and she wasn't going to lose this decent man over a stupid party.

Malik leaned over her counter and kissed Ebony passionately on the lips. "Goodbye, my queen," Malik said after the long kiss. "I'll give you a call when I have a chance." He gave her another peck on her full lips and then began to make his way to the door. As he walked out the door he heard Ebony's voice in the distance. "Goodbye, my king," Ebony replied smiling from ear to ear like a schoolgirl.

When Malik, Kel, and Larenzo were finally back outside of the building Kel began to make fun of the couple that were so very much in love. "Oh, please don't leave me, my king." Kel continued to mock the couple, "I don't know what I would ever do without you. Kiss me my queen. Ha! Ha! Ha!" Kel and Larenzo burst out laughing after the terrific impression of Malik and Ebony.

"That shit ain't funny," Malik said trying not to laugh at the impression of himself. "You'll understand when you meet that special woman and fall in love, my brothers. You'll see. Besides, Ebony and I have an understanding. She's my queen and I'm her king. Now a king can have a few mistresses on the side as long as he respects the woman that has his children. She understands that other women are going to try to sleep with me. She doesn't care as long as I don't bring home any disease and don't get any girls pregnant. What I need one of these other girls for anyhow? Ebony is the perfect all-natural woman of my dreams. Watch, one day I'm going to marry her. Now, let's go to this party."

"Man you acting real soft right now," Larenzo jabbed still laughing loudly and pointing at Malik. "You don't have to prove to me that you love her. I ain't got nothing to do with it, but you know that broad Shawna is going to be at the party. Word up, man if you ever cheat on Ebony, she's gonna cut your balls off."

The three men got into Malik's mother's Cadillac Sedan DeVille parked at the end of the street. The vehicle was a thing of pure beauty. The Cadillac was a '85 classic model with twenty-inch rims. It was painted midnight blue, and the windows were tinted jet black. Other students commonly referred to the Cadillac as the "pimp-mobile." But to Malik, his mother's '85 blue Cadillac was his baby; his pride and joy. He had spent hundreds of dollars of his candy selling money to completely remodel the classic vehicle. Other than Ebony, Malik's mother's car was his one true love.

When Malik turned the key in the ignition the car seemed to almost purr. Malik paused for a second just listening to the car's motor running for a while. After he was thoroughly satisfied he put the car in drive and began to make his way to Red's house. Kel sat in his usual position in the front passenger seat while Larenzo stretched out comfortably in the back seat.

"I can't wait for this party," Malik said as he expertly drove the big car in and out of traffic. "I've been waiting all summer break for this party."

Larenzo chuckled loudly agreeing with Malik, "Yeah man, me too. Make a stop at the liquor store so I can get a bottle of Tequila for tonight." Larenzo simply loved the taste of Tequila, and he couldn't think about going to a party without a bottle of Jose Cuervo's finest gold blend. "Have you seen the rest of the guys, yet?" he asked as the car slowed down in front of the liquor store.

"Naw, but I'm sure Bobby, Midget Moe, and J.C. will show up at the party later on tonight if they're not already there," Kel responded as he arranged a few stray phone numbers into his electronic black book. "They wouldn't miss one of Red's parties if their life depended on it," Kel said laughing out loud. "Shit! You know how I feel about it? If they don't show up; more women for us."

CHAPTER 2

Red's Party

It wasn't too much longer before the three men arrived at Red's house. His house was located a few blocks away from the university in the middle of the slums. The rent was low and he lived in a two-bedroom home by himself. The exterior to Red's house was painted a yellow and white color, which had faded through the years. A rusty fence surrounded his property and his lawn. Red had no driveway and he didn't have a car. Most of his lawn was dirt and gravel because of the large amount of cars continuously being parked there. The small part of his lawn that wasn't dirt and gravel was overgrown with weeds. The trio of men realized that Red was here because they saw J.C.'s brand new Honda Acura and Bobby's black Nissan was parked in front of Red's porch. J.C.'s Honda was painted dark blue with tinted windows and had New York license plates on it.

Two dogs ran loose chasing each other without any collars on around the neighborhood. Across the street from Red's house was a boarding home which housed four flirtatious girls whom also attended Blanding University and loved to party. On one side of his house laid the ruins of an old crack house that had burned down two semesters ago. On the other side of his house was a run down home that belonged to a elderly couple. The elderly couple had been living in the home for many years and even though they had the resources to move they refused to leave there home. The husband suffered from total hearing loss in one of his ears and partial hearing loss in the other. His wife on the other hand, could hear very well but she never complained about the noise that came from Red's loud parties. As a result, the police were never notified and Red's parties were never broken up early.

The three men opened the door to Red's house and casually walked inside. Red left his door unlocked purposely because he believed no one was dumb enough to try to rob from him. He always said if they robbed from me they wouldn't have much to take anyway. The inside of the house was as plain as a hotel room that one finds on the highway. The tile floor was without carpet and a small black and white television screen sat on the floor playing cartoons. The walls didn't have any pictures on them and the windows didn't have any blinds covering them. A large wooden table used to play cards on sat in the middle of the dining room/living room area. Around the table sat Red and the rest of the small group of friends that Malik, Kel, and Larenzo had come to love as brothers. Card games were a favorite past time for college students and this group of college students had mastered several of the games but none of the other games were as satisfying as Spades. For the students who spent time at Red's house, the game of Spades was a serious sport.

A small group of mostly male students had already begun to show up at Red's house. In the center of the dining room Bobby, Red, Midget Moe, and J.C. were in the middle of a heated card game of spades. A small stash of five-dollar bills was bunched up in a pile on the side of the table. Bobby and Red were winning, but from a distance Larenzo could tell that midget Moe was beginning to cheat. Moe was a good spades player but he was an excellent spades cheater. Midget Moe was palming extra spades when the other team wasn't looking. If someone else caught him cheating there would surely be a fight. A few girls were in the kitchen stirring liquor into a giant container of punch.

Red was the first person to speak when Larenzo, Kel, and Malik walked into the room. "What's up?" Red said looking away from the game for only a split second. "What ya'll bring for the party?"

Red was visibly older than the other students that attended the university. He was a light skinned brother, almost yellowish in color. He had gray eyes and his hair was braided in long dreadlocks, which hung to the middle of his back He was dressed in a bright red t-shirt, a pair of black jeans, and brand new red and black Air Jordan's on his feet. A red bandanna was tied around his head draped casually under his dreadlocks. Red was originally from New Jersey, and rumor had it that he was affiliated with a well-known gang there, hence the name and preference in clothing color.

Red was a career student at Blanding University with no intention of graduating anytime soon. No one knew exactly what his age was but he had been at the school for at least six years and everyone on the campus knew his name. He wasn't a gangster in the original

sense of the word. He didn't sell drugs or beat people up but he did
carry a .45 caliber pistol with him hidden in the back of his pants at
all times, even when he went to class, and he wasn't afraid to use it.
Before he came to Blanding University he was in and out of trials still
pending in New York, New Jersey, and Virginia. Red decided that
South Carolina was as good a place as any to stay out of trouble and
in the meantime escape having to go to trial for an assault charge he
received in New Jersey a few years ago.

   "You know I brought some good ol' Jose for the Back-to-School
Jam tonight." Larenzo said as he held up the large bottle of Tequila
in his right hand. "If you got some salt and lemons this bottle alone
should get like twelve to fifteen young ladies drunk as hell." Larenzo
would know. He was an expert when it came to getting women at
parties as intoxicated as possible. He felt in some way that it was a
natural result of a successful party.

   "No doubt. Put the bottle in the freezer with the rest of them."
Red said without looking up from the game again. His suspicions
were suddenly aroused because he saw Midget Moe looking at the
bottom of the deck when he thought Red wasn't watching. Now
Red was staring at Midget Moe through the side of his eyes with a
hateful sneer on his lips.

   Midget Moe's excellent peripheral vision had picked up the hateful stare in the eyes of Red. "What? I ain't cheating." Midget Moe
said very defensively like a kid who was caught with his hand in the
cookie jar. Midget Moe threw down his cards on the table face down
and said, "I'm not gonna play if you keep suggesting that I'm cheating. Shit, I'm your boy. C'mon, would I do that?"

   "You better not be or else I'm gonna fuck you up, Moe!" Because
of the anger in his voice, Red's natural New Jersey accent appeared
when he spoke. Midget Moe picked up his hand and finished playing the game after Red's threat of bodily harm. Midget Moe was
originally from the surrounding slum neighborhoods around the
campus and through the years he had become somewhat of a hustler when it came to card games and peoples emotions. He knew
when it was time to quit and as a result he wouldn't try to cheat Red
and Bobby anymore...this game.

   Red had good reason to beware of Midget Moe. Morris Houldwell
or more commonly known as "Midget Moe" to his close friends was

not a man looked at for his incredible reputation for honesty. Moe was the type of man to steal candy from a baby if he could make a profit from it. Moe had three children, two baby mommas, and a girlfriend on the side. He was only twenty-two years old. For Moe life was a card game. There are winner and there are losers, and no matter what anyone else says cheaters do prosper. For Moe everything was a potential money scheme and everyone was potentially a victim, everyone that is except for him.

Midget Moe was the color of unlit charcoal. He had a bush of curly black hair, which grew like a fluffy cotton ball on his head. Midget Moe was completely clean-shaven and possessed the smile of a politician and the slick tongue of a car salesman. When he smiled he showed a brilliant shining set of teeth except for one chipped tooth in the front that he acquired fighting in his youth. As for his height, Midget Moe wasn't quite a midget in the true sense of the word. Moe stood only five foot two inches tall. Even with his specially made sneakers on, which were designed to make him appear taller, he was still visibly smaller than all of the other men and most of the women.

JC glanced at his spades partner and then grabbed the score in disgust, "Who got next because this game is about over?" JC inquired after realizing Midget Moe wouldn't be able to cheat any more.

"Naw bro, don't throw ya hand in. You might as well finish up the game it's almost over." Bobby said looking at JC preparing to throw his hand in and quit the game. "Ain't no money, like ho money, but I'll take yours anyhow. I'll make this beating as painless as possible." Bobby said as he began to count the stack of five-dollar bills that was crumbled up on the table.

Directly across the card table was Midget Moe's teammate JC. JC was the newest member of the group of friends. He was slender and supple, mostly bone and muscle, with a little bit of youth still present about his face. He was a second semester freshman from Brooklyn and had stitches from a stab wound to prove it. He was dressed in an official New York Knicks basketball jersey and a pair of navy blue jeans. On his feet he wore black socks and a pair of black high top Addidas. A black dooragg covered his naturally wavy hair. A long platinum chain hung around his neck with a large medallion connected lying heavily on his chest. The chain and medallion alone cost more than two months of Red's rent. On his exposed right arm was a tattoo of a crucifix on a basketball with the symbol for R.I.P. with a long list of names belonging to his deceased friends that lived in Brooklyn. He had lost all of his old friends in New York two years ago in a brutal shootout at the Rucker's basketball tournament.

To deal with the pain of the lost, JC practiced day and night on his already excellent basketball skills. Two months after the shootout JC was propositioned by a recruiter for Blanding University, with a full scholarship. It was odd for a black university to actually get a good basketball player. The best players in the country usually went to white schools where they would get more publicity. But JC was different, he hadn't planned to even go to college before the shooting and now his whole life had been rearranged in a manner of days. JC simply took the first option that was offered to him.

He was still only eighteen years old but like most young African Americans JC had already lived a full life. He never wanted to leave the city for some small "country-ass" town in the Deep South. Nevertheless, his mother had decided to get JC out of the city for a while as a chance to hopefully start over. Playing basketball for Blanding University would give JC the chance to one day, maybe impress a NBA scout. Just a freshman, JC was already a starting guard for the school basketball team and he realized that his past dreams of one day going pro, could very well become reality.

Larenzo had befriended him one night last semester over a game of poker. JC had betted a hundred dollars on a College Basketball game simply because the star of the team was from the same part of Brooklyn he was from. A hundred dollars was a lot of money to a college student especially for a bet on a basketball game. JC was a big money spender and usually he won these incredibly large bets. Larenzo liked his style instantly, and that very night Larenzo introduced him to the rest of his friends. He was the very first freshman that the rest of the guys accepted into their ranks.

The last member of the spades playing quartet was Bobby King. Bobby was a sophomore math major originally from Pennsylvania. Bobby King claimed to be the descendent of a long line of genuine pimps. His father was a legendary Negro pimp by the name of King Cat Daddy and his mother was a Caucasian bottom whore. Bobby grew up being pampered by his father's other hookers. The other prostitutes took Bobby to the park, fed him, and even bathed him. If it were up to his dad, Bobby would have followed in the footsteps of his father and his father before him. By the age of seven Bobby King had already mastered the walk, talk, and the flashy clothing of a pimp. Bobby grew up witnessing his father and other pimps beat women and taking their money. There's no question that Bobby would have eventually became a full-fledged pimp if it weren't for King Cat Daddy's brutal death. When Bobby was still young, the police in a routine traffic stop killed his father just for a good laugh. After they viciously beat him to an inch of his life they shot him twelve times.

After the murder of his father, Bobby realized that even legendary pimps eventually die. His mother gave up the career of prostituting and turned her life over to God. His mother soon after, became a nun at a local church and Bobby began to take care of himself at the age of fourteen. He would never admit it, but deep down he still admired his father greatly. As a result, Bobby picked up many of the characteristics of a pimp without even trying. He had the gift for gab. He was blessed with the uncanny ability to attract women of all ages and races with his words. He was always dressed very well and he kept his fingernails cleaned and trimmed.

Bobby was dressed in a pair of gray slacks with a gray designer Ice Berg shirt on. He wore a pair of designer leather shoes, which was shined to the point where you could see your own reflection in them. A small thin gold chain carrying a gold crucifix hung around his neck. He was a light skinned brother thanks to his mother's Irish gene pool. His clothes fit him well, not like the baggy style of his friends at all. His haircut was very low and neatly taped up. And when he smiled he showed a single dimple in his left cheek. He was very attractive even on his "off" days.

"Hey Danielle, fix me a drink!" Bobby yelled at one of the girls stirring punch in the kitchen. "Hurry up, damn. I ain't gonna ask you again." Bobby spoke with a command quality in his voice when he talked to women. There was cockiness about him when it came to females and he knew it. He had a baby momma, which he lived with but on various occasions he would sleep around on her.

A beautiful young girl wearing an enormous amount of makeup appeared out of the kitchen. She rushed over to the table and as she walked, her butt switched from left to right inside a very short mini-skirt. She handed Bobby a large cup of Hennessey, "Here you go, Bobby. Just like you like it with extra ice in it." She smiled as she handed him the drink and bent over so she could show off her shapely breast. Her breast seemed about to pop out of the tight-fitting shirt as she bent over. She tried to kiss him on the lips but he moved his mouth away from hers.

"I'm a pimp," Bobby casually stated looking away from her. "What I look like kissing some ho on the mouth. I don't even kiss my girl-friend in public. What makes you think I'm going to kiss some other ho?" Bobby was openly cruel when it came to the feelings of average women and he didn't care who knew about it. Only his girlfriend and his daughter escaped the attention of Bobby King's when it came to the disrespect of women. Danielle was just the most recent victim in a long list of names when it came to his discontent of the female gender.

She blushed slightly embarrassed from the exchange. Realizing that she had been rejected in front of everyone she rushed back off into the kitchen where she continued stirring the alcoholic punch. All of the other men watched her ass as she walked away, everyone except Bobby King. Danielle was a groupie. She had been passed along sexually by many of the guys that were playing cards even now. Sure, Bobby had slept with her also, but even the thought of show-ing affection to her in public sickened him.

Something about women covered with makeup, showing off their breast disgusted Bobby. She reminded him of a hooker. He had grown up all of his life surrounded by these sorts of women and he hated it. They didn't necessarily have to be prostitutes to be whores and he knew it. A woman such as Danielle would be another man's dream girl, but for Bobby she was just another dumb whore who wasn't getting paid to have sex.

As the spades game eventually came to an end so did the daylight hours. When the sun finally fell from the horizon the back-to-school party began. All of the lights in the house were cut off and a neon black light was turned on. A personal D.J. began to spin records and by eleven o'clock Red's house was overflowing with people dancing and drinking. The entire student body had showed up and the party soon spread outside to the front and backyard. Within hours the house was filled with the smoke of marijuana and the friction created from the body heat alone made the house a literal sweatbox. Already the party was a complete success. A senior was kneeling in the bathroom in front of the toilet. It wasn't unusual for someone to "spill there cookies" at one of Red's parties. No one even seemed to pay attention as the senior loss his supper in the toilet and on the bathroom floor. Reggae music blasted in the background as everyone began to grind on each other in the dimly lit living room area, everyone that is, except for a shadowy figure sitting quietly by on the back steps of the house sipping on a can of soda.

A little bit before midnight, the group of freshmen that Malik, Larenzo, and Kel had met earlier had finally made it to party. The inside of the house had transformed into a packed dance floor. In a blend of ecstasy and rhythm the students danced with each other to the flowing beats of the music. The erotic dancing resembled more like people having passionate sex standing up, other than just dancing. Most people inside were dancing. Those who weren't dancing were having actual sex in Red's two bedrooms. Grunts and moans of pleasure could be heard from Red's locked room. Red had taken two girls in there earlier in the night. Outside of the door two guys had their ears to the closed door listening intently to the grunts coming from the other side.

Outside of the house a small group of men were shooting dice in the backyard. A large pile of money had been placed under a small rock and like usual; when money was involved Midget Moe was in the middle of it. He was in rare form that night as he hustled the group of young students surrounding him. "Lucky seven! Lucky seven!" Midget Moe exclaimed as he rolled the pair of dice against the house. "Yes! Pay me my money! Pay me my money!" Midget Moe yelled as he rolled another seven. Moe had already made well over two hundred dollars that night and his night didn't seem to be slowing down at all. Of course, the dice were purposely filed down unevenly so they would roll seven every time.

Everything would have gone fine for Midget Moe but unfortunately not everyone takes losing so graciously. One of the guys that had his money on the dice game was a student by the name of Travis. Travis was a junior from Charleston, South Carolina. He had seen this scam run on people before by his older brother and he wasn't going to be taken like so many others. He had watched skeptically as Midget Moe won money over and over again through the night. When Moe rolled seven again for the fourth time in a row, Travis reached down and snatched his money from underneath the rock. "Hell no! Little man, I'm not paying you anything." Travis said as he counted his money and quickly placed it in his back pocket. When Travis spoke the shine from his gold teeth glistened off of the moonlight. "You ain't slick. No way I'm going out like these other suckas," Travis said as he looked down his nose at Midget Moe. "I'm not paying you shit! You shaved those dice you four foot goofy ass motherfucka."

"Hold on Travis." Midget Moe said as he tried to calm Travis down rationally. "You put your money down like everyone else. If you think I'm cheating don't play anymore but that money in your hands is mine." Midget Moe only came to Travis' chest but he showed as much courage as any man. "Now give me my money before I have to jump up there and beat ya ass." Midget Moe said confidently now staring up into the eyes of Travis.

"I'm not paying you shit!" Travis said in reply to Midget Moe's threat. When Travis turned his back to Midget Moe to walk away a red-hot anger sent shockwaves through Moe's five-foot figure. Midget Moe quickly grabbed a partially empty beer bottle that was on the ground and jumped up smashing the bottle across the back of his head. When the bottle broke against Travis' skull, the large crowd of gamblers that had surrounded Moe instinctively took a step backward. Obviously stunned by the attack, Travis stumbled forward but somehow he managed to stay on his feet. A mixture of ice-cold beer and warm blood dripped from the head of the young gambler.

Midget Moe ran up quickly behind him but Travis was already regaining his senses. Travis swung a wild right hand at Midget Moe but Moe was able to duck under it easily. Midget Moe punched Travis hard in the stomach and Travis fell to the floor in pain. When Travis fell to the floor Midget Moe ran over and began to fiercely kick him in the chest and face. Bobby and Larenzo who were watching the whole fight take place ran over to the aid of Midget Moe, and helped him stomp Travis to an inch of his life. The more the three of them kicked Travis, the more blood poured from his mouth. It wasn't before too long that Travis was literally lying in a pool of his own blood. When Travis stopped moving all together the three men stopped kicking him. Only his light breathing gave anyone the indication that he was still alive. Midget Moe rummaged through his pockets and took the money that he had won back.

"Didn't...I tell...you not...to fuck...with...me?!" Midget Moe was out of breath and his words came out in short syllables. Midget Moe stood kneeling over the lifeless body of Travis as he gulped large quantities of air.

After the fight many of the party guests left. The sight of that much blood had scared many of the girls off and when the girls left the guys soon followed. An ambulance was never called because they would ask too many questions. If a hospital were notified about the fight they would surely call the police. The police would show up at the house and want to make charges against Midget Moe and the others. Red never really liked Travis that much and he hated the police more than anything. To make sure things stayed quiet around his neighborhood Red asked two students to pick Travis up and take him to his dorm. The two students laid Travis' bloody body in front of the door to his dorm that night. He would probably stay there until a janitor or a R.A. eventually woke him up early the next morning.

By four-thirty in the morning most of the crowd was either intoxicated or unconscious. The majority of the people that were at the party had either left when the fight in the backyard started or were in a drunken stupor laid out on the floor. Larenzo was one of the few exceptions to the rule. Larenzo was partially intoxicated but he was still fully functional. Larenzo wobbled as he walked through the hallways, barely holding himself up, a bloodstain was still visible on his Timberland boots from the fight earlier that night. Larenzo inspected the damage, as he staggered through the wreckage that used to resemble Red's home. The dance floor was sticky from where someone had spilt his or her drink on it. Empty cups of liquor and cigarette butts were scattered everywhere. The bathroom was especially atrocious. Vomit was smeared on the walls, floors, and in the toilet. An overweight student was fast asleep, lying in the tub, in the fetal position looking quite pathetic. All of the liquor bottles were empty including the Tequila that he brought.

"Damn good liquor." Larenzo said to himself as he stared at the empty bottle in amazement.

"Yeah, it's some powerful stuff." A voice from another room answered.

Larenzo was startled at first by the unknown voice answering him. He believed that everyone was fast asleep and he would be able to talk to himself in privacy. Larenzo prided himself on never being caught off guard so he quickly regained his composure and said, "Yep, it sure is. Who's there?"

A figure emerged out of the shadows of a room in the back. The figure belonged to a scrawny guy younger looking than Larenzo. He was dressed in a white t-shirt tucked in a pair of beige khakis. On his feet he wore a pair of scuffed brown penny loafers. Automatically, the figure reminded Larenzo of the few preppies that had attended his High School. He was maybe an inch taller than Larenzo but he slouched slightly and as a result he looked much smaller. He was light-skinned almost the same complexion as Bobby and his light brown hair was cut short like he was in the army and naturally curly. He only had light peach fuzz growing on his chin and his awkward appearance sort of reminded Larenzo of a big kid. The figure seemed nervous for some reason, and his hands hung at his sides almost as though he didn't know what to do with them. His eyes were large as he stared in amazement at Larenzo.

"You don't really remember me but I remember you," The figure began to speak "My name is John Spencer. You came to my class last semester and got Tiffany Allison's phone number. After Tiffany, I saw you at Clark Hall tongue kissing Valencia Williams behind the bushes. Then in front of the Pitt, a week later, I saw you smack Cynthia Mack on the butt in public and she didn't even curse you out. You're like a legend at Blanding University and it's only your second year." John Spencer spoke very properly, not like the rest of the guys that attended Blanding University. He had an almost sophisticated tone to his voice.

"I'm flattered that you been following my long career of womanizing but I don't even know you." Larenzo said plainly. "What the hell are you doing up this time in the morning anyhow? You need to stop following a nigga around and get some sleep." A sound of aggravation was in his voice as he spoke. It was clear that Larenzo believed John Spencer to be some crazy stalker whom had somehow waited up all night to hunt him down. Larenzo began to walk off when John Spencer ran up behind him and grabbed Larenzo softly by the shoulder.

Larenzo jerked his shoulder from John's grasp with ease. "Don't touch me, man!" Larenzo commanded John, his voice became higher from the anxiety of the physical act itself. "I don't know you and you damn well don't know me. So I suggest you let me go and stop following me!" Larenzo was mostly upset that a man that he didn't know had just touched him. His shoulder seemed to be somehow contaminated by the touch of the stranger.

"I didn't come here to follow you around," John said pleading with tears in his eyes. "I admire you and I came here to ask you for advice." Larenzo could tell right away that he was sincere. It surprised Larenzo a little that someone would ask him for advice. Sure Larenzo was considered a ladies man throughout the campus but he never imagined that people would ever ask him for advice on being popular or something equally improbable such as that.

"Advice on what?" Larenzo asked. His anger began to subside as his curiosity grew.

"I want to know how to keep my girl from cheating on me." John said with his head down, almost as if he was ashamed of the statement. "I love my girlfriend and I think she loves me too but I know that she isn't faithful. She's never in the room when I call her and she doesn't even hold my hand in public anymore." John Spencer was actually sobbing as he continued his story. Droplets of water emerged in his eyes as he spoke and his voice became cracked. "I want you to teach me how to become smooth like you. I want her to love me like she used to." John sniffled a little bit then he wiped his face with his white t-shirt.

"Look, I can't help you man. You're in love and you're crying. I don't have any expertise in that field." Larenzo said very coldly as he looked the pathetic figure of John Spencer up and down. "You need a hug or something. I don't do that shit. Maybe you should get a good psychiatrist or something along that line."

Larenzo began to walk off from the sobbing man when John began to plead for help one last time. "Larenzo, you're my last hope. Please help me. My girl's name is Janet Stub. You might remember her. You used to date her roommate last semester." John said in a last ditch effort to keep Larenzo from walking off from him.

When Larenzo heard the name he stopped dead in his tracks. He did recognize the name of John's girlfriend. Larenzo didn't usually remember all of the names of the women that he had ever met but this one girl stuck out more than others. Last semester he was visiting Trish, one of his various "girlfriends," in her dorm and he met her roommate. She was a gorgeous light skinned girl with the body of an hourglass and the face of a model. Her name was Janet Stub. He remembered her name because when she mentioned her last name she would always slap herself on the ass. She used to say it was because her last name was the word butts spelled backward. She was a part time dancer now at Tony's strip club on the outskirts of town. Larenzo had seen the girl dance plenty of times, and he thought that he knew the girl well, but he never imagined that she actually had a boyfriend. One look at John, and Larenzo knew that Janet hadn't told him of her college career choice.

Larenzo turned around and stared at the pitiful figure of John Spencer standing before him. Larenzo knew instantly that Janet Stub was way out of John's league. Chances are she had probably given him a little bit of sex and now he was pussy-whipped. Deep down in Larenzo's cold heart he felt sorry for John. Maybe it was the fact that John's girl was a stripper. Or maybe it was the fact that Larenzo had never seen a grown man cry so freely before tonight. Whatever it was, Larenzo smiled at John and said in a pleasant tone, "Well the first thing that we have to do is get you some new clothes. What are those...penny loafers? You got to be kidding me."

CHAPTER 3

Party Aftermath

The next day was as bright as the day before. Larenzo was the last to go to sleep the night of Red's party and he was the very first to wake up the next day. During his freshmen years, Larenzo's body had become accustomed to sleeping only a few hours a night. Everyone else that spent the night at Red's house was still trying to sleep off there hangovers. Early in the morning, Larenzo jogged to the campus and tried to register for classes. The late fee for registering had went up an additional twenty dollars since yesterday. Nevertheless he stood in line for ten minutes until he finally spoke with the lady in charge of late registration.

There was nothing peculiar about the lady who sat behind the large table at the front of the line. She was a wrinkled middle-aged lady who was slightly overweight. Her hair was colored brownish-gold and a pair of glasses hung loosely at the end of her reddish nose. Larenzo didn't have to even look up to describe her. All of the workers at the university looked the same. Most of them were overworked, underpaid, and the stress of their job showed on their face.

"What do you want?" The lady in charge of registration snapped at Larenzo when she saw he was next in line. It was 9am and she had already had a busy day.

"This is the registration line," Larenzo replied trying to be as polite as possible. "I want to get registered." He then presented the class schedule that he needed to officially be considered a sophomore. She straightened her glasses on her face and began to type some information into the computer. She paused for a moment to look up from her computer with an odd look on her face. Then she jabbed the enter button and a printout began to slowly roll out of the older model printer.

"Here you go Mister Baker. This is your schedule but before I can approve it I need seventy dollars and your school ID." The registration lady gave an obvious fake smile as she spoke.

"I don't have seventy dollars and my school ID was broken during the summer break." Larenzo said trying to sound as pitiful as possible. He wasn't used to asking for anything and he wasn't sure how convincing his begging actually looked.

"Well that's not my problem Mr. Baker," the registration lady said very coldly. "You need to go to Allen Hall and get a ID card first." The lady said as she waved her finger at him. "Then you need to go to the financial aid building for a loan payment on the late fee charge. Then you need to verify and process these classes through your department advisor. But before you can do anything you have to get an identification card so I can verify that you are a student at this university. Understand? Next please." The registration lady said casually dismissing Larenzo and calling the next student in line.

"Hey wait. I don't understand! Why can't you just call Allen Hall and verify that a ID card is already stored with my name and information on it!" A tone of aggravation was clearly noticeable in his voice as he continued to speak to the registration lady. "Every time I register there's always some new shit you guys pull. Why can't we ever get everything we need in one building like the white schools? Why is it that we can't get the same service that they do?" Larenzo said slamming his fist on her desk.

"Sir, don't make me call security," the registration lady interrupted Larenzo's speech abruptly. "It's university policy, sir. Don't get upset at me; take it up with the Dean of the school. Maybe he cares? Like I said earlier, <u>Next Please</u>." The registration lady said decisively ending her argument with Larenzo.

Truthfully, Larenzo expected this from Blanding University. It was the run-around technique and he was by no means a stranger to it. The financial aid building was on the complete opposite end of the campus. Many people believed that Blanding University used this technique to make sure students became acquainted with the campus area and to keep the students in shape. Larenzo believed that Blanding University designed it like that on purpose just to make registration as difficult as possible.

Larenzo took his time and strolled to Allen Hall, occasionally stopping to talk with a few young girls he knew. Larenzo finally reached Allen Hall, where he attempted to obtain his identification card. Allen Hall was a one-floor building whose only purpose was making

ID cards. When he reached the door there was a long line of students, as well as teachers, standing in line waiting for replacement ID cards. Identification cards were important cards at Blanding University for several strange reasons. If you were in a car they wouldn't allow you to drive on campus without one. To visit someone else's dorm you would have to have own one. Even if you wanted to get food from the cafeteria they would ask to see your ID card. For Larenzo the whole idea of an identification card was ridiculous. He didn't believe he needed an ID card at all. He was very well known by teachers, students, and even the security guards around the campus.

A full hour later Larenzo emerged from Allen Hall with a brand new identification card in his wallet. When he stepped outside the searing heat of the South Carolina sun began to beat down on Larenzo. It was already around midday and the sun was at it's strongest. Even with Larenzo's baseball hat tilted over his eyes the sun was blinding in its radiance. Larenzo wiped a few beads of sweat from his forehead and began to walk to the financial aid building located on the far east side of the campus. The insects of the small South Carolina town had become an unendurable nuisance as they swarmed in front of his face. Larenzo cursed to himself under his breath as he slowly sauntered to the financial aid building.

When Larenzo finally made it to the building and his heart leaped for joy when he thought about the air-conditioned interior of the building. He reached for the doorknob of the glass pane door and pulled on it softly at first. When the door didn't bulged he gave it a harder tug and then a fierce yank. In complete misery, Larenzo put his face to the glass door and read the sign that was on the other side. The sign read: OUT FOR LUNCH.

A growl of anger slowly grew in Larenzo as the realization that he had walked from one end of the campus to the other in the South Carolina heat, just to find out that the workers in the financial aid building were out to lunch. A combination of rude workers, hot humid weather, and running around from one building to another had driven Larenzo to the edge of his patience. "Argh!!" A primal yell came from the lips of Larenzo Baker. "Of all the damn time to go to lunch! Would it be too much of a fuckin trouble for one lousy person to stay on duty when everyone else goes to lunch!" Larenzo cursed loudly to himself as he began to walk back to his dorm room located in the middle of the campus.

Halfway to Monroe Hall, an unfamiliar car drove up beside Larenzo as he sluggishly walked down the sidewalk. The car was a green BMW with shaded windows. The car stopped suddenly in front of him and at first Larenzo thought that it might have been someone wanting to get retaliation for the beating that him, Midget Moe, and Bobby gave Travis last night. Larenzo stepped back cautiously with his hands up like a boxer preparing for anything. He was too tired to run from anyone so he decided that if it was Travis or one of his friends he would just have to fight him alone.

Instead of a group of guys jumping out of the car door, the shaded window to the BMW rolled down. The figure of John Spencer was smiling happily like a kid with a new toy inside the expensive car. "Hey Larenzo. It's me, John Spencer. You remember me from the party. Do you need a ride somewhere?"

Larenzo gave a sigh of relief as he realized who was behind the steering wheel of the car. "Woo," Larenzo exhaled when he saw John's friendly face. "Don't you ever scare me like that again. What's wrong wit you sneaking up on a nigga like that? I thought you was that chump that I stomped out last night." Larenzo said relieved that it wasn't Travis and a bunch of his friends.

"Take me back to Red's house." Larenzo said as he opened the door to John's car and hopped in. Larenzo could feel the air condition flow over his body like a mother's gentle kiss as he sat back in the car. Larenzo was originally from Chicago and he wasn't used to the humid weather of South Carolina yet. When the air condition enclosed around his body he naturally relaxed and closed his eyes. By the time Larenzo opened his eyes again John's car was pulling up at Red's house. From outside, the house looked like a hurricane had swept through the front yard. Beer cans and empty plastic cups were scattered all across the lawn.

Larenzo walked through Red's front door first followed closely behind by John Spencer. The inside of his house looked worst than the front lawn. It was clear that nothing had changed since four thirty this morning. Empty plastic cups and puddles of dried up liquor were everywhere. John looked around the living room nervously standing in the open doorway of the house. A look of shock was present on his face as he stared at students still sleeping peacefully from last night's party. Except for Bobby, all of Larenzo's friends were still present. It wasn't surprising that Bobby wasn't there because he was, after all, a family man. He wasn't married but he did have a steady girlfriend and a newborn daughter at home. He had no doubt left late last night to join his girlfriend.

"Shit, close the door nigga. This ain't a barn." Larenzo said to John.

John closed the front door to Red's house and took a small step into the home. "Um, It doesn't look like anyone is awake." John said nervously looking around at several people still sleeping on the couch and on the floor. "Maybe we should come back later on."

"Hell no. It's almost noon they'll wake up soon," Larenzo said as he calmly stepped over a student who was sleeping on the floor. Larenzo was no stranger to the aftermaths of good parties. He tipped toed through the hallways of the house on his way to the kitchen. JC was asleep on a couch in the living room with a young girl curled up beside him. Malik had fallen asleep sitting up against a wall in an almost meditating position. A half smoked roach set undisturbed in an ashtray beside him. Shawna, the girl from the steps of Clark Hall, laid on the floor with her head nestled in his lap. Larenzo walked by Red's partially opened door, which had been locked late last night. He could see that Red was still fast asleep with the naked bodies of two beautiful dark skinned young ladies sleeping quietly on either side of him.

The heat from outside had dehydrated Larenzo and he knew that there was a small possibility that there would be beer left over in the kitchen. "Hey John, do you want some beer? There's a little left over from the party last night." Larenzo inquired as he poured some foam filled beer from the giant keg in the middle of the kitchen.

"No thank you. I don't drink alcohol." John answered.

Larenzo chuckled a little bit when he heard John's proper answer. "Did you just say, no thank you? Where are you from John?" Larenzo asked with a slight look of scorn on his lips. The whole situation disturbed him a little. Larenzo wasn't used to hearing black people speaking so properly. He was also not accustomed to black men not drinking alcohol.

"I was born in Fairfield Connecticut," John said smugly to Larenzo. "I graduated from Heartland High school before I attended college. This is currently my second year at Blanding University." He was very proud of his hometown and it was obvious from the way he spoke that wherever Fairfield was located it was mostly a white neighborhood. He was still nervous but he maintained a very upright posture to his stance. He held his head up high and when he spoke to people he always seemed to look down his nose at them.

Looks of disgust developed on Larenzo's face as he listened to John speak. Larenzo thought that John sounded more like an English butler than a college student attending an African American University. "Listen to yourself. You sound like you're in a interview for a job or something." Larenzo said looking at John oddly. "If your gonna hang around me you got to relax a little. And you're gonna have to drink." Larenzo opened up the refrigerator and grabbed a can of beer. Larenzo quickly shook the beer and tossed it at John.

"But I don't drink." John said nervously as he caught the can of beer clumsily with both hands.

"Hey, that's the rules. If you don't relax when you're around me and drink some beer I can't help you keep your girlfriend from cheating on you." Larenzo said very plainly. "I don't really give a fuck about your relationship with your girl. If you don't drink that beer you can leave right now and we can act like we never even met each other. Or you can drink that beer and we can go about getting your girl to fall deeply in love with you."

John stared down at the cold silver can of Budweiser sitting in his hands. He looked up from the can of beer to see if Larenzo was just fooling around. When he glimpsed upward he saw the determined eyes of Larenzo Baker staring right through him. John knew right then that Larenzo was very serious and the only way that he could get help from Larenzo was to drink from that can of beer. John Spencer swallowed a gulp of his own spit uncomfortably then he opened the top to the can of beer. When he opened the top of the Budweiser can, beer exploded all over the face and clothes of John Spencer.

Larenzo burst out laughing when the built up pressure of beer exploded spraying alcohol all over John. "I can't believe you fell for that one." Larenzo said still laughing uncontrollably. He laughed so hard that tears began to swell up in his eyes.

"Honestly, I can't see how you can find humor in this situation." John said simply.

Hearing John's statement made Larenzo laugh even harder. Larenzo laughed so loudly and freely that he woke one of the slumbering houseguest. JC, who was asleep on the couch, with a young lady lying comfortably beside him, woke up and yawned lazily. Dried up drool had accumulated on the sides of his mouth because he was sleeping with his mouth open.

"A man can't get any sleep around here," JC said wiping the sleep from his eyes. "What time is it?" JC inquired as he reached for his watch lying on the floor beside him.

"It's time to get your lazy ass up." Larenzo jokingly said to JC.

"Anyway, what's all the ruckus about Renzo?" JC said looking at John.

"Ain't nothing," Larenzo replied quickly. "I would like to introduce you to John Spencer from Connecticut. He's having female problems. I'm gonna let him chill with me and the guys for a couple of days."

JC took a moment to stare at the trembling figure of John Spencer. Drenched with beer and standing very uncomfortably in the doorway, JC couldn't help but giggle at his awkward appearance. "He's having female problems? He looks like a female," JC said pointing at John jokingly. "Look at him. He's wasting all of the good beer on the floor."

"I'm sorry. Larenzo told me to open up the can and it...never mind," John, realizing that he was simply confusing the situation more, stopped explaining. "Well, can you help me now?" John asked plainly as he held the open beer can in his hands.

"Yeah, I'll help you. Just stop fucking begging me." Larenzo smiled as he spoke. Truthfully, John's constant whining had begun to bother Larenzo. For a moment, Larenzo wondered if he had taken up too big of a responsibility promising to help John Spencer.

It wasn't before too much longer that everyone began to awaken and things started to return to normal. Everyone had soon gotten up and the house was again alive with the sounds of conversation and laugher. Many of the girls that had slept over began to leave for class. Malik woke up and left for lunch with his girlfriend. He had promised to meet her for lunch and he was already five minutes late. Kel woke up a little bit later and took a shower in the vomit filled bathroom. Midget Moe soon followed scratching his head as he tried to wake himself up. Red woke up last and walked into the living room looking very bewildered. The two women who slept with him last night, now fully dressed, followed closely behind and left through the front door. Red shook his head when he saw the mess that was left over after the party.

"Every single time," Red said pausing slightly as he glanced at the wreckage that used to resemble his living room. "Every single damn time I throw a party the house gets torn up. C'mon guys, let's clean this place up." Red said motioning with his hands for his friends to help him begin cleaning. "You too new guy," Red said looking at John. "No one leaves until this house looks the way it did two days ago."

Since Red's house wasn't that clean two days ago, it didn't take long at all for the small group of friends to get the house organized. Kel kicked out all of the women who weren't helping clean. Larenzo and Midget Moe began picking up the cups and empty beer cans. JC began to sweep and mop the floors and Red took on the responsibility of cleaning the bathroom. After the floors and the bathroom was cleaned up Kel, Midget Moe, Larenzo, and JC sat down to play a game of spades. John Spencer simply pulled up a chair at the table and waited for Larenzo to finish.

Larenzo and Kel played on one team against Midget Moe and JC. Kel and Larenzo were the reigning Spades Champions at Blanding University, and considered themselves unbeatable. Even with Midget Moe's occasional cheating, the game was fast and brutal. As with all card games that took place at Red's house, it was filled with trash talking, profanity, and card slapping. Kel and Larenzo, as usual, left the card table victorious.

CHAPTER 4

Relationships

Malik's mother's Cadillac quickly sped toward the campus at break-neck speeds. Malik swerved through traffic recklessly as he made his way to the campus. He glanced at his watch and momentarily lost control of the steering wheel, almost hitting a parked car. He quickly gained control again, realizing that he almost wrecked his mother's car and slowed down just a little.

Malik wanted to treat Ebony as though she was something rare. To him she wasn't like other girls on the campus. She was special. She was an all-natural black woman and she deserved the best. He hated breaking promises to Ebony. It made her feel like he wasn't treating her like she deserved to be treated and he hated it. Malik truly loved her with his heart and soul and deep down it upset him that he had became drunk and fallen asleep last night over Red's house. Malik also didn't like telling Ebony untruths. He told her that he was going to call her last night when he got home and he didn't call. Now, he was supposed to meet her for lunch at 12:30 and he was late. Most of all he didn't like to see the look of disappointment in Ebony's eyes. She would say that she understood, as is a woman's role, but Malik knew that not being able to depend on her boyfriend bothered her greatly. He knew that she deserved a man who could give her everything she wanted and he was determined to be that man.

It was 12:42 before Malik finally parked in front of the cafeteria. He rushed into the cafeteria and his light hazel eyes darted around the room, scanning for his girlfriend. The cafeteria was packed as usual; the same students filled the building everyday at the same time. Malik thought once again of sheep grazing peacefully in a pasture and he laughed to himself. The mass of students talked loudly between each other eating happily on government prepared welfare food. The school fed the students just enough to keep them alive and the food was never very nutritious.

Malik smiled when he heard Ebony's voice over the roar of the rest of the student body. He practically leaped in the air when he spotted Ebony from across the room. She had nearly finished half of her lunch and a partially empty plate of food was across the table from her. A feeling of horror spread through his body followed quickly by a sensation of jealously. Feelings of anger built in his body when he saw her half eaten plate of food. She had always waited for him in the past. Usually she would wait for him before she ate, even when he was a few minutes late, this time she had eaten lunch without him and to make things even worse, with someone else. The sensation of jealousy ran through his mind when he imagined another man eating beside his girlfriend. His eyes lit up with genuine joy when he saw that a female friend of hers filled the seat occupied across the lunch table from Ebony.

"Over here Malik," Ebony yelled across the room to Malik. "I want you to meet one of my new friends." Ebony stood up from her chair and motioned for Malik to come and join them.

Malik walked over quietly and sat next to his girlfriend and kissed her on the cheek. When he kissed her she turned her head slightly, like she was embarrassed that he had kissed her in public. He knew that she was upset with him for being late, but he never imagined that she would ever turn her head from one of his kisses. He would have been angry, but he then realized that he was still in the clothes, which he wore yesterday and that he didn't brush his teeth this morning. He checked his breath, blowing into his palm, when he didn't think either of them was looking. A little embarrassed about the situation himself he simply sat back in his chair quietly.

"Malik, this is Cynthia. Cynthia is a freshman from California and this is her first time in South Carolina. You don't mind if she eats with us? She lives across the hallway from me in the dorm," Ebony said smiling gleefully.

Malik took a moment to look Ebony's lunch companion up and down. Cynthia was a very beautiful lady only nineteen years old. Her hair was jet black and braided in long strands down her back. Her skin had a golden tone about it that resonated from her body. Her large innocent brown eyes had a little bit of eye shadow above them like pictures of Egyptian queens. A ring stylishly protruded from above her left eyebrow. Her body was shaped very well. Her breasts were large and curved perfectly in her tight white tank top, which was cut so her flat stomach and navel piercing were exposed. Her plump lips were curvy and very attractive.

"What's up Cynthia?" Malik said trying not to undress her too much with his eyes as he spoke. Malik tried to remind himself of how much he loved Ebony when he glimpsed Cynthia's body. She was very beautiful, but Malik refused to allow his eyes to roam toward her luscious breast or her plump alluring lips anymore.

"Cynthia this is Malik Brown, my boyfriend." Ebony said finishing the introductions. An enthusiasm was present in her voice that Malik hadn't heard in a long time. The last time that he recalled hearing that tone in her voice she was introducing him to her parents. Malik glanced at Ebony as she spoke, managing to take his eyes off of Cynthia's well-developed body.

"Hello Malik, it's good to meet you," Cynthia said as she extended her hand to Malik. "I've heard a lot about you and it's all good." Cynthia smiled as she spoke like a salesperson would. Malik thought her smile was large, bright, and flirtatious in its friendliness. When Cynthia smiled Malik noticed for the first time that Cynthia had a small silver tongue ring.

"Pleasure to meet you." Malik said courteously as he shook her hand. At that exact moment, Ebony's facial expression changed from extreme happiness to what Malik believed was a hint of jealousy. Realizing the change in her appearance, Malik decided to force himself not to look at Cynthia for the rest of the lunch.

The trio spent the rest of the lunch basically in silence. Within a few minutes, both of the females had finished their lunch and Malik then escorted them back to the dorm. Once outside of Clark Hall, Cynthia gave Malik an intimate hug and then hugged Ebony closely. "I'll see you upstairs later Eb," Cynthia proclaimed as she ran up the stairs and into the dormitory.

Malik watched in silence as Cynthia ran up the stairs and into the dorm. Once she had disappeared behind the walls of Clark Hall, Malik turned all of his attention toward his girlfriend. When he turned around to look into Ebony's large bedroom eyes, he saw only aggravation and anger building up in what are usually passionately filled eyelids. Her whole demeanor had changed within seconds. Malik was caught off guard by the look of pure hatred now boiling in Ebony's eyes. Only mere moments ago, Ebony seemed to be happy to see him and now she was furious with him for some strange reason. Her stare wasn't the only aspect that bothered Malik, Ebony crossed her arms over her chest and her lips curled up in an almost sneer like pose.

"What?" Malik exclaimed, acknowledging the obvious anger present in the eyes of his girlfriend. "I know you're mad about something. Just tell me what I did." He used the little boy voice that she loved so much. Usually, the voice would have been enough to get his way, but there was something else in the tone of his voice. There was a definite sincerity present in his voice. He genuinely cared about Ebony's feelings and it was apparent by the tone of his voice that he didn't have any idea what he did wrong.

Noticing his tone of sincerity, Ebony smiled slightly trying not to forget her anger. When he spoke like that Ebony couldn't help but fall in love with him all over again. She tapped her right foot on the ground impatiently and stared at him angrily. His thin face with his keen nose, and his deep hazel eyes, was a black woman's fantasy. His eyes were always the catcher for Ebony. They were entrancing in their fullness and with one good stare he was always able to make her do anything he wished.

Ebony quickly turned her head from Malik's piercing gaze and puckered her mouth in a tight frown. "Don't look at me like that. You know damn well what you did. Or better yet, what you didn't do," she squinted up her nose and looked at Malik with a new intensity in her eyes more fierce than before, then continued. "Malik, you didn't call me last night and you said you were. Then you show up at lunch late and your drooling all over my friend. One top of everything else, your wearing the same clothes you had on yesterday and lipstick is on your collar. How could you embarrass me like that in front of Cynthia?"

A feeling of shock ran through Malik's spine when he heard her accusation. He checked his collar and sure enough there was a tinge of red lipstick on the collar of his shirt. He knew instantly where the lipstick originated. Memories of Red's party vividly rushed back into Malik's mind. When he was dancing with Shawna last night she rubbed up against his shoulder and since he fell asleep at Red's house because of the excessive amount of alcohol and marijuana in his system he forgot to call Ebony. He didn't have sex with Shawna last night; she slept beside him on the floor. But he knew that Ebony wouldn't understand the truth no matter how far fetched it was. His mind raced for a reasonable explanation for the lipstick on his collar but he couldn't think of anything.

On the verge of tears Ebony began to run up the stairs in front of the dorm. When she rushed pass Malik he gripped her by the arm momentarily keeping her from leaving. "I got really drunk at Red's party but I didn't do anything." Malik blurted out the truth explaining unconvincingly, "Let me explain Ebony. I would never cheat on you. You got to trust me." Malik was almost pleading now; the strong black militant persona, which usually described him so well, had disappeared. In the black militant's place stood only a man in love trying to make the woman he loved believe him.

Ebony yanked her arm from his grasp and ran up the stairs to her dormitory. When she reached the doorway of the building she turned around and looked at Malik's pitiful figure standing at the bottom of the stairs. Her voice was trembling as she spoke, "Malik I trusted you and you threw it all away when you cheated on me. I hope she was worth it." With those final words, tears began to roll down Ebony's full cheeks. When the droplets hit the ground she spun around on her heels, walked through the doorway and slammed the front door to the dorm.

At that exact moment on the other end of town, another member of the group of friends began to have relationship problems of his own. Bobby lived in a cozy two-bedroom apartment a few blocks away from the campus with his girlfriend Terry and his seven-month-old daughter Sheena. Bobby was late for his Calculus class already and he knew that bickering with Terry would only make him later. Her voice could be heard echoing through the walls of there small home, "Bobby are you listening to me? You never listen to me!"

Bobby ignored her loud shouts of anger as he prepared to leave his home for class. He began to speedily pack his book bag on his bed while he argued slightly with his girlfriend. His girlfriend was a light skinned beautiful woman a little bit younger than him. She had given birth to his child and still she maintained the small youthful figure that first attracted him. As she yelled at him, her usual pecan skin complexion turned red with anger. Their seven-month-old daughter crawled on the floor playing with some toys in their bedroom. She had experienced these sorts of arguments before between her parents. For the toddler these sorts of fights had become routine. She played happily with her Barbie doll ignoring the yelling of her parents.

Bobby's girlfriend, Terry, was so upset that her face actually turned bright red as she yelled hysterically at him. Her hair had a natural red sheen to it, which perfectly blended with her blushed complexion. Small freckles covered by a light shade of makeup slightly appeared on both of her cheeks as she chased behind Bobby from one room of the small apartment to another. Bobby hated arguing with his girlfriend in front of his daughter. It reminded him of his mother and father fighting in his youth. They would argue about pointless trivial things only to make up later on in the week. It was ridiculous when he was a child and now he was arguing with his girlfriend in the same ridiculous fashion. To him the whole discussion seemed pointless. Who really cared whether he vacuumed the floor before class or after he returned? A look of frustration formed on his face as his girlfriend's voice began to get louder and louder to an almost shrieking sound.

Bobby had cheated on Terry plenty of times before but the arguments were never about that. She never found out about any of his several escapades with different women. Bobby was too much in control to ever allow her to find out about his one-night stands around the campus. No, for Terry the arguments were always about paying a bill late, housecleaning, or not paying her enough attention when she was talking. Bobby realized that he loved her because he had never taken that much grief from any other women in his life.

Without yelling at Terry in any type of way, Bobby picked his daughter up from the carpeted floor and kissed her lovingly on the cheek. "Sheena, I want you to take care of Mommy, okay baby. She's mad at Daddy but he doesn't have any time to play with her. Daddy has to go to class and make you proud of him. Bye bye, Sheena. Say bye bye for Daddy." Bobby said using his best baby voice for his daughter. Showing her two baby teeth, his daughter smiled from ear to ear then said trying to imitate the words bye bye but it sounded more like buh bah. Bobby grinned when he heard the attempt at speech escape from her infant lips.

His daughter smiled joyfully when Bobby held her high in his hands and talked to her in a baby voice. His daughter resemblance to Terry's facial features was uncanny. She even had a small set of freckles on both of her cheeks. When his daughter would look into Bobby's face, her light brown eyes filled with a gold light, if but for one moment. Bobby would have thought that he didn't contribute any genes to the baby at all, but Sheena did have a small dimple on the right side of her mouth when she smiled. He was certain that she had inherited that dimple from him and joy filled his heart whenever he saw her smile. It was that smile that kept Bobby from ever truly considering leaving Terry. Bobby loved his daughter more than life itself and on occasion when he felt like leaving his girlfriend he would look into the almond shaped eyes of his daughter and realized that he couldn't live without her.

"Bobby, I asked you to vacuum the carpet this morning and it's still not done. All I'm asking you to do is help me out a little bit around the house. I can't even get that much from you! Now you're ignoring me again." Her eyes blazed with fury as Bobby ignored her statement. "Don't you dare ignore me when I'm talking to you. I hate that!" Terry's head bobbed from side to side as she yelled at him. Bobby knew that she hated when he ignored her but he didn't see any easy way out of an argument with her, besides simply walking away from her. Bobby threw his book bag over his shoulders and turned to leave for class. When Bobby turned his back to Terry an uncontrollable fury engulfed her small body forcing her to react. She ran in front of him standing between him and the front door. "You think that you can just leave me here with Sheena and everything will be alright. Don't ignore the problem Bobby. There's a definite problem in our relationship and I won't let you just walk out this door like you walked out on your responsibilities to this family." As the words left Terry's mouth a menacing look came to her face. Terry's words were as cruel as she knew how to make them. She was determined to make Bobby stay in the house however she could.

"I don't have any time for this, Terry. I'm late for class," Bobby began to speak but Terry's yelling drowned out any chance of his words being heard.

"Bobby you always treat me like this," Terry continued. "I'm sick and tired of being your personal slave! If you…"

"Get the fuck out of the way!" Bobby cursed cutting off her flow of words. His anger was finally getting the better of him as the profanity slipped easily from his lips. He didn't like raising his voice to Terry and he liked cursing at her even less. It felt like he was losing control of the situation, like he was losing control of the relationship.

"Why don't you make me get out the way," Terry said continuing her constant nagging. "I put off my career. I put off school. I put off a year of my life to have your child and now you treat me like I'm a housemaid that you can just boss around." Terry's anger was building to a climax and she didn't even try to deny the sensation slowly throbbing in her. She pointed her finger inches away from Bobby's eyeball as she cursed obscenities at him. "You stingy bastard! I had a life before I met you and now you want to just turn your back on me like you did your other girlfriends. I'm not one of those other bitches, I'm the mother of your child." Tears were in her eyes as she spoke. Bobby wanted to laugh at the ridiculousness of her statement. So easily did she call herself a bitch that she didn't even register her own words?

Bobby had heard enough of her crying and nagging. He shoved her gently on the shoulder so he could reach the doorknob. When he touched the doorknob Terry balled up both of her fists and pushed Bobby hard in the chest. The force of her push caught Bobby off guard and he stumbled backward. Flashbacks of his youth took over Bobby King's mind. Bobby reacted instinctively to the push and swiftly slapped Terry hard across the face. Terry fell to the floor instantly when the back of his hand collided against her fragile cheek. Her body crumbled to the carpeted floor of the apartment and curled up defensively in a fetal position. A combination of pain from her face and a hurt originating in her soul had weakened her knees dropping her body at his feet. She held her mouth trying to stop the blood trickling from her busted lip. The thought that Bobby would hit her was far more painful than any slap he could ever give.

"Terry!" a shout of panic escaped from Bobby's lips when he saw what horrible act he had done. He had struck her down like she was a common tramp on the street trying to steal a dollar from him. As soon as his hand slammed into her soft face, visions of his father slapping his mother rushed into his mind. He was three maybe four years old when it happened, only a child, but he remembers it vividly like it was yesterday. He knew that it was pimp instincts passed down genetically from his father and grandfathers. A curse passed on through the generations that he had to fight with every waking second of the day. Bobby hated the fact that he had to fight these instincts every time he argued with Terry. Then a terrible thought ran through his frantic mind. What about his child? Would these images of torment torture her in the future as she dated? Would she remember the time that her daddy hit her mother?

He glanced at his daughter playing on the floor quietly a few feet away from her mother. Sheena was staring right at him. As he gazed into her innocent eyes, a sensation of weakness flooded over his body. He had never hit her before and he decided right then that he would damn well never hit her again. His right hand began to tremble as he contemplated the seriousness of his actions. He had tried very hard to not be like his father but some habits are harder to break than others.

Bobby loved Terry with all of his heart but it seemed that for the briefest of moments his natural instincts took over. It was almost as if he didn't mean to hit her at all. The loud noise of her yelling and the fact that he was already late for class combined with the fact that he didn't want to get into a fight while his daughter watched had become too much for senses. All of these factors added up creating a tension filled environment. The tension had gotten the better of Bobby King this time. These were just a few thousand excuses that came to his mind all at once why he hit her. But no matter how many excuses he could come up with, none of them seemed good enough to explain why he would hit his girlfriend of three years and the mother of his child. He hated the fact that he had hit Terry and for the first time since he was an adolescent, Bobby King dropped to his knees and cried tears of sorrow.

When Terry saw that Bobby was kneeling on the floor crying beside her it made her weep even more. When she cried harder Bobby cried harder and together they sat on the floor crying. The whole experience was rejuvenating in its pureness. The more they cried it seemed that the tears cleansed away the sins of the deed and with it came a sort of redemption. They embraced, and in that intimate hug of tears, all of their recent sins were washed away.

Terry had never seen Bobby cry before and she realized then that he would never lay his hands on her again. Bobby had always carried himself as a pimp and he would have never imagined crying in front of a woman before. The sensuality of the experience was more than he could take and no matter how hard he tried he couldn't keep the tears from falling from his eyes. With a large amount of difficulty, Bobby began to speak, "T...Terry, I love...love you and Sheena more than anything else in the world. I would never hurt you on purpose. I swear to God that I'll never hit you again. Please forgive me." His voice was cracked and trembling.

"I love you too." Terry said affectionately as she burst into tears once again.

Bobby never made it to class that day. For the rest of the evening Bobby and Terry embraced each other sobbing softly in each other's arms. Their daughter even crawled over and sat quietly with the couple. For Bobby, his family meant more to him than anything else on the planet. His family meant more then class, and more than various one-night stands, and if his girlfriend wanted him to stay with her that's where he meant to stay.

CHAPTER 5

Lesson #1

By three thirty in the afternoon, Red's home was cleaner than before the back-to-school party ever occurred and the spades game that was being played slowly came to a finish. An hour later, Larenzo and John had made their way back toward campus. Larenzo stared out of John's car window moodily as John's green BMW drove swiftly back onto campus. John spoke in a friendly tone about the weather and how very much he loved Janet. Of course, Larenzo faked paying attention as politely as possible. At that exact moment, Larenzo decided that John's constant blabbing and incessant whining over his girlfriend had become too much for his senses to deal with any longer.

"Hey John," Larenzo said interrupting John Spencer in mid-speech. "Would you shut the fuck up about the heat? It's South Carolina in August, of course it's going to be hot outside. Do me a favor and drive by Haines Hall. I'm gonna give you your very first lesson."

Haines Hall was an upper classmen dormitory. It was the largest female dorm on the campus and also the largest skyscraper in the small southern town that Blanding University rested in. It housed over two hundred young women inside it's brick walls at all times day and night. It was designed like a huge fourteen story tower that reached up disappearing far into the blue sky. The dorm was commonly referred to as the "castle" because of the quality of women that resided within. The castle was home to the cheerleading squad, student body officers, and the Homecoming Queens of Blanding University.

John parked in front of Haines Hall and looked at Larenzo curiously. John had never been this close to Haines Hall before and his uncertainty showed in the beads of sweat beginning to grow on his forehead. His grip tightened on the steering wheel as he parked the car in front of the female dormitory. Larenzo got out first and then John slowly followed his lead.

"What are we doing here?" John nervously mumbled after a short pause. "Janet lives in Allen Hall." Fear was clearly present in his trembling voice as he spoke. Larenzo could hear it in his voice and when he did, he knew that this was going to be a long day. Larenzo understood that John was scared but John needed special attention that only Haines Hall could possibly provide for him.

"Alright John, you asked me to help you get your girlfriend back so I'm gonna help you." Larenzo said as he confidently gazed up at Haines Hall in all of its glory. "This, Mr. John Spencer is Haines Hall," Larenzo said using a voice that made the building sound like a big deal. "There are exactly two hundred and nine young and horny African American women that live inside. You, on the other hand, are a young African American man. You understand what I'm getting at?"

"No." John answered honestly.

Larenzo gave a long sigh when he heard John's answer. He knew then that his earlier assessment was correct; this was going to be a whole lot harder than he intended. Larenzo looked at John's nervous figure and quickly critiqued his clothes. "Nope. That will not do at all," Larenzo shook his head as he looked at John's clothing in disgust. "Listen, this is the big leagues kid." Larenzo said sounding like a baseball coach rooting his players on. "You have to look at yourself as though you're a hunter and women are the big game. Before we can go inside you have to pull your shirt out of your pants. To properly hunt women you have to be completely calm at all times and you don't look at ease at all."

John quickly pulled his white t-shirt from his khakis and looked at Larenzo feeling unsure about his new style. To him he looked sloppy with his shirt hanging out of his pants, but he wouldn't tell Larenzo what he thought for fear that he wouldn't help him anymore. "Are you sure about this?" John said tentatively with his arms out.

"Yeah. Better, but not quite perfect." Larenzo said still staring at John's clothes. "One of the most important things women look at are your shoes. A man's shoes say a lot about him and woman know this fact. When a man's shoes are scuffed or worn down a woman sees that and automatically knows that he doesn't care about his appearance or he doesn't have a car and is walking. Both are bad. If you don't care about yourself what makes her think that you'll give a damn about her. And if you don't have a means of transportation you won't be able to take her anywhere." Larenzo paused for a second trying to think of anything else he might have forgotten, and then he continued. "Also the newer your shoes the better. Women keep track of the new male shoes more than guys do. Take Red for example, he buys the newest Jordan's before they even come out. With me, I don't have as much money as he does, so I either buy Timberland boots or Addidas classics. Those types of shoes never really go out of style and it's hard for them to get scuffed."

"Now look at your shoes," Larenzo said looking down at John's foot apparel. "You got a pair of penny loafers on. You can't pick up any women in those. Here, slip on my boots," Larenzo said as he slid off his boots easily and handed them to John. "Well what are you waiting on? Don't worry about it; I got an extra pair of sneakers in a friend's room in this dorm. I'll be alright, now take off your shoes."

A look of doubt ran through John's mind when he saw the large military style boots in Larenzo's hands. "But Larenzo it's August," John said shyly staring at the boots. "Don't you think that it's a little bit too hot to wear boots in this weather?" John inquired.

John's question disturbed Larenzo greatly. Larenzo was already considering not helping John and now that he was questioning his authority, Larenzo became angry with him. "Do you want me to help you or not?" Larenzo said aggravated that John had questioned his sense of style. "What? Are my shoes not good enough for you? Trust me. Women like it if you're a little different from everyone else."

John didn't question Larenzo anymore as he took off his shoes and laced up Larenzo's boots. Larenzo's boots were a larger shoe size than John's penny loafers, yet John put them on without complaining. John wiggled his toes happily in the boots trying to get a feel for the larger shoes.

"Okay. Now you look comfortable. How do you feel?" Larenzo said as he looked at John's new look.

"I feel comfortable." John said untruthfully.

"You're lying." Larenzo said inspecting John, closer now than before. "But you do look comfortable and for right now that's what counts. Now that you're dressed for your first lesson we can finally begin. Now there is only one main rule to remember when you're trying to understand the opposite sex. Women are emotional creatures and that they want to have sex with you as much as you do them. The only thing that they're waiting for is for you to approach them. Now you also have to remember that how you approach them is as important as <u>whom</u> you approach." Larenzo paused for a moment to see a confused look emerge on John's face.

"I know that I'm going at an accelerated pace. You'll just have to trust me." Larenzo said reassuringly. "Now your very first lesson will be learning that women are emotional creatures by nature. They don't think rationally like us, and in that fact, men have always had the advantage in the battle of the sexes. When you have sex with a woman, if you do it right, you not only please her physically but emotionally as well. Once you're in their emotional cipher they'll do absolutely anything for you." A glimmer of light shined in Larenzo's eye as he spoke. John on the other hand, stared up at the "castle" in complete awe.

"Pay attention," Larenzo commanded. "Why does your girl cheat on you?" Before John could speak Larenzo had already answered for him. "You have no idea why your girl cheats on you, but I do. See John, your girlfriend is a woman and as a woman she has been taught since infancy to manipulate the minds of men."

"No. Not Janet." John blurted out. "We love each other. It's just on some occasions she seems so distant, like she's thinking about leaving me." John stated honestly. His words had once again nearly brought him to tears.

The sight of John on the brink of tears sickened Larenzo. Larenzo believed that a man should never cry no matter what the situation was. It just wasn't proper for a black man to cry in public, especially over a woman. Even worst than the idea that a grown man could cry that easily was the fact that John always used the word love to describe his relationship. Just the mention of the word love made Larenzo want to vomit. Larenzo had fallen in love years ago, manipulated by a woman, and then cast into the winds when his usefulness was finally over. To Larenzo, Janet Stub was just some faceless stripper who had manipulated the mind of some poor kid. But according to John, the Janet Stub he knew was a different person entirely. She was a vibrant young lady whom he loved and planned to spend the rest of his life with.

A look of revulsion flashed across Larenzo's face when he heard John mention the word love again. When Larenzo heard the word love mentioned again he speedily continued his lessons. "Lesson two. Don't ever use the word love ever again. It's a female word. Many men view it as a weakness, and women beg for you to use it. The very first time you use the word in front of your girlfriend, she thinks that she has you. Remember that the word love for a woman equals the word commitment. So even if you do think that you might be falling in love, never admit it to her.

"Love is a manipulation word. For example, it might start off like you saying I love your cooking but for the woman their subconscious registers it the same as saying you love them. You might not have even told them that you loved them but they'll believe you did. Before you know it they'll be saying that they love you too. Here's where women use this little fact to their advantage. When someone tells you that they love you, your natural impulse is to say I love you too. It's something that our grandparents and mothers instilled in us since we were young. We might not even think that we're in love but we'll say the phrase because that's what we've been taught. Understand?" Larenzo asked to make sure he didn't lose John's attention.

"I think so." John said nodding his head yes.

"Good. Now that you have the basics, I can begin to help you," Larenzo said grinning slyly. "In every relationship there is a manipulator and there's someone who gets manipulated. In order to keep Janet from cheating on you, you must take the role as a manipulator in the relationship. Currently, you're in love with her but in order to save your relationship you have to separate yourself from love completely. Once you've fallen out of love you'll be able to better control the relationship."

Larenzo became very serious as he continued the rest of the lesson, "Now your very first assignment on your way to falling out of love is to have sex with someone else." A wicked glimmer of light shined in Larenzo's eyes as he spoke. "It's really a very simple theory. When Janet realizes that other women on the campus desire you sexually she'll start paying you more attention, hence paying her other men less attention." Suddenly, the wind seemed to get cooler and John shivered slightly when he saw the look in Larenzo's eyes. John had never seen that look in a man's eyes before. The look in

Larenzo's eyes was that of determination. It was this look of determination that chilled John Spencer on that warm August evening.

A million thoughts rushed through John's mind at that moment. What if Larenzo was right and the only way for him to save the relationship was for him to cheat on her? Was this the only way to keep Janet faithful? Before today John Spencer would never have imagined that he would ever contemplate cheating on his girlfriend. John realized that he loved Janet too much to ever seriously consider it but for right now he was going to go along with Larenzo's plan.

"But why did you choose Haines Hall over all of the other dorms?" John asked staring up at the magnitude of the enormous building. The sheer height of the building against the light blue evening skyline was enough to intimidate anyone who wasn't a veteran to Haines Hall. For John, the sight of Haines Hall seemed even more frightful. If Janet even found out that he was in Haines Hall looking for women it could very well mean the end of his relationship.

"The reason why I picked Haines Hall is simple. No matter what anyone says, women do talk about sex. Since you obviously haven't slept with any other women on the campus your street value hasn't been measured yet. It's like building a resume. You need experience first. Depending on who you receive experience from, your street value goes up. Haines Hall has the most popular and the best looking women on the campus. If you sleep with a few of them you'll be known across the campus in no time at all," Larenzo explained still smiling wildly.

Larenzo motioned for John to follow him and together they journeyed into Haines Hall a.k.a. "the castle." Haines Hall was the newest and largest dorm on the campus. A gush of air-conditioned wind comforted their heat-exhausted bodies as they entered the "castle's" hallowed hallways. The inside of Haines Hall was well lit unlike the gloomy male dormitories. It also had wall-to-wall blue carpet, and a big screen television, with a VCR on top, sat in the corner. Taped reruns of soap operas played silently as Larenzo and John walked toward the front counter. Unlike the other dormitories on the campus, Haines Hall was exceptionally clean. It was estimated that the university spent a quarter of a million dollars of its already miniscule budget, to build, maintain, and furnish the dormitory.

Even with only a pair of white socks covering his feet, Larenzo walked calmly with a slow stride to his step. His confidence soared as he approached the R.A. in the main lobby. John, on the other hand, tentatively paced behind the confident figure of Larenzo.

The R.A. glanced up from her desk as Larenzo strolled towards her. Larenzo only half-heartedly smiled at her when he saw who it was. He had slept with her the previous semester and now he could barely remember her last name. Their relationship ended when she took the job of R.A. and had a chance to witness firsthand how many women Larenzo had become sexually acquainted with in Haines Hall alone. "Hey Larenzo. I love the new style," she said cockily looking at Larenzo's shoeless feet. "Who do you want to page downstairs tonight?" she inquired in a voice that hid her true envious feelings. She was a dark skinned woman about five foot five. She wore a silk blouse and her hair was cut short and bobbed around her ears. Her makeup was plastered on and she had the fragrance of chocolate about her. She peered at Larenzo through a pair of wire-framed eyeglasses that sat on the edge of her nose.

As he stood in front of her, Larenzo could feel her eyes running up and down his body. A sense of pride spread through Larenzo at that moment. For a second he felt like a prize wining racehorse sent out to stud. He realized that she still wanted him even after he neglected to call her for weeks at a time. Larenzo knew that he had treated her wrong in the past, but the sex was excellent and sometimes sex is what keeps women going back to a man that they know is no good for them.

Larenzo smiled deviously and his voice became slightly lower. "What up Nicky? Call Crystal Kerry down from the tenth floor and tell her to bring the sneakers that I left upstairs in her room," Larenzo said flirtatiously to her. He enjoyed playing with the minds of women, and he was good at it. He didn't intend to talk to her again but he still enjoyed the reaction he could get from her by simply showing her a little bit of interest.

She relaxed instantly, her memories reliving the time that they spent together when she heard his voice. The woman wet her lips, then picked up the phone and called upstairs to Crystal. "Hey Crystal, I got Renzo downstairs. Yeah, he wants you to bring his sneakers down, too. Okay bye. She'll be down in a moment," the woman said staring into Larenzo's eyes intensely.

"Appreciate it. I'll wait over here," Larenzo said coldly. He felt uncomfortable all of a sudden as she stared at him through her glassy eyes. Her stare made her appear desperate and her sexual appeal seemed to disappear in that desperation. Larenzo and John sat on a nearby couch in front of the elevator and waited patiently for their visitor to arrive.

It wasn't too long before the elevator door sounded and Crystal Kerry walked out. Crystal was the head cheerleader for the university, a member of Alpha Kappa Alpha sorority, and the sophomore class secretary. Crystal Kerry's skin was like smooth golden brown sugar. Her youthful breasts, firm and tender, stood straight out without any sag. Her long silky dark brown hair hung to the middle of her back. She was dressed in a pair of low-cut boxer shorts, which fit snuggly around her thick thighs, and in a tight white cheerleading t-shirt. Her nipples protruded slightly from underneath the shirt. Her feet were covered with white sneakers, which she often used when she cheered. At first sight, she aroused both Larenzo and John with her revealing outfit.

She smiled at Larenzo when she stepped off of the elevator. In her right hand she held a pair of black sneakers dangling by the laces. Still smiling at Larenzo she put her left hand on her hip and cocked her head to the side arrogantly. "You got some nerve Renzo. You didn't call me all summer break and you didn't even invite me to the back-to-school jam. Now you decide to show up unexpectedly and the first thing you ask for are your sneakers." As she spoke her neck bobbed and twisted from right to left angrily.

Dumb ghetto bitch, thought Larenzo Baker. All she wanted was someone to pay her attention. She wanted Larenzo to beg and apologize for not calling, and he knew that she would then have sex with him anyhow. Larenzo had played these mind-games with girls like her for years. Larenzo believed that women played these little mind games to help them feel better about themselves. She wanted him too think of her as a prize that must be won, not a free sample whore that he could have sex with whenever he was around.

Larenzo motioned with his hands for her. "Crystal, come over here baby. You know I been busy."

Before he was done speaking, she had begun to walk over to him. She walked with her head high in the air, with a proud step, knowing well that she was in her prime. She walked more like a princess than a student. "Why do you even have a cell phone if you don't turn it on?" she inquired still a little angry at Larenzo's complete disregard of her.

With skillful hands Larenzo reached around her waist and began to slowly massaging her lower back between the top of her buttocks and the small of her back. It was one of her many secret erogenous zones. Her entire body relaxed as his fingers sensually massaged her hot zone freely. Larenzo knew every sexual portion of her lean body and he realized that she couldn't stay angry with him for long. As he steadily massaged her back he pulled her close to his body and slowly nibbled her on the ear, allowing his tongue to linger around her earlobe caressing it gently. The sensation of Larenzo's tongue inside the inner sanctuary of her ear sent a sexual chill down Crystal's spine. After the long kiss on her ear Larenzo whispered some words to her and then took his sneakers from her hand patting her lightly on the ass.

Crystal blushed slightly as Larenzo took his shoes from her and slid them onto his feet without lacing them up. Obviously holding her breath during the exchange, Crystal exhaled gently before she began to speak. "I don't know why I put up with you Renzo?" she said in a little lost girl voice, fully realizing that Larenzo was no good for her.

"You know why," Larenzo said with confidence very softly in her ear.

"Yeah I do," she whispered admitting the truth to him. "Now who's your cute friend?" Crystal said inspecting John from the top of his curly head to the black soles of Larenzo's boots. John stood completely motionless not saying anything as Crystal stared at him. "Is he a freshman?" Crystal asked not recognizing his face from any of the football games or parties.

"Naw," Larenzo answered quickly. "He's not a freshman, he's a transfer student from Connecticut." Larenzo said with a straight face lying easily to Crystal. It was death to be a freshman at Blanding University. Larenzo realized that freshmen rarely ever were accepted by the upper classmen. On the other hand, if he had told her that

John was a sophomore like herself, and that she didn't know him, the consequences would have been terrible. She would have thought of him as unpopular, which would have also equaled death. For Larenzo's plan to work perfectly, John would have to play along and trust him.

"This is my boy, John, and I want to show him a good time while he's in Haines Hall. He's gonna be chilling with me. Could you hook him up with one of your cheerleading friends for his first night at Blanding?" Larenzo's words were more of a request than a question.

Crystal's eyes looked John up and down once again, and then she said, "Sure. I got the perfect girl for you." Crystal was staring now at John's newly acquired boots. "Her name is Mary. She's on the cheerleading squad with me."

"Is she upstairs?" Larenzo asked becoming impatient.

"Yeah. She's in my room," Crystal said.

"Great. Then sign us up," Larenzo responded quickly.

John shook his head dumbfoundly. Things were happening too fast for him. In mere minutes he had followed Larenzo inside "the castle" and met face to face with one of the most popular girls on campus. For a moment, John simply stood motionless with his mouth open in amazement. Then as if his senses suddenly rushed back to him, John began to speak, "Are we going upstairs?" John asked trying very hard to hide his fear of Haines Hall.

"Hell yeah, we're going upstairs." Larenzo said ecstatically pressing the up button on the wall panel.

Crystal turned to the RA in the main office and waved, "Nicky, I'm taking Renzo and his friend upstairs." Crystal grinned an artificial smile as she spoke making sure to show all of her well-kept teeth. Her smile had a dazzling whiteness to it, which came from long periods of brushing every night before a game. Nicky sat forward in her chair and waved happily at Crystal. Other men had to sign a roll sheet and give the RA a form of picture identification. But for Larenzo and his many of his friends, the rules were always bent, sometimes even broken. Since Larenzo was so well known on campus, Nicky allowed him free access upstairs even though it might one day cost her the job of RA. As the trio walked into the elevator, Nicky tried not to imagine how Larenzo had used her sexually and tossed her to the wind when he was done with her.

Crystal, Larenzo, and John quickly entered the small elevator. Crystal pressed the button for the fourteenth floor. Commonly referred to by the residences in Haines Hall as "The Penthouse." The elevator shook a little bit when it started to move. "I hate that girl," Crystal said still smiling from ear to ear. "Larenzo, you know she's got a thing for you? She's been spreading rumors around campus that she slept with you and everything. The bitch is just jealous over what we have together."

Black women always seemed to smile at each other and then talk about each other when no one else was around. Crystal assumed that Nicky was lying about her sexual encounters with Larenzo because he had never told her about them. According to Crystal, she didn't believe that Larenzo would pay Nicky any attention because she just wasn't popular enough. Nicky wasn't on the same popularity level as Crystal. She wasn't on the cheerleading squad or a member of the student council. She was just a lowly RA working downstairs in Haines Hall. As a result, when Nicky said that she had slept with Larenzo Crystal took the statement as a lie. Larenzo never told her whether or not he had ever slept with her. Crystal always assumed he didn't sleep with her because Larenzo never acknowledged that he did. As a result she would never know. Larenzo simply smiled slyly to himself when he heard her statement.

Bing. The elevator sounded when they reached the floor. The sounds of loud R&B music penetrated the walls of other student rooms as the elevator door opened. The floors upstairs in the dorm were just as nice as the lobby downstairs. Dark green carpet covered the floor and a smaller version of the big screen downstairs sat in the corner. Several doorways were visible from the elevator. The doors had the names of the girls that lived inside taped on them. Crystal took Larenzo by the hand and led him to her room. John, being a rookie to the inside of Haines Hall, followed closely behind.

Crystal led Larenzo and John through a dimly lit corridor and into her room. The door creaked open and the stale smell of left over popcorn assaulted them. Her room was a disaster area. Clothes were scattered in large mountains on the floor and spread across her bed. Pompoms and other cheerleader paraphernalia were hung everywhere on her white walls. Her friend sat on Crystal's roommate's bed watching music videos on a small television set. The sounds of sexy R&B music lightly played in the background.

Crystal's friend was a very thin light skinned young lady. Her skin was very pale almost like that of a Caucasian; her eyes were green, and her hair, brunette with soft highlights of blond. She could only have been one hundred and twenty-four pounds soaking wet. Her fluffy hair hung down to her shoulders and her dark green eyes danced with delight when she saw John walk into the room. Her facial features appeared to be that of an Anglo-Saxon, yet her body splendidly displayed her African heritage. To John she seemed so tiny yet so very well put together. It was really no wonder that she made the cheerleading team. She seemed fragile yet there was definitely a sexual magnetism in her movements and in her eyes.

Crystal quickly introduced her friend and John, "Mary this is John. John this is my friend Mary." John shook her hand nervously. His palms were beginning to sweat, and he had hoped that she didn't notice. "Why don't you guys get to know each other better? I think me and Larenzo have something to talk about?" Crystal gave Mary a devilish smile then glanced back at Larenzo. Mary knew what the look was for and grinned like a schoolgirl instantly when she saw it. Larenzo realized what the look was intended for also, and laid back in Crystal's bed confidently putting his feet on her covers.

"C'mon John. Let's go to my room," Mary said in a very high-pitched voice pulling slightly on John's shirt. "I got something to show you." Mary basically dragged John out of the room, allowing Larenzo and Crystal to be alone. John left without saying a word of defiance but the feeling of betrayal on his face spoke for him. John didn't want to be left alone in Haines Hall with some woman he didn't know. To him it didn't matter how beautiful the girl was, she was a stranger, and he felt that Larenzo had somehow abandoned him.

When John and Mary left the room, Crystal turned off the lights creating a dim shadowy atmosphere with only the sun from the small window as light. With incredible speed, Crystal leaped on top of Larenzo's body like a horse jockey straddling him on her bed. The small bed squeaked under the weight of both of their bodies. Her body heaved back and forth with sexual enthusiasm. Crystal leaned forward pressing the softness of her breast against his muscular chest.

Crystal's hands wandered across Larenzo's body caressing and encircling his privates. Her heavy pants of breath signaled to Larenzo that she was well past ready.

"What about your roommate?" Larenzo asked.

"Study hall. She won't be back for hours." Crystal answered her hands caressing him harder up and down.

"Crystal, I didn't carry a condom on me," Larenzo said blowing the mood.

"It's okay daddy, I'm on the pill," Crystal replied moaning slightly as she talked. "Besides, I trust you," Crystal seductively said as she closed her eyes, lying back in the bed. Larenzo always wore a condom during sex but this time was different. Already he was fully aroused and he did trust Crystal...well mostly. It's difficult to trust anyone with your life on the line with the different STD's out. Her eyes had the look of truth in them; she probably was on birth control pills. He was sure that no one else on the campus was sleeping with her, but there was always a possibility that someone from her hometown was still sleeping with her. He took a deep breath and his eyes filled with sexual tension.

Larenzo and Crystal sensually undressed each other admiring one another's body. The only article of clothing left on Larenzo was his White Sox baseball cap. He never took off his hat even during sex; his hat was like a trademark for him. Her nipples, large and brown, extended yearning for more contact pressed against Larenzo's firm chest. Larenzo gripped Crystal from underneath her kneecaps and aggressively laid her on her back. Her muscle-toned legs wrapped around his waist anticipating the long hard thrust; which were sure to come. Larenzo shoved his organ inside of her roughly, causing her to grunt with delight. When the first sharp thrust connected with Crystal, her body convulsed in pain and her eyes fluttered with passion. A look of boredom spread across Larenzo's face as he checked his watch for the time. Larenzo had mounted Crystal and was pumping harder and harder into her warm wet insides. His robotic motion was completely void of emotion and passion.

Crystal's eyes rolled to the back of her head as she dug her fingernails deeply into Larenzo's back and neck. The pain from the scratches didn't slow Larenzo down at all; in fact, the painful sensation of her nails clawing at his back turned Larenzo on more. Suddenly Crystal's features changed as if in a dream or a mirage. Larenzo realized that he was no longer having sex with Crystal Kerry but with the image of Joy Summer, a young girl from his English class last semester. He pumped faster in her than before. Crystal's body shook violently as she began to climax. She tried to yell, verbalizing the experience, but her voice disappeared, lost in the moment. Realizing that the moment had arrived, with one grinding thrust and two shorter pumps, Larenzo also climaxed spilling his semen inside of her.

Afterwards, Larenzo ran his hand through her hair, playing with the silky texture of it. The vision of the lovely Joy Summers was beginning to fade and Crystal's face began to materialize. The apparition of Joy Summer had slowly disappeared like a phantom in the night. Larenzo didn't want the beautiful image of her flickering away so quickly. He had dated Joy the very first semester of college and deep down he knew that he still cared for her. Out of all of the women in Blanding University she was the one that got away. He dated her for three weeks straight and they never had sex once. She was a virgin and she wanted them to wait till the time was right. But that time never arrived. They broke up on bad terms, on account of him sleeping around. Now every time he had sex with someone else, no matter how pretty the woman was, he was tormented with visions of Joy. Larenzo gazed into Crystal's eyes, thinking that he might see a small glimmer of Joy's beauty still there, but when he stared into her eyes he only saw Crystal's light brown eyes staring back at him. Larenzo gave Crystal an innocent peck on the lips, like a father kissing his daughter goodnight. Larenzo hated long wet kisses on the mouth. It was too intimate of an experience for him. He drew back for a moment.

"What do you think John and Mary are doing?" Larenzo asked jokingly.

"Ha, Ha," Crystal giggled out loud still a little bit out of breath. "I hope they're enjoying themselves as much as me."

Larenzo laid his head on the pillow beside Crystal's naked body. The image of Joy Summer was now completely gone. Only the content face of Crystal Kerry remained under the sheets with him. She snuggled closely beside him, slightly rubbing her soft buttocks against his withering shaft. His head swam with confusion and Larenzo closed his eyes, sleeping peacefully next to Crystal.

Across the hallway in Mary's room, the situation looked quite different from Crystal's room. Mary had stripped off all of her clothes in an attempt to captivate John's interest. John, entirely undisturbed by her nudity, sat in a chair talking on the phone to his girlfriend as Mary laid on top of the covers with only a thong on. She rolled over on her belly completely exposing the roundness of her ass. Mary had failed in her attempt to seduce John. Discouraged in the fact that her feminine wiles weren't enough to tempt John into having an affair, she buried her head in her pillow sexually aggravated at the night's events.

Half an hour later, Larenzo stirred out of his restful slumber. After he woke up completely from his nap, Crystal signed Larenzo and John out of Haines Hall. At the front door of the dorm Crystal hugged Larenzo passionately and kissed him softly on the cheek. Then she turned to John and hugged him also. "Goodbye guys," Crystal said smiling friendly at them. "Larenzo, I guess that I'll see you in about another week when you need something," Crystal said handing Larenzo a wad of cash and kissed him again, this time on the lips fully.

Larenzo smiled and said, "Yeah, thanks for everything. I'll call you in a couple of days."

By the time Larenzo and John emerged from Haines Hall it was already nine thirty. The day had slipped away, turning into dusk. The night sky was filled with stars and the moon hung high over their heads. Larenzo yawned loudly as they walked back toward the car, still a little tired from his sexual escapade. "Hey Larenzo what's she give you the money for?" John inquired staring at the wad of cash in Larenzo's hand. Larenzo opened up his hand and began to count the money in his hand. There was sixty dollars in his palm in crumbled up ten dollar bills. "Shit, this is money for registration tomorrow. I ain't been in class yet."

"So how was it John?" Larenzo asked once they reached the car. "How was what?" John asked.

Larenzo paused for a moment believing that John was only joking when he asked the question. Maybe he was trying to be a gentleman and not give any details about his night. Larenzo decided to press the question a little more. "How was Mary? You know. Did you have fun fucking Mary?" Larenzo asked getting straight to the point. "Don't tell me you didn't sleep with her. Please tell me you slept with her. I saw that look in her eyes! She wanted you bad as hell!"

"I didn't sleep with her," John answered truthfully. "We had a conversation and she said that she respected my decision to stay faithful to my girlfriend. Then she took a shower and went to sleep."

"She took a shower? Then she went to bed!" Larenzo asked astonished at John's ability to ignore her obvious signals. Larenzo's curiosity grew and he asked more questions. "Well, what did she wear to bed?"

"Just a pair of panties," John said frowning. "She said that she liked to sleep in the nude."   A look of shock froze on the face of Larenzo. He knew that Mary was one of the best looking women on the campus and he had basically dropped her in John's lap. The idea that a man could turn down a beautiful woman, mostly naked lying in her bed, was too much for Larenzo's mind to comprehend. Larenzo stared at John in astonishment, and then his astonishment turned into suspicion.

"What are you gay or something?" Larenzo asked suspiciously taking a step away from John. "Because I ain't ever heard of any man turning down a fine piece of ass like that before. If you're a homo or something just tell me. I can't let you hang wit me or nothing but at least you should let a nigga know. You'll fuck around and mess up my reputation." Reputation was always important to Larenzo. It was what separated the few from the many at Blanding University. Reputation was the difference between a nerd and a local star.

"I'm not a homosexual," John said in his defense. "Mary is a very attractive lady. I'm just not ready to sleep with anyone else yet. I got a chance to talk to Janet, though. She's finally back in her dorm." John didn't have any bias feelings toward homosexual people but he definitely wasn't one of them. The idea of cheating on Janet hurt him deep in his heart. He knew that he would never entertain the notion of cheating on her again.

"Whatever nigga. You just ruined all of my plans." Larenzo said disgusted at John. "I hope you're fucking happy. Nigga just take me back to Red's house."

John and Larenzo walked back to John's BMW. Once inside the car Larenzo slammed the passenger side door angrily. The idea that John had passed up sleeping with a beautiful woman to talk on the phone with his girlfriend pissed him off. John started the engine and began to drive back to Red's home. John Spencer's attitude became serious when his car door slammed shut. Noticeably offended at his actions John began to speak. "Could you please reframe from slamming my door?" John said very properly. "And while you're at it, I'm also very insulted at the constant use of the word nigger in my presence. As African-American men we should have more respect for each other than using that word of bigotry."

"Nigger?" Larenzo said with a perplexed look on his face almost as if the word was poison. "I didn't call you a nigger. I called you a nigga, wit the letter A at the end. There's a big difference between the two words. The word nigga is a term of endearment. It's a word from the street, used to describe a group of people oppressed by society. When black people call one another nigga it just means that we've all struggled through the same shit. Now the word nigger is some racist shit, used by rednecks that use to make our ancestors pick cotton. There's a big difference."

"Okay, I apologize...my nigga." John said slowly making sure not to pronounce the last word with an –er ending. He said the word in syllables like a foreigner learning a new word for the first time. Larenzo glanced at John with a look of amusement. It was clear that John had never said the word before.

Larenzo laughed a little to himself at the ridiculousness of the way John spoke. "Yo, do me a favor and never say that word again. You sound like a fucking white boy. You don't say it with enough emotion. Listen, that's a ghetto word and if you're not from the ghetto it just ain't gonna sound right." Larenzo lay back in the seat, closed his eyes and smiled. Tomorrow Larenzo was sure that he could get registered, and on Tuesday he would attend his first day of class. Within a few minutes, John's BMW pulled up in front of Red's house.

CHAPTER 6

Dreams Shattered

At that same moment a few blocks away, Malik Brown was in his bedroom at his mother's home waiting by the telephone. Malik's room was filled with pictures of Ebony constantly reminding him of her beauty. His bed and dresser was covered with teddy bears from a collaboration of years of Valentine Day gifts. He had argued with Ebony earlier that evening and now he was waiting for her to call him. Whenever they would argue she would always apologize for yelling later on that night. Usually it would only take a few hours for her to calm down and call him, but this time was different. It was already nine forty-five at night and his phone hadn't rung. He checked the caller ID again making sure that he hadn't missed her call when he went to the bathroom. Nothing had changed.

His mother stood in the kitchen baking a cake for the next day's desert. A youthful beauty of a middle aged woman, Mrs. Brown watched her son's tense behavior in silence. She had a blend of gray strands of hair mixed with her original long brown hair. She wore an apron and spent most of her time in the kitchen. "Malik, did you have a argument with Ebony again." Mrs. Brown's voice sounded reassuring in her southern accent. "Boy, you know that girl loves you. You and Ebony have been going with each other for years now. She'll call you soon enough, just stop waiting by the phone you look like a long lost puppy." Whenever the couple argued, Mrs. Brown saw that look of despair in the eyes of Malik. Helpless to ease the pain of her son, Mrs. Brown simply watched Malik suffer from heartache. Giving advice about women to a son was a job for the father. She was a single mother, Malik's father had run off years before, and she was bringing Malik up all by herself. She didn't really miss him anymore but on nights like this one having him around would have made life a whole lot easier.

Ring. Ring. Malik jumped at the phone snatching it off the hook and answering it quickly, "Ebony, please let me explain." Malik blurted out not waiting to see who was one the other line. Malik sighed sadly when he heard the voice on the other side. "Mom!" Malik yelled to the kitchen. "Pick up the line its Aunt Barbara on the phone." Malik angrily hung up the phone after his mother picked up the phone in the kitchen. A feeling of doubt ran through his mind when he realized that it wasn't Ebony calling. He even thought about calling her after his mom got off the line with his aunt but his pride wouldn't allow him. He put his hands to his head and slowly rubbed the temples on either side of his head. "No. She'll call me. I just have to wait," Malik said to himself over and over again.

It was ten o'clock when Malik's doorbell rang. Mrs. Brown rushed to the door and answered it. When she opened the door, Ebony was standing on the porch; her eyes were filled with tears. Mrs. Brown tried to hug her but Ebony stepped back cautiously not allowing Mrs. Brown to touch her. The look on Ebony's face said a million things at once without saying a word. Dried up tears could still be seen on her cheeks. Her nose was red from where she had used a dry piece of tissue to clear her nostrils. Her chin trembled a little when she looked up to see Malik's mother standing in front of her. "Hello Mrs. Brown," she said hesitantly. "Can I please speak with Malik?" Her voice was soft and cracked as if she could burst into tears at any moment.

"Malik you have a visitor at the door!" Mrs. Brown shouted to the back rooms where Malik's bedroom was located. Then she left the doorway so the couple could have their privacy. Malik leaped out of his bed overjoyed at the news. When Malik heard the doorbell ring he knew that it had to be Ebony. It surprised him a little that she came to his house because she didn't own a car. It really didn't matter that she didn't call him. He realized that she couldn't stay away from him for too much longer. They were soul mates and it was irrational for soul mates to stay mad at each other. He checked himself in the mirror to make sure that he looked all right and dabbed a small amount of cologne on for effect. Then he rushed to the front door.

When he reached the door he instantly knew that she didn't come to apologize. The look in her bloodshot eyes shocked him. Malik had known Ebony for most of his life, and half of that time he had spent as her boyfriend. Out of all of that time he had never seen the look in her eyes that he saw at that moment. Her dark brown eyes were enraged with fury. She was fighting for control as tears began to swell up in the corners of her eyes. Just the sight of her eyes sent a feeling of apprehension through his body.

"Ebony, I know that you're mad at me but you got to know that I would never hurt you," Malik said sounding as persuasive as possible. From the look in her eyes he knew that it wasn't going to help him this time. It was obvious to Malik that she wasn't paying attention to anything that he was saying. He knew that he was wasting his breath but the only way he could ever get her back would be to talk to her. "I'm sorry baby," Malik finally said in his little boy voice that she loved so much. She smiled slightly for a second, reminding him if only for one moment of how they use to love each other. Then her face quickly transformed back into her crueler version with hatred in her eyes.

"You're not sorry! Malik, I loved you and you threw it all away!" She continued her voice like venom. "You can't get back something like that. You can't make things right again just by saying you're sorry. Sometimes it feels like you don't love me as much as other shit in your life. That car, Red's parties, and even other women seem to come before me. Look, I don't want to fight. I didn't think that you would mind if I came here to collect my stuff." She growled with resentment as she spoke. Ebony shoved past Malik and hastily walked to his bedroom. Malik could tell from her walk that she wasn't playing around. She marched as she moved toward the bedroom. Her head remained still and her arms stayed to her side.

Once inside Malik's room she began to take the various cards and presents throughout the years into her hands. She ripped her pictures off of his dresser and yanked the teddy bears from of his bed. Within seconds, she had gathered together an assortment of teddy bears, pictures, and love letters in her arms and began to walk out of the door. Without the colorful presents for decoration, his room looked like an empty shell of its original glory.

Before Ebony could walk away, Malik grabbed her by the arm and pulled her close. He stared in her tear filled eyes and spoke very softly, "Ebony, don't do this. I love you, and you're my queen. How can I be a king without a queen?" His words were very sincere and his face was full of compassion and understanding. He stared in her eyes for a signal, and for a moment Ebony loss the hatred that was building up for so long. The room became silent and a feeling of affection could be seen slowly emerging on her face. She wet her lips as if she was contemplating getting back together with Malik. Suddenly, a car horn honked breaking the silence, and ruining the magic of the moment. Ebony shook her head as if waking from a dream and said, with tears once again in her eyes, "That's my ride. I have to go."

Ebony yanked her arm from his grasp and ran out of his house. Malik chased after her, but he knew that there was nothing else he could possibly do. When Malik reached the front doorway to the house he stopped running. She rushed out of the house and jumped into a light blue Honda that Malik had never seen before. He couldn't tell who was driving the vehicle because it was so dark outside but he already knew to whom the car belonged. The license plate on the back of the vehicle was from California, and Malik would put money on the driver being none other than her friend Cynthia. He had lost Ebony, and he wasn't sure he would ever get her back again.

Depression flowed through Malik's body when he saw the car pull off quickly. His queen had just run out of his life, and there was nothing that he could do to prevent it. Never before had Malik felt so alone than at that exact moment. He didn't even have even any pictures or letters to remember her by. He sniffled a little bit, but his African male pride held back the flow of tears. Ebony had stripped his room of all of the presents and pictures, but she would never strip him of his manhood. Alone and depressed Malik walked back to his empty room.

"Son, are you all right?" Mrs. Brown said when she saw the tortured look on Malik's face. "Do you want to talk about it?" she inquired thoughtfully trying not to be too intrusive. Malik's mother had spied the whole thing from the kitchen window and her heart went out to him.

"No," Malik answered plainly. "You wouldn't understand."

Later on that night Malik was awakened by a horrible crash followed closely by the sound of his mother's car alarm. Malik jumped up quickly grabbing a baseball bat from underneath his bed and headed toward the front door. His mother had been awakened by the blaring sound of the alarm, also. With her long robe wrapped around her and a hairnet sitting on her head she too hurried on her way toward the front door. "Get back to bed mom!" Malik shouted at her. "I'll handle this!" She screamed when she saw the bat in her son's hands. Then she rushed back to her bedroom and prayed that Malik would be okay by himself.

When Malik opened his front door he couldn't believe his eyes. He shook his head at the scene. His mother's Cadillac was keyed on both sides and a giant brick had been thrown through the front windshield. His most prized possession on the planet had been violated and there was nothing that he could do about it. Malik saw a car speedily driving off in the distance but he couldn't tell what type it was. It was too dark and the car was moving too fast. It really didn't matter. In twenty years nothing had ever happened like this before at his home. He didn't want to believe it but he knew exactly who was responsible for this. Malik would have never dreamt that she would ever do anything like this.

The next day Malik Brown walked to Red's home early in the morning carrying a small bottle of Crown Royal. He didn't mind walking at all; in fact he preferred it, as he took huge gulps from the liquor bottle. The fresh air and exercise helped him concentrate on his failing relationship with Ebony, and since he didn't have use of his mother's car he didn't have to worry about being pulled over for a DWI. Besides, being without a car allowed him to enjoy the beauty of nature in its perfect fullness. He walked across town without barely a single glance up. By the time he reached Red's house he had already finished the whole bottle and discarded it in the front lawn. Before he knew it he was walking through Red's front door. As usual there was a game of Spades being played in the living room and various women were running around the small house. Some were beginning to cook in the kitchen and some were dancing to music being played in the background. Others still were watching television on the couch. Malik collapsed on the couch beside a young lady and put his feet up ignoring the world around him.

Almost everyone that he cared for was in Red's house. All of the gang was present. Kel, Larenzo, Midget Moe, JC, and even Bobby were present. Everyone was present except for the one person he cared about the most, the person who had occupied so much of his time in the last two days. Ebony was missing. With the alcohol settling in the pit of his stomach, Malik's thoughts drifted to his fight with Ebony. He tried to forget about her but the pain of being without her was becoming too much of a burden to bear.

Once in the privacy of Red's house, Malik took out an already rolled blunt from his pocket and lit it. The marijuana smoke filled Malik's nostrils and hovered in a small cloud around his head. He coughed a little from the smoke after he took his first few puffs from the brown blunt. Malik could feel himself drifting away from the reality. With half of the blunt gone Malik could feel the marijuana invading his mind, breaking down all inhibitions making him care less and less. The normal distractions of Red's house didn't disturb Malik at all. His eyes closed and he could see colors. Beautiful blends of swirling blue, green, and purple dancing around each other when his eyes shut. All of the problems that he had from day before become insignificant compared to the swirling light of the colors. Malik smiled when he saw those colors, and when he opened his eyes a few moments later they only opened slightly, like that of Asians.

Now fully feeling the effects of the drug, Malik found an ashtray sitting on the floor beside him and put out the blunt saving it for later. He let his head fall back against the pillows of the couch, no longer having the strength to hold his own head up. Malik stayed on the couch somewhere between reality and a dreamy unreal state until he was awakened by a female's voice. The voice belonged to one of the young girls who were sitting next to him.

"Malik. Malik. Wake up Malik." The girl's voice came to him like a lighthouse beam shining through a fog. "Don't you want some spaghetti? The food is already ready." The girl had a tone of concern in her voice as she spoke. Spaghetti was a favorite food eaten by college students at Blanding University. It was cheap to make and it fed a lot of people at one time.

Malik lifted his head slowly and scanned the room with bloodshot eyes. The Spades game was over and several people had already begun serving themselves. The smell of the food made Malik's stomach growl. Malik was no stranger to the munchies and now his body craved the spaghetti and tomato sauce like never before. *"How long have I been out of it?"* Malik thought when he observed the plates of food being eaten by the other students.

Malik stood up quickly stumbling as he began to walk. He staggered to the kitchen and found a full plate of food waiting for him.

His mouth watered as he looked down on the food. Without waiting to sit down at a table, Malik began devouring the spaghetti in the kitchen. The hot sensation of the food flowing down his throat was satisfying. No. Not just satisfying, but truly exceptional like that of the fruit of gods. He swallowed the food on his plate hastily, spilling sauce on his shirt and pants. Unashamed of his greediness, Malik wiped his mouth with his sleeve and burped out loud.

Malik was fixing a second plate of food but he was distracted by the smell of a familiar aroma drifting through the air. He sniffed in the air like a dog trying to place the scent and then it came to him...marijuana. Malik dropped the plate spilling the sauce on top of the stove and floor. He rushed from the kitchen to the living room and a fury like none he's ever experienced before filled him. Pure anger balled up Malik's fist at the sight of it. A girl sitting on the couch had picked up his blunt and was smoking on it. Just the sight of the girl licking and pulling on his drug drove Malik to new heights of fury.

"Put it down!" The words were a sharp command. The music stopped suddenly and everyone in the house became silent when Malik yelled. Malik ran up to her and stared straight into her eyes. His half opened eyes were filled with the intensity of a madman as peered down at her. She could smell the wrenching stench of a mixture of alcohol and marijuana on his breath. Malik spoke with an anger in his voice that she had never heard before.

"You greedy fuckin' bitch!" He yelled snatching the drug from her hand. "You didn't even ask me if you could smoke it. You just take whatever you think you can? Every time I turn around a fucking bitch is taking something from me." Malik's stare changed from no longer anger but that of pure abhorrence as he watched the delicate features of the girl. She reminded him of Ebony and he wasn't sure why.

"I didn't think that you would mind," the young girl replied. "I just took a tiny puff. I thought that you'd share."

Her words echoed through his mind pounding against his skull until he finally couldn't take it anymore. Malik's left eye twitched a little when he spoke. "You didn't think I would mind!" He yelled hysterically. "I'll show you how much I fucking mind!" Malik said as he lunged at her. He had heard that statement over and over again by Ebony, and this time it was enough to finally push him over the edge. In fear her body fell backward toward the couch, trying to escape, but Malik leaped on top of her. His hands quickly wrapped around her neck, his thumbs pressing hard into her larynx. She tried to scream but the sound came out only as a gag of help. Malik screamed out an conglomeration of obscenities at her as his hands tightened around her neck.

Everyone in the house stared in complete awe as Malik began to strangle the life out of the young girl. Only Kel rushed over to the aid of the young girl, perhaps saving her life. Kel grabbed Malik's arms in a wrestling hold and dragged him in another room separating Malik from her. Her face had turned a hideous shade of purple from the lack of oxygen. The girl gasped for breath when Malik's fingers were finally pried from her neck.

Many of the people in the house ran to the aid of the young girl when Malik was dragged off of her. The simple viciousness of the act stunned everyone in the house. The majority of the people in the house gathered around her checking on her, seeing if she needed a drink of water.

Only Red shrugged his shoulders indifferently and looked away. "Bitch shouldn't have smoked the man's stuff," Red said coldly. He didn't have any remorse for the girl on the couch at all. She was just another bitch to him, not worth the time and effort of worrying about. Red usually didn't have a worry in the world but something did worry him that day. Malik's behavior worried Red. It was uncharacteristic for the calm, leveled- headed, black militant to attack a "sister." Red knew that there was something definitely wrong with Malik. Red turned his back on the sobs of help coming from his couch and walked to his room where Kel had dragged Malik.

When he walked into his room Malik was sitting on his bed with his head buried in his hands. Kel stood by his side smoking on a Black & Mild cigar. A look of aggravation was plastered on his face as he looked down at Malik. Red walked over to Malik and put his hand on his shoulder. "This shit ain't like you, fighting women and shit." His voice was calm and friendly. "So tell me what's up, Malik?" Red inquired caringly like a father asking a son.

Malik shook his head "no" for a moment. Malik's mouth hung open almost as if he were searching for the words to explain his behavior. Red waited patiently, making sure not to rush him. Malik looked up at the faces of Kel and Red and began to speak, "I broke up with Ebony." He paused for a moment as if the words were a great weight lifted off his chest. "We had an argument yesterday. She thought I cheated on her and then she threw a brick through Mom's windshield," Malik confessed. His hand shook a little as he spoke, struggling to maintain his composure.

"I'm sorry about what went down in there, Red. I'm drunk and when she just took my shit I flipped. I'm stressed out right now. Is she okay?" Malik asked about the girl, feeling sorry for his actions a few minutes before.

"Yeah, she'll be alright," Red replied. "Bitch was just shaken up a little."

Kel looked at Malik with more compassion now then before. "Look if you wanted to jump on a bitch, then take your aggression out on Ebony. But if you do still want to be with her, which is what I think, you should go see her and tell her how much you love her. Now do you love her?" Kel inquired easily. Kel considered himself the mediator of the group. He would consult all of his friends on there personal problems whether they wanted his advice or not.

"Yeah. That's my queen. I've always loved her." Malik said quietly.

"Well if you feel that strongly about her you should go to her tonight and apologize. It's the only way. She'll take you back. Pay for your mom's Cadillac and everything will be like before."

Malik nodded his head in agreement with Kel's statement. For Malik, the idea of being reunited with Ebony was like a fantasy come true. Sure it would be difficult but Kel's words seemed to make sense to Malik. If she was his true love then he should be able to explain away a little lipstick on his collar easily. Malik took a deep breath, trying to inhale as much unpolluted air as possible, to clear his thoughts. "You're right," Malik said standing up. "I'm going to see her and reclaim my queen."

When Malik stood up the room began to spin. Kel caught his body before it hit the floor, an aftereffect of the weed and alcohol. Straightening up, Malik pushed himself off of Kel. "I'm okay," Malik said reassuring Kel that he could stand by himself. He made sure that he was fully under control before he began for the door; Malik took small steps taking his time, making sure not to fall again.

"I need to get to her and tell her how I feel. I need a ride on campus," Malik said slurring his words, a sort of desperation present in his voice.

After JC heard the story, he was only too happy to give Malik a ride to campus. The shadows began to get long outside, and smell in the air signaled the start of a thunderstorm coming from the horizon. It was late in the evening when JC's Honda pulled beside the curb of Ebony's dorm. It was already six o'clock, and with all of her classes done, Malik knew that she would be in her room. Ebony lived on the second floor of Clark Hall, and from the front steps Malik could see that someone was in her room. The blinds were closed and the soulful sounds of jazz music seeped from her window.

Malik rushed into Clark Hall completely disregarding the RA standing at the front desk, and made for the stairs. "Sir, can I help you?" the RA said stepping in the way of Malik. "Can I help you, sir?" she repeated herself. Her voice sounded cruel like that of one truly in authority. He couldn't allow this woman to stand in the path of true love, and he didn't have enough time to explain his actions. Anger flashed on Malik's face as he shoved her out of the way. She fell to the floor not because he shoved her that hard, but because the look on his stone-hard, hostile face scared her.

JC, who was right behind Malik the whole time, stopped to pick the RA up from the floor. JC looked the RA directly in the eyes and began to apologize for Malik's behavior. "I'm sorry about my friend. He's kind of hyper right now and he needs to talk to Ebony. So I would appreciate it if you don't notify the authorities on this little matter," JC said handing her a folded fifty-dollar bill. "Why don't you take off for the rest of the evening? Take another lunch break or something. Act like you never saw us, okay?"

The RA smiled when she saw the fifty-dollar bill in his hands. It was more money than she would have made that night anyhow. She looked around the lobby to make sure that no one was watching then said, "Okay. I never saw either one of you come inside but you better not get caught or say my name." She then took the money out of JC's hand and turned her back happily humming a tune to herself. JC smiled at the ease of bribing the security at Blanding University. For JC it was a good investment, not only could he help a friend, but he could walk into Clark Hall whenever she was working from now on. To him fifty dollars was a good exchange for free reign in Clark Hall.

JC ran up the stairs after Malik. Malik had already stopped in front of Ebony's door. His fingers fumbled through his keys searching for the right on. He had a copy of hers made months before they'd both forgotten about. "That's it," he said triumphantly holding the right key in his fingers. He squeezed the key in the lock and turned it. The door crept open and Malik could tell that there were two figures underneath the sheets of Ebony's bed.

The lights were all off but a few candles were lit giving the room a romantic atmosphere. A familiar aroma was in the air, which both men recognized instantly. It was the smell of sex. What Malik saw next was enough to drive a man to the edge of madness. Shock came to Malik's face when he walked into the room. His jaw dropped and he blinked his eyes several times as if he could change what he saw if he only closed them again. Ebony's head popped from under the covers first with a look of shame in her eyes. Then another head emerged from the covers. This head belonged to Cynthia, her friend from California. Malik couldn't believe what he was seeing with his own eyes. His soul mate, his future wife, his queen, was having sex with another woman.

"Ebony?" Malik questioned in amazement, trying to understand the scene in front of him. Malik's light brown skin became as red as a tomato as he stared at Ebony and Cynthia lying in bed. Ebony had a look of guilt plastered on her face and Cynthia had a look of complete satisfaction on hers. Perhaps it was the result of the sex or maybe it was the fact that Malik was seeing them together that turned her on. Either way, it was a scene that Malik never would have believed possible, and just the sight and smell of it was enough to drive his already unstable mind to unknown heights of anger and lust. How easy it was to go through life thinking that you knew someone's innermost thoughts and then waking up and realizing that you don't know anything about that person. A reddish haze blurred his vision as he continued to stare at them, their bodies wrapped intimately intertwined in each other.

Malik clenched his fist so tightly that the knuckles began to turn white. His first instinct was to pounce on top of the women and beat them to death with his bare hands, feel there fragile bones crush under his fist, and feel the very life squeeze out of them as they choked for breath. To hear there frantic screams of pain for mercy. Visions of pain and hate ran through Malik Brown's mind at that moment, but he never acted on those impulses. Instead his eyes turned cold and his face became expressionless.

JC had never seen that look in Malik before, and something about it scared him. JC knew that look only too well. It was the look of a man who had lost everything and no longer cared for the outside world. "C'mon Malik, let's get out of here," JC said looking at the couple lying on the bed together. "She made her choice, I hope she's happy." JC wrapped his arm around Malik's shoulder and led him away from the door.

"Malik wait!" Ebony stated, covering her exposed body quickly with the sheets from the bed. "I made a mistake. Can't you see that I still love you and I think we can make things work again? You're still my king." She ran up to him and leaned forward like she was trying to kiss him. Malik inched back from her without saying a word and spat in her face. Then Malik turned his back to her and walked out of the door.

It was drizzling by the time they reached the street. It only seemed right that it would rain on a night like this. That way if Malik did cry no one would notice his tears. But it wasn't tears that came from Malik's eyes that night. There was coldness in those eyes that would freeze any tears he'd have. JC could still feel a coldness coming from Malik as they walked to the car. He was sure that Malik would be forever changed after this. Malik didn't cover his head from the rain or hurry to the comfort of the car like JC. Malik didn't smile, frown, or show any type of emotion at all. Malik looked like a cold-hearted soldier coming home from a war that was lost. Beaten and battered he refused to die physically but ended dying emotionally.

Once they reached the car Malik pulled out the drug-filled blunt from his pocket. He lit it and took a long pull of the intoxicating drug, inhaling the mood-changing fumes. Malik closed his eyes and once again pictured the beautiful colors dancing around him. JC thought about telling Malik not to smoke the drug in his car but he didn't. Malik deserved the small amount of pleasure he received from the marijuana smoke. He had just lived through a traumatic time in his life and any comfort he could find was good. At that moment, the only comfort that Malik found was in the brightness of those colors. The drug helped entrance Malik, absorbing him into another reality all together. It took him to a reality where he didn't have to think about Ebony and Cynthia enacting in unnatural ways, where he could just close his eyes and enjoy the lights. As the drug took affect on Malik's senses he could only think of the beautiful, colorful lights.

It rained as the car pulled away from Clark Hall. A thunderstorm of tremendous proportions swept through the small southern town, shaking the very foundations of many of the buildings in the neighborhood. The wind howled and the rain came down in torrents washing through the streets. Most of the inhabitants in the town were asleep, nestled together in their homes awaiting the passing of the storm. Only the few "troublemakers" of the town would go out on a night like this. Late on a Wednesday night, only one place stayed open through this tempest: Tony's strip bar on the edge of town.

CHAPTER 7

Pay Back

Tony's bar was filled every Wednesday night with under aged students drinking alcohol and throwing one-dollar bills at strippers dancing on stage. The dimly lit club reeked of cigarette smoke and sweat. Young men from all across town would meet to fondle and drool over the woman that worked there. At the bar a dancer casually stripped gyrating her body in front of a group of students. A stack of one-dollar bills were in her g-string as she twirled around inspiring the young men to give more and more of their parents' money.

One of those young men was Midget Moe. Midget Moe had been at the club for a few hours already. A half empty glass of Crown Royal sat in his hands, and the blank stare of drunkenness was visible in his eyes. Midget Moe looked up at the tall figure of the woman in front of him happily. He loved taller women and the high heels worn by the strippers combined with the liquor in his system turned him on even more. Of course, most women were naturally taller than Midget Moe. For Midget Moe the stripper persona was irresistible. The gold anklet, the glossy painted toenails, the tattoo of a tiger's paws on her thigh, and the way she curved her back so her ample buttocks protruded turned Moe on. Midget Moe showed the girl a wad of cash and motioned with his finger for the young lady to talk with him.

"Let me talk to you for a second," Midget Moe said to her tossing the money at her feet. "How 'bout you wrap them long legs around me somewhere a little bit more private." The stripper smiled when she saw the pile of dollar bills on the bar. Most of the night she was only getting a few one-dollar bills at a time. This was an occasion that she could make a large amount of money without all of the extra work. She looked at Midget Moe with oriental lidded eyes, painted heavily with mascara, as a paycheck for the next week and grinned.

"Sure daddy," the stripper said flirtatiously to him. She pulled herself closer to him and whispered in his ear, "Let's go to the Boom-Boom room. I'm gonna give you the best time of your life." She kissed him on the forehead and took his hand, headed toward the Boom-Boom room.

Strippers were of the norm in Black Universities across the country. Pleasing men was an easy job, and the pay was excellent. What the women lost in respect they gained in immediate cash flow. Many of the employees at Tony's bar were female students at Blanding University just trying to get enough money to pay their tuition. Other strippers at the club were there simply because that was all that they knew how to do. In one of the several small dimly lit back rooms, labeled the "Boom-Boom room," women would take men and perform sexual favors with them for twenty-five dollars each. One of the strippers working in the "Boom-Boom room" that night was Janet Stub, the girlfriend to John Spencer. She was completely naked and was entertaining two men at the same time. One of the men was Travis, the very same man who was brutally attacked at Red's back-to-school jam. His face was only slightly healed from that encounter, still showing cuts and purple bruises.

"Hey, big boy," she said teasing Travis, giving him a lap dance. "C'mon over here to momma," she said to the other man grabbing him by the belt and pulling him close. She had been stripping at Tony's for almost two semesters now, and she had lost all of her shyness around customers long ago. Even the disfigured appearance of Travis' face didn't keep Janet Stub from entertaining him. She was a working girl, and she didn't care how she got the money. For Janet, stripping was just a way to pay her tuition and some of her credit card bills. The two men moaned in ecstasy as they humped away on her. "Oh my god! You're one of the best pieces of ass I've ever seen," one of the men said to her. "Don't you think so Travis?"

"Hell yeah, Corey!" Travis answered, enjoying his lap dance thoroughly.

Midget Moe walked in holding the hand of the tall stripper that was dancing on top of the bar. He plopped down on the couch across from Janet Stub and Travis. Since Janet was on top of Travis, Midget Moe didn't get a clear view of him. The stripper from the bar licked Midget Moe's neck and laid on top of him straddling his small waist. Midget Moe closed his eyes and began to immensely enjoy the private lap dance.

Midget Moe didn't take notice of the two men enjoying themselves across from him, but one of the men did notice him. Travis' friend, Corey pushed Janet Stub away from him and tapped Travis on the arm. Corey nodded his head toward the figure of Midget Moe lying on his back with his eyes closed. Travis' eyes became alive with built- up revenge. He hesitated for a moment, and then he pushed Janet off of him completely. She fell to the cold floor looking up at Travis in amazement. A customer before had never shoved her off, and the experience was shocking, if not totally embarrassing. Travis stood up smugly and took out the chrome plated nine-millimeter pistol that was holstered in the back of his belt.

The pistol glistened from the dim lights in the boom boom room. Janet looked up into the bruised face of Travis and there was no mistake about it. There was murder in his eyes. Janet let out a scream of panic and tried to make it back to her feet. Before she could make it to her feet, Travis fired his gun. The bullet missed the head of Midget Moe by mere inches imbedding itself in the wall beside him. Travis had never shot that gun before and the power behind the weapon startled him. Midget Moe tossed the stripper off of him and dashed for the exit. Right before Midget Moe made it to the exit of the boom boom room, Travis managed to fire a second shot. The second shot hit Midget Moe in the right shoulder blade completely spinning him around in a 360-degree turn. Midget Moe cursed loudly, "Shit!" The bullet burned when it entered his shoulder, ripping through flesh and bone both. In excruciating pain, Midget Moe regained his balance and broke for the door. Travis would have fired again but Janet Stub ran in his view.

The club erupted in chaos after the two deafening gunshot blasts. The music stopped playing and everyone began to run for the front door. The commotion of everyone rushing for the door at the same time caused a chaotic riot of people pushing and shoving each other. It was still raining outside of the club. The rain came down so hard that it was difficult for anyone to even see ten feet in front of themselves. Everyone was having difficulty except for Midget Moe. Since Moe was smaller than everyone else in the club, he easily disappeared in the swarm of the crowd. Midget Moe was running for his life and pure frantic desperation kept his feet moving, dipping in and out of the crowds, and speedily making his way to the car.

Travis ran after Midget Moe, stalking his prey through the crowd like a true predator. Midget Moe made it to the parking lot without being shot again. His shoulder dripped blood profusely leaving a trail on the concrete. Travis waved his gun in the air from left to right as he followed the trail like a wild game hunter. Midget Moe had almost made it to his baby momma's car when more gunshots rang out in the night. Bullets whizzed above Midget Moe's head. Travis wasn't a great shot but Moe didn't know how much longer his luck was going hold out.

Midget Moe was in so much intense pain that he doubled over because of it, slowing him down a little. Moe could feel his heart pumping faster and faster almost as if it were going to burst in his chest. Midget Moe was used to the adrenaline rush of someone always chasing after him. As a hustler it was expected that someone would always be after him. He knew the feeling well, but never before had he been shot. In excruciating pain, Midget Moe staggered towards the car falling to the ground, reaching for the door in pain. The only thing racing through his mind was that if he made it to the car he might actually survive through the night.

Travis could hear police sirens in the distance but he knew that they wouldn't get to the crime scene in time. He took a deep breath and steadied his aim. This time the bullet hit Midget Moe in the leg. The force of the impact made Midget Moe collapse to his knees but Moe didn't quit. He crawled to the car on his hands and knees praying for salvation to come from some higher being. *Dear Lord, don't let me die.* Using the very last bit of his willpower Midget Moe stood up on one leg and hobbled to the car finally reaching the door. He opened the door and reached for the .357 Magnum revolver hidden underneath the driver's seat.

When Midget Moe's fingers wrapped around the heavy weapon two more gunshots exploded from Travis' gun. One missed Midget Moe hitting the car the second hit Moe in the back. The blast took Midget Moe completely off of his feet throwing him inside the vehicle. Moe gave a low moan when the bullet punctured his back. He was alive but just barely. He could feel his life's energy ebbing away from him. Midget Moe coughed up dark blood and tightened his grip on the gun. "You mothafucka," Midget Moe yelled gathering enough strength to turn around and fire a shot. Midget Moe raised his weapon, but it was too late. Travis had already taken aim and two more bullets hit their target. One hit Moe in the neck and another bullet smashed into Midget Moe's forehead. He died before his body hit the pavement. Blood and brain fragments splattered all over the inside of the car.

Travis shot Midget Moe three more times just to make sure that he was dead. The extra gunshots were senseless but it made Travis feel better. He could now hear the sound of police sirens much clearer than before. Travis ran toward his friend's parked car with Corey already sitting in the driver's seat. Hopping into the passenger seat, they drove off quickly into the night.

As the two drove at breakneck speeds down the streets it became clear to Travis' friend that Travis didn't know what to do next. Panic rose on the face of the driver as he stared at Travis in horror. "Stupid! Stupid!" Corey yelled out more to himself than to Travis. Midget Moe's murder had been completely unprepared and sloppy. He didn't think that Travis would kill Midget Moe. At best he thought that they would only beat him up a little. Maybe even pistol-whip him, but the idea of murdering Moe never came to his mind. He was sure that everyone in the club saw their faces and the cops would be knocking on their dorm room door before the night was over.

Travis was too busy remembering the bliss he felt when he squeezed the trigger ending the life of Midget Moe. Ever since the back-to-school party at Red's house Travis had lived for nothing else than to kill Midget Moe. He hated Midget Moe. Revenge fueled this hatred and that hatred helped Travis blank out the results of the gunfight at Tony's Club. It didn't matter that the cops were probably on the scene already. It didn't matter that everyone in the club recognized his face. And it didn't matter that he might go to jail for the rest of his life. The only thing that did matter to Travis at that moment was the fact that he had gotten revenge. In that fact Travis' body relaxed and a sinister smile came to his lips.

"What are we going to do?" the Corey said worriedly, talking to Travis. "Why did you have to kill him? I know that the cops are going to pull us over. I just know that the cops are going to pull us over. I'm too young to go to jail. We could have just scared him. We didn't have to kill him!" The man rambled on full of sorrow on the verge of tears.

"Shut the fuck up!" Travis commanded. "Look we're just gonna have to hide out for a while and keep our mouths shut. We'll have to get rid of the car too. It's hot and the police will be looking for it. Now the club was dark so I'm sure no one saw my face. Besides the stripper no one else knows what we look like. I've seen the stripper before; she's a student at Blanding. She won't say nothing."

The two men parked the car in the backyard of a friend's house. Cory walked back to his dorm room, but Travis didn't go home to his dorm room that night. There was too much of a risk that he might get caught in the middle of the night. That's when the cops usually get you, when they think that you're asleep in your bed at four in the morning. He wandered the street on foot until he finally decided to spend the night at another friend's home off campus.

Bobby heard about the shooting the next day from one of his girls that worked in the strip club. She was upset that the police shut down the strip club after the shootout occurred. She wanted to give up school entirely and work the street, but Bobby didn't pay her pleas for employment any attention. The only thing he wanted to know was whether she was sure of whom she said died that night. He didn't believe her, questioning whether she saw what she knew that she saw. A million questions rolled through Bobby King's mind at that moment. Maybe it was a mistake. Maybe it was someone who looked like Midget Moe. Maybe he was only hurt real bad and was in the hospital now. But deep down Bobby knew the truth. She was telling the truth and no matter how much he tried to deny it he would have to face it sooner or later. It was a natural reaction for some people to go through denial when they heard of tragedy striking. That was Bobby's immediate way of coping with the lost of his friend.

With time, Bobby accepted the fact that his long time friend Midget Moe was dead. The only thing left for Bobby now was revenge. The stripper said that she didn't know who did the shooting but Bobby had a good idea. Midget Moe had hustled plenty of guys out of their money in the past, but no one had seen Travis around for a couple of days. Bobby knew that Travis would try to gain his revenge one day, if not on him, then on Moe or maybe even Larenzo, it was only a matter of time. That day Bobby went to Red's house and told the guys the horrible news.

The next few days were difficult for the group of friends gathered together at Red's house. The house didn't seem the same without Midget Moe around. No longer were the sounds of card playing and cheerful music heard in the home. The sounds of music were replaced by only the deafening silence of sorrow. Midget Moe's funeral was on a rainy Thursday. The funeral was very plain. The pews of the small Baptist church were mostly vacant as the diminutive body of Midget Moe set in a dull black rectangular casket. His face was powdered and plastered together to hide the bullet wounds, which had violently ruptured his body. His arms were folded across his miniature chest solemnly. Only his mother, stepfather, two baby mommas, and a few of his very close friends showed up. Even after the funeral, the group just didn't seem the same. It would take time to heal from the pain caused by his death.

In the coming days, everyone dealt with the death of Midget Moe in their own unique way. When Larenzo heard of Midget Moe's death he took his baseball cap off in regret. Larenzo never took off his hat for anyone and the fact that his hat was in his hands now showed how much he cared for Moe. Larenzo wasn't new to the deaths of close friends, and he knew that the police wouldn't do anything to catch the perpetrators. There was evidence to implicate Travis but no one would come forward and identify him. If justice was to be found it would have to come from the street, of that Larenzo was sure.

Malik didn't say much at all when he heard of the death of Midget Moe. He simply poured out a little bit of liquor from the small bottle of rum he had hidden in the pocket of his baggy army fatigues. Dealing with his despair in his own private way, Malik lit another blunt inhaling the drug. The cold emotionless look on his face was still present from when he spat in the face of Ebony. Since that night he barely ever spoke to anyone, much less showed any amount of emotion. His drug habit had taken a turn for the worse since that day. He now averaged four blunts a day, instead of one. Trying to maintain his high throughout the week began to get expensive, and the lights that he used to enjoy so much when he first started smoking began to fade more and more each day. It got to the point that his whole day seemed devoted to getting those lights to appear again. Malik had even stopped going to school all together, since his teacher kicked him out of the room for closing his eyes during class. With the death of Midget Moe, Malik fell deeper into his lonely depression.

JC became enraged when he heard the news. Kicking and screaming through the house, JC cursed the very ground that Travis walked on. JC didn't show up at Midget Moe's funeral. Years before JC promised that he would never go to another funeral again unless it was his own. Instead JC sat on the couch at Red's house rocking back and forth, scratching at the tattoo of dead friends on his arm. He tried to clear his mind of the image of Midget Moe lying in a coffin six feet under the ground with dirt on top of him. He had witnessed that scene too many times already with his other friends. He refused to see it again. The loss of another friend was almost too much for his young mind too deal with.

There were only two ways that Kel knew of forgetting the pain of losing a loved one, exercise and sex. Kel tried to work out in the gym first, doing pushups and running around the track several times. He was a Physical Education major, and working out was the only way that he knew how too deal with lost. Whenever he worked out his body, his mind forgot about the pain. Even when Kel worked out he smoked Black & Mild cigars. It seemed to him that no matter how much running or lifting he did, he couldn't forget about the pain he had from losing Midget Moe.

After exercising in the gym didn't work for him, Kel decided to devote his time to exercising in the bedroom. Kel attacked the female dorms on the campus night after night, sleeping with two or three girls in an evening. His favorite dorms were Haines Hall and Jenkins Hall. Much like his best friend Larenzo, Kel enjoyed having sex with cheerleaders and female freshmen. Medical reports prove that sex is the best stress reliever. If the medical reports were true, Kel had to have been the calmest person on the planet.

Red, on the other hand, dealt with the death of Midget Moe much differently than the rest of the guys. His face turned cold when he heard the news. The police reported that it was a gang war that spilled over into the streets. The police always made crimes that took place at Black Universities sound much bigger than what they truly were. "Gang war," Red laughed sarcastically. He knew that the little Southern town that the university resided in had never seen the results of a true gang war, not like the kind they had in New Jersey. Red knew the truth. It was just a poor dumb kid who was trying to get revenge on Midget Moe.

"They want a war, I'll give them a fuckin' war!" Red said coldly after the funeral. There was a grim almost deathly look on his face. Red went back to his house and walked into his room. Inside the dresser drawer by his bed, Red pulled out his twin .38 automatic pistols and checked the bullets in both of them. "When I catch Travis, he's a dead man!" Red proclaimed as he tucked them in the back of his red colored dress pants. Red had made up his mind to murder Travis whenever he saw him, but he didn't have any idea where to look.

Larenzo walked in Red's room when he heard the man talking to himself. "I know a way that we can get him," Larenzo said with a devilish smile. "I've been thinking about it since that night. I talked to a friend of mine that works in the University's Hall of Records. She says that Travis has been reported absent from all of his classes for the last couple of weeks, but his name hasn't been kicked out of the system yet." Larenzo paused for effect.

"So what does that mean for me?" Red asked sounding very confused.

A short interval passed during which Larenzo went quietly to Red and placed a hand on his shoulder. Red didn't acknowledge this tiny gesture of intimacy at all. "Well," Larenzo continued, "Don't you get it? If he hasn't been kicked out of the system yet, it means he was approved for independent study. Independent studies are offered to students who suffered a tragedy and can't return to their classes. Like if your roommate dies or you break both of your legs. He hasn't been skipping his classes this semester. He's been taking them at home and is supposed to turn in the work later on in the year."

"You're beginning to really piss me off," Red said cutting off Larenzo. "Larenzo, please explain to me why I should give a fuck where he's taking his classes. Or if he makes the Dean's List and all that other shit. I want to know how I can find him, so I can kill the son-of-a-bitch!" Red said angrily.

"Do I have to spell everything out to you? Listen, if you're taking independent study courses for Blanding University you are obligated to hand your work in personally at the end of the school semester to the department chairman. In other words, at nine o'clock in the morning on the last day of school Travis will have to go to Dr. Johnson's office on the third floor of the Mathematics building." Larenzo smiled at the precision of his plan.

"My friend also said that Travis put in for a transfer slip after this semester was over. So that means that if we don't kill him in the next couple of months he'll get away with it." In Larenzo's mind the plan was perfect. They knew exactly where Travis was going to be and when. Now it was only a matter of waiting patiently for the right time to strike. Four months was a long time to wait for a revenge but if they wanted the murder done right they would have to.

CHAPTER 8

Baby Momma

The next few weeks inched by slowly for the remaining friends. For the most part, life went on as usual. In time, sounds of joy came back to Red's house and things slowly reverted back to normal. It was nine o'clock in the morning.

Yawning loudly, Larenzo fought the desire to close his eyes and fall asleep in Shakespeare class. Shakespeare class always managed to put Larenzo to sleep sooner or later. It wasn't that the class itself was boring. Larenzo was an English major, and as such, he was intrigued by Shakespeare's unique ability to entertain crowds throughout the centuries. No. The fault wasn't in the greatness of the literary work itself. The fault lay in the professor of the subject. Larenzo solely blamed his behavior on the instructor. Dr. Fredrick taught English 201, and no matter how hard Larenzo tried he was never able to stay awake through the whole class period. Dr. Fredrick was an older looking teacher from Nigeria, and the tone of his mundane foreign voice alone was enough to put anyone asleep.

Dr. Fredrick walked through the rows of the classroom slowly reading from a large book as he started his lecture. "Today class, we will examine in detail the full implications and the extraordinary use of the LOVE theme as used in Shakespeare's plays and sonnets." Dr. Fredrick paused for a moment to write the word "LOVE" on the board. "The word love for Shakespeare dealt with so very much more than mere fornication and other various sexual encounters. In Shakespeare's time, William Shakespeare used the theme of true love as a pair of characters completely created for each other in every way possible. Most characters in his plays are stuck in a repressed phallic stage. Their mates are generally described as there animus, or perfect partner, someone whom the character would give up their life for, someone whom they would kill for..." Dr. Fredrick's mundane voice trailed off as Larenzo's eyes eventually closed.

The more Dr. Fredrick talked the more sleep began to overcome Larenzo. Today was worse than other days for Larenzo. He could hardly keep his eyes open, exhausted from staying up late the night before, and playing video games with JC. Now he could feel his body beginning to slowly shutdown. Larenzo sat only a few rows from the front and he was sure that Dr. Fredrick was watching him closely. Unable to fight off sleep any longer, Larenzo allowed his head to drop down on his chest as he nodded off. Thanks to Dr. Fredrick's intervention, the sleep didn't last long at all.

Dr. Fredrick walked over to Larenzo and slammed his giant textbook on the desk causing Larenzo to jump up startled. The classroom snickered a little when the instructor began to speak with Larenzo. "Mr. Baker, I would appreciate it if you did not hibernate in my classroom. This is a learning environment. If you do not want to learn you are welcome to leave. I do expect for not only you, but all of your fellow classmates, to take heed of this warning, for it is the final one I shall give." Dr. Fredrick said slowly in his foreign accent making sure to pronounce each word carefully.

The initial shock of the book slamming on the desk had startled Larenzo back to his senses. "Dr. Fredrick, you know you're right and I think everyone should take close heed of that warning," Larenzo said cockily. "That's why I'm going to ask you to excuse me to the restroom so I can fully awaken myself. That way I can totally enjoy the whole experience of your exhilarating lecture." The classroom giggled at Larenzo's sarcastic remarks.

Before Dr. Fredrick could answer, Larenzo got out of his chair and rushed off to the bathroom. Once in the bathroom, Larenzo splashed cold water on his face. He yawned loudly and stretched, finally wiping his face with a brown paper towel. Larenzo knew that Dr. Fredrick would be steaming mad at him when he returned. As a result, Larenzo took his time making his way back to the classroom. The hallways were empty and as Larenzo casually walked down the corridors back to Dr. Fredrick's classroom he noticed that the other classes were full. Perhaps it was curiosity or maybe just boredom, but Larenzo glanced into several of the classrooms recognizing many of the students inside.

The classroom next to Dr. Fredrick's was only partially full. A youthful teacher was standing in front of the students. Larenzo watched as the class silently took notes, and that's when he saw her. She was writing notes on a piece of paper and she had a habit of slightly sticking her tongue out in between her soft lips when she was deep in thought. She was thin and no taller than five foot six inches. Her smooth skin was the complexion of cool coconut. Her long silken brown hair hung past her shoulders and her eyes were the color of golden honey. She sat completely still at her desk with her skirt rising slowly up her smooth legs. If he let himself Larenzo could drop into a trance staring at her sleek legs or those deep honey colored eyes. In total awe of her beauty, Larenzo simply mouthed the word ... "Joy."

At first, Larenzo's heart seemed to flutter when he laid eyes on her. His mouth became dry and he could feel his knees become weak. He hadn't seen her face this whole semester except for in his dreams and when he was having sex with other women. To Larenzo, Joy Summer was, by far, the sexiest black woman on the campus, if not the world. Everything about Joy fascinated Larenzo. Her deep honey coated eyes. The touch of her tanned skin. Even the scent of vanilla in her hair drove Larenzo to extremes of lust. Joy Summer was a virgin her freshman year of college and it was this pureness that attracted Larenzo to her more than anything else. In Larenzo's eyes she was nothing short of a goddess sent from the heavens to be worshipped. She was the peak example of feminine exquisiteness in its most uncorrupted form. She was the one woman on campus that he wanted to have more than anything else, yet avoided his every advance.

Larenzo shook himself out of his hypnotic stare at Joy. Satisfaction flooded through Larenzo as he glided back to Dr. Fredrick's English class. Once in the class, Larenzo sat at his desk, and this time instead of falling asleep, Larenzo daydreamed of one day reuniting with Joy Summer. The rest of the class period was uneventful and generally went by quickly for Larenzo after he saw Joy in the next classroom. When the period was over Larenzo rushed from the class searching for Joy. He looked up and down the hallway but he didn't see her small, well-shaped figure anywhere. The class next door had let out early. "Damn it!" Larenzo said cursing to himself. A glimmer of panic was in his eyes; he had come too far to lose her again.

He sprinted down the stairs and headed toward the Pit in the center of campus. That's where he saw her again. She was strolling peacefully on the sidewalk with one of her female classmates. Joy was cradling her books in her arms like she was holding an infant. She didn't walk. She seemed to glide down the sidewalk, full of grace in her every step like that of a princess. Her lip-gloss glistened in the sun. Her tight fitting skirt hugged her rear as she walked. Larenzo couldn't hold back his passion any longer. He swiftly ran up behind her and tapped her on the shoulder, startling her, slightly making her jump.

"Joy, I missed you," Larenzo blurted out quickly when she turned to see exactly who it was. "I miss us." Larenzo said more honestly than ever before. Larenzo's heart pounded so hard that his chest began to ache.

Her eyes, when she glanced up at Larenzo were bright and happy at the words of authentic sentiment, which flowed from his lips. She tried not to, but she smiled at his words, blushing. Her smile was captivating in its sweet sensuality and pureness. "Hi Larenzo," Joy said softly. "You know that you hurt me a lot. But I kinda missed you too." Her voice sounded like a classical sweet melody to him.

Larenzo smiled back at her. He was glad that she was still talking to him after all that they had been through together. "Well, maybe we should talk about it over some breakfast in the Pit." Larenzo said offering his arm like a gentleman but she didn't accept it.

"No." Joy said reluctantly.

"No?" Larenzo repeated surprised at the answer.

A frown crossed Larenzo's face, but he didn't let her see how much her answer affected him emotionally. Larenzo seemed a little bit bewildered at the response, he was sure that she still had strong feelings for him but she didn't show any. Larenzo prided himself as a man of confidence, and Joy's unexpected reply hurt his feelings, ripping the confidence from his image.

Joy smiled at the look of momentary doubt in Larenzo's eye. She wasn't used to that expression in Larenzo's usually cool demeanor, and deep down it reminded her of the young man that she first met a year and a half ago. "I have to go to my dorm but you can call me some time," Joy said smiling flirtatiously. She took out a piece of paper wrote down her phone number and then handed it to him.

"I'll be home tonight around eight o'clock. So if you want me...use it."

"I sure will." Larenzo's voice trailed off as the two women walked toward their dorm. For a minute Larenzo stared at the phone number written in bright pink ink. The piece of paper read: For Joy call 553-7549. It was the number to her dorm room. Larenzo gave a half smile at the youthful word play on the piece of paper.

That night Larenzo lay in his bed, calling Joy. He set up a time to meet. Larenzo used his cell phone so he made sure that the conversation was quick and to the point. After Larenzo hung up his emotions swelled with visions of marriage and delight. Larenzo jumped into the cold shower of Munroe Hall ignoring the icy temperature of the water.

On the other end of the phone, on the opposite end of campus in Townsend Hall, the emotions were much different. Joy's roommate, Stacy sat on her bed and glared at Joy in disgust. "How could you consider going out with that creep after what he did to you last year? He had his chance and he blew it! Why don't you talk to that nice football player that keeps calling you? What's his name, you know...Steve?" Stacy said staring at her roommate who obviously still had feelings for Larenzo.

"I don't want Steve," Joy answered casually. "I don't want a jock who doesn't care about me as a person. I want Larenzo. I've always wanted Larenzo, even before I knew what I wanted. Stacy, you wouldn't understand the connection that we have. It's like being on a diet and wanting a dessert you can't have. Larenzo is my chocolate cake." Joy paused for a moment then she continued. "It's like having something you know is no good for you but you want it anyway. And you know that it will hurt you in the end but it just doesn't matter."

The next few weeks for Larenzo and Joy were spent filled with blissful delight as they became reacquainted with one another. Frolicking gleefully through life, their pasts began to be forgotten, and with it, the anguish of the breakup. Holding hands walking together at night, under the moonlight, Larenzo and Joy began to once again feel comfortable around each other. If it were possible they would remain in this utopia, forever content with the present, blind to the past.

But no matter how marvelous life seems, utopia is never forever.

Time passed quickly for the couple as it usually does for those whose hearts is happy. Before they knew it, it was already time for midterms. It was the middle of a Wednesday and the campus was alive, students were thriving wholesomely intermixing with each another. Hundreds of students would hurry to their various classes with number two pencils held in front of them like medieval soldiers off to war holding swords. Teachers prepared lesson plans, dreaming of well-deserved vacations, knowing well that the four month long task of educating was halfway over.

For the majority of the student body at Blanding University midterms week is a time to reminiscent over the mistakes they made prior and promises to do better in the future. Last minute studying and worrying about their courses ran ramped through the campus. Most of the student body made preparations for taking the tests, most, but not all. Red was one of the members of that minority. He didn't care whether he passed or failed the tests. Red strolled casually into his calculus class ten minutes late. The instructor glared at him with a look of loathing, but didn't say anything as Red made his way to a desk and began his test. Midway through the test Red got a strange sensation. He looked around scanning the classroom. That's when he noticed it, or more to the point he didn't notice it. The seat beside him, which Kel usually sat in, was empty and a strange quietness covered the class. Sure it was of the norm for Red to miss a day, but it was an oddity for Kel to miss a class much less a midterm examination.

Red didn't care that Kel missed the test and that his midterm's grade would be horrendous. No, Red's worries were far more selfish than that. Frantic fears that Kel might have been in trouble ran through Red's mind. He had already lost one friend during the semester, and he didn't want to lose another. After the test was done, Red called Kel's dorm room searching for his missing classmate. Ring. Ring. No answer. Red checked at his house but no one there had seen him in a few days. Then Red searched through the campus for Kel, but no one seemed to know where he was. Red was walking by Haines Hall and just when he'd all but given up on finding Kel, Kel found him.

"What up, Red?" Kel yelled out running out of Haines Hall with a large smile on his face. "Heard you was looking for me. Yo, look I know that I missed Mrs. Perry's calculus test but I've been real busy for the last couple of days. Besides, my uncle is a doctor and he already wrote me a excuse note. What's going on, my nigga? What I missed in class?" Kel said still extremely happy as though he didn't have a worry in the world.

There was definitely something very peculiar about Kel's behavior. His eyes were filled with merriment. Red hadn't seen Kel like this since before the murder of Moe. In fact, Red had never seen Kel quite like this before. His facial expressions seemed to shine; it was as though there was a lantern under Kel's skin shining brightly. He was a child reborn, living life to its fullest, forgetting all of the pain and suffering that he had experienced in the past few weeks of his life.

"Where the fuck you been?" Red said aggravation beginning to build in his face. He stared at Kel suspiciously for a moment longer, then continued. "Ain't no one seen you around my house in days. You don't play cards with the fellas anymore, and now you're missing midterm test. Talk to me Kel! What's really going on?" Red said in a mellow voice hiding his true frustrated feelings.

Kel stood in front of Red with a look of shock on his face. "Nothing is up," Kel said defensively. "For the first time in a long while I actually feel good. I've been chillin' with Crystal Kerry for the last couple of days. Besides, Mrs. Perry can kiss my ass. I got her medical excuse; I'll take the goddamn test when I feel like it. I'm just tired of mother-fuckers bothering me over little petty shit. I'm stressed and I'm just trying to chill out. I'll stop over your house later on tonight and play some cards, but if you don't see me its because I'm chilling out with my girl."

"Your girl?" Red paused for a long time but Kel didn't answer at first. Then he spoke, or rather laughed, at the absurdity of the statement. "I thought Crystal Kerry was Renzo's chick. He knows that you been beating Crystal's back out when he's been gone? I guess that you already told him that you've been kicking it with his old broad like that."

"Told him?" Kel repeated Red's statement in disgust. "I don't have to tell him about every girl I'm sleeping with," Kel said as he lit a Black & Mild cigar. "I mean, shit, it ain't like he was going with her steady or nothing like that." Kel threw his arms above his head wildly, almost violently. "He's been spending so much time with that bitch, Joy, that I haven't had a chance to talk to him anyhow." The use of the word bitch from Kel surprised Red more than anything else he said. Kel never called women bitches and the fact that he called Joy one made Red realized that there was more to the situation than met the eye. A tinge of jealousy was present in his voice.

Kel let out a sigh as he blew a puff of smoke in the air. The discussion with Red had drained Kel of his exuberant attitude and left him weary. Wanting to end the conversation, Kel checked his watch. "Look, Red, it's getting late and I got to take Crystal to the store. So I'll just talk to you later. Okay?" Kel said quickly, stopping the conversation rudely. Then he scurried back into the front door of Haines Hall and up the stairwell.

"Damn shame," Red said as he watched Kel hurry back to Crystal's room.

That night, Red's house was filled with students. Loud Rap music pounded through the walls all the way to the street. It was like the death of Midget Moe never happened. Peace and tranquility had finally come back to Red's hollowed home. For an instant it seemed that the theory that time erases all worries was valid. Malik sat on the couch. His mind drifted off as he smoked on a blunt peacefully. JC and John Spencer played a basketball videogame sitting on the floor of the living room. Shawna and the rest of a small group of girls were in the kitchen cooking a giant pot of Ramen noodles. Bobby was sipping on an alcoholic beverage trying his best to ignore the admiring stares and whispers from a few of the girls in the kitchen. Larenzo was talking on the phone with Joy, and Red was having sex behind his locked door with a young lady. It seemed as though everything in the world was right once again, but no, there was something missing. The card table was bare. That was it! The sounds of card playing weren't there. It was that joyful noise of blended laughter and arguments, which was still missing in the house. After Midget Moe's death no one played Spades anymore. It was almost as though without his cheating antics there was no reason to continue playing.

The bareness of the card table depressed Larenzo greatly, and for a moment he actually considered leaving Red's house and visiting Joy. That idea quickly fled his mind when he heard the doorbell ring. The sound of the doorbell startled everyone in the home. Everyone usually just walked into the house without announcing them-selves first. No one had ever used the doorbell before and the loud rattling noise that it had made everyone present flinch. Everyone sat silently, gawking at the doorway curiously to see who was ringing the bell. Bobby thought that first thought that it was a door-to-door sales-man, but then he realized that a salesman wouldn't come to that neighborhood. "The door is open!" JC yelled not taking his eyes off of the video game in front of him.

"It's probably a fucking Jehovah Witness," Malik said blowing mari-juana smoke in the air.

It was obvious that no one was prepared for who walked through that door. With a squeak of the doorknob Crystal Kerry walked through the doorway first. She stepped softly knowing full well that everyone in the house was staring at her. She didn't mind, though, in fact she enjoyed the attention she received. She was used to it. "Hi everyone," Crystal said giving a halfhearted wave at the crowded liv-ing room. "Kel said that we should come by and visit. We brought some gifts." Her voice was soft and friendly like a child exploring new territory. She had been to Red's house before, but only on a few occasions at his wild parties. This was the first time that she had ever walked into Red's house without being at an official party.

Kel staggered through the door next, in his arms were three big bottles of liquor. "Let's get the game started!" Kel exclaimed full of excitement. Kel seemed like his old self again. Kel smiled and hopped slightly as he walked, happy that he was once again back at Red's house. He was back home. Larenzo hadn't even noticed that he hadn't seen Kel in a few days. Bobby grabbed a couple of the bottles preventing Kel from dropping them. "I feel like cutting some body's ass on the card table," Kel said as he pulled out a deck of playing cards and threw them on the wooden table. "Who's going to be first?"

A spark of happiness rose in Larenzo's eye when he saw the deck of cards hit the wooden table. "Hell yeah," Larenzo announced hap-pily. "That's what I'm talking about! Lets get a classic game on, Kel and me versus Bobby and JC. Winner takes all!" Larenzo pulled out a few balled up one dollar bills from his pants pocket and placed them on the table.

Just the mention of money made JC turn his attention from the video game to the card table. "I'll match that bet," JC said quickly staring at the few dollars lying on the table.

"No you won't," Kel said quickly shaking his hand at JC, pausing. "These our my cards and my rules. We're not gambling during this game. I don't need to hear any crying when me and Crystal beat ya'll ass."

"No gambling? Shit, I'll sit this one out," JC said as a scowl came to his lips. Kel's words seemed to strip all delight from the face of JC. Just the idea of playing cards and not making a friendly bet took all of the pleasure out of the game. JC hadn't bet on anything since Midget Moe died, and now that he couldn't wager any amount of money on this game the notion of playing lost its appeal.

"I'll play with Larenzo," Bobby said sitting down at the table first.

"We're not on the same team?" Larenzo whispered to Kel as if the words were filled with mystery. He couldn't believe his ears. It was absurd for the two Spade champions to play against each other. Kel and Larenzo had played as teammates on the Spades table for so long that the idea of playing against each other seemed wrong in some way. Larenzo didn't like the teams at all, it was like going off to war to battle your brother. Something wasn't right and Larenzo got an ominous feeling before the first card was thrown on the wooden table.

Before long, the card game started and a bottle of gin that Kel brought was opened. Bobby and Larenzo played against Kel and Crystal, but the game took place mostly in silence until the last hand. Thanks to Kel's expert card playing, and a few bad hands for Larenzo and Bobby, Kel and Crystal only needed one more good hand to win the game. They bid five for the win. A solemn silence ran through the table as everyone looked at their cards. Kel looked worriedly at his hand. Then he looked at his partner and saw that she wasn't looking at her cards at all anymore; she was staring at Larenzo.

Bobby looked at his cards and smiled from ear to ear, "We're going pound for the win!" A small look of doubt flashed across Larenzo's face, but he had confidence in his partner so he smiled also. The next few minutes were filled with trash talking and nail biting. The last cards remained and Larenzo realized that Bobby and he were going to win the game. Larenzo stood up from the table and slammed a joker down ferociously. "You two bitches can get the fuck off of the table, because this game is over!" Larenzo said triumphantly.

Kel's bushy eyebrows shot up at the statement. Kel stood up also and slammed his fist down on the wooden table making it shake slightly. "What'd you just call her?" Kel said. His arms trembled from anger. Kel wasn't used to losing and when he heard the profanity slip so easily from Larenzo's lips, it disturbed him.

"I called both of you bitches." Larenzo repeated his statement. "Don't catch feelings now because you're losing. You should have played on the same team with me when you had the chance." Larenzo spoke calmly as though he didn't see the major problem.

Larenzo's harsh words hit a nerve and Kel's face grew dark with fury. "I don't give a fuck what you have to call me! But never ever call her a bitch again in your life! She deserves better than that. Take it back! Tell her she's not a bitch!" Kel demanded.

Larenzo shrugged his shoulders at the ridiculousness of the entire situation. To Larenzo he was just talking trash to the opposite team, as is the right of the winners over the losers. He knew that he couldn't apologize to Crystal. It would have been simple enough to say 'I'm sorry', but Larenzo knew that he wouldn't say those words. His pride prevented him from saying it. Saying those words would have meant admitting that he was wrong to have called her out of her name. His reputation demanded that he stay stubborn even if it meant ending a lifelong friendship.

"I ain't taking back shit! I wish I would apologize for talking shit on the card table. Did you forget where you are? We originated talking shit on the table!" Larenzo stated with anger now in his voice. He had had enough of Kel's rampant accusations and unreasonable requests. Larenzo threw down his remaining two cards on the table, and stared intensely, locking eyes with Kel. "What'd you want to do, fight me over this bitch? She was my bitch way before you ever thought about sticking your dick in her!" Larenzo said flinging his middle finger in the air in defiance.

"I don't talk about Joy!" Kel said scowling as he mentioned her name. "I would appreciate it if you don't talk about Crystal."

"This has nothing to do with Joy!" Larenzo replied angrily.

Bobby stood up between the two men, separating them from each other. He was well respected by both Larenzo and Kel and at that moment he was the only one capable of separating the two. His voice was calm and collected as he began to speak, "You guys are like brothers. It's not right for you two to be fighting like this. It's just a game and in the morning both of you are going to regret some of the stuff that you said tonight."

For a moment Bobby's words sunk into the psyches of the two lifelong friends, and nothing but silence could be heard. A bitterness swept through the room like a sandstorm. Kel stood stubborn as ever, his skinny arms folded across his chest. His nostrils flared with rage and his eyes closed to mere slits like daggers. Across the table stood Larenzo, his chest out with pride. His brown eyes slanted downward cockily at the smaller Kel. Larenzo's hand twitched with expectation of a fight. A look of sorrow was found deep in his eyes, but he kept his emotions hidden, bottled up like a secret.

"You're both pathetic!" an intoxicated Malik Brown proclaimed breaking the silent stare down of the two men. Malik's eyes were barely open as a result from the heavy drug use. When he tried to stand up from the couch, he lost his balance slightly, almost falling. "Pathetic to believe that women are worth fighting real friends over." He chuckled too himself. "We are black men. Men are sons of suns, and as suns it is our right - no our responsibility to shine light on the universe." He paused to sip some liquor from his glass.

"Shut up! You're high and not making any sense." Larenzo said turning his anger toward Malik.

"Hey at least he's not smoking cigarettes. That shit will really kill you." JC said trying to make light of the argument before it could go any farther.

"I may be high... but I know what I'm talking about." Malik laughed, a hollow laugh like one who is in pain, yet hides his scars. Malik put his blunt out stamping the fire out in an ashtray. "Listen to my words. It is unnatural for man to fall in love. That is why black men cheat on their women. In ancient African culture, a man could have as many women as he could afford. See, the original man realizes that instinctively, man is a sun. Every culture on the planet has worshipped the image of the sun in one shape or another. The Egyptians, Aztec Indians, Jews, and yes even Christians." He half smiled, and then let it go perhaps realizing he was rambling off the subject.

"Man is the sun and woman are the earth," Malik continued. "Even you've heard the expression Mother Earth. See, as a sun we might want to focus our radiant sunlight on just one planet in our solar system. But if we do, that planet, no matter how large it is will eventually dry up and die. That is why, we as men, can't give all of our attention to just one woman. They simply can't handle it; eventually they will dry up and die inside, turning into desolate wasteland shells of their former beauty."

Kel threw up his hand dismissing Malik's statement as drunken ranting of a hurt lovesick man. "You need to get help. That drug shit is melting your brain cells. I'm leaving. Peace!" Kel said, upset and confused as he walked toward the front door.

Malik shook his head ponderously and sighed. "Look at the effects of love in its purest, foulest, vile form. How it destroys friendships and stabs at the heart..." Malik gave an evil cackle from the pit of his gut, like a mad scientist uncovering the secret of everlasting life. His blood-shot eyes opened widely, and he smiled showing all of his teeth. "Maybe you should leave? Leave your friends that you've known for years to be in the arms of just another harlot! Both of you think that somehow the right woman will make your dreams come true and your fantasies become reality. You need to both listen to me. I may be high and I may be drunk, but I know the evil that is woman, and I know that to find peace, we as suns, will have too find it in our friends."

"Kel, listen to me," Larenzo stated pleadingly. "You've been my best friend since the seventh grade. You are my brother. We go back to Transformers and comic books. Don't ruin our friendship over some girl that doesn't care about either one of us."

Kel left Red's house without saying anything in response, Crystal Kerry on his arm. Pity rose on the intoxicated face of Malik when Kel slammed the door behind him. Malik's closed eyes squeezed tight, "Alas, both you will soon see the error of your ways." After Malik spoke, his body collapsed back onto the couch wearily, almost as if his legs gave way from the strain of holding up his body.

Larenzo tilted the brim of his hat attempting to cover his eyes. The argument with Kel had rekindled feelings that Larenzo thought were buried forever. In anger, Larenzo flung the deck of cards across the table, scattering them across the floor. He had known Kel since they were in elementary school and now his friendship might have just ended over a Spades game and a damn girl. Larenzo felt like crying but his tears never came. His pride was stronger than that.

That night Kel laid in Crystal's bed alone, restless with thoughts of betrayal running through his mind. Crystal was in the shower humming happily as she bathed in the warm water. Kel never wanted Larenzo to find out about him and Crystal like that, not in that sort of environment. In the quietness of the Haines Hall dorm room looking down upon the rest of the campus Kel thought of different ways that he should have handled the situation better. *"Maybe I shouldn't have asked him to apologize? Maybe I shouldn't have brought Crystal to Red's house? Maybe I should call him and say I'm sorry?"* The internal questions burned into his brain like poison fire. And just as soon as the questions of doubt developed in his head, an old streak of stubbornness arose from his subconscious denying the possibility of any wrongdoing. *"No, I can't be wrong for being with the person I love. I won't believe it! He was wrong. He was wrong to mistreat her! Larenzo has always been wrong for the way he treats women!"*

Kel's thoughts brooded on the validity of his actions from earlier that night. He had been friends with Larenzo for years and the idea of not speaking with him sickened Kel. All Larenzo had to do was apologize and Kel would have forgiven him. No, Kel knew that Larenzo would never apologize, not in front of a group of people. His damn pride would keep him from doing that heroic deed. Kel had Crystal now and that is what really counted. It was obvious that Larenzo never really wanted her to begin with; she was just another woman that he occasionally used for sex and money. At that moment, Kel made up his mind that if Larenzo couldn't treat Crystal like she deserved to be treated he would happily take the job. With his mind definitely made up and his conscious clear, Kel closed his eyes relaxing on the satin sheets of Crystal's bed slowly falling into a deep slumber.

Half hour passed, before Kel was awakened to the sensation of light kisses on his forehead and chin. He knew from where the kisses were originating before he even opened his eyes. "Crystal," Kel said still partially asleep, his voice raspy and hoarse. Kel opened his eyes to see the beautiful features of Crystal Kerry staring back at him. He kissed her fully on the lips and caressed her face lovingly within his hands. "I was dreaming about you," Kel said wetting his lips.

"I know." Crystal replied. "You called out my name when you were sleep. It was so cute."

Her comment made him blush a little, his face flashing a wide grin for her to see. It made him feel good to be awakened with soft kisses. Crystal was dressed in only a white towel, which was wrapped around her golden brown body like a tight fitting dress. Droplets of warm water still glistened off her body. Her hair was wet and combed backward in shiny straight strands. The heat and smell of the shower still lingered in the air of the dorm room. Crystal sat on top of Kel's waist and fingered his small muscular chest slowly. She was beautiful: sitting calmly on top of him like an angel staring deeply into his eyes. It was perfect. Kel wouldn't have traded that moment for anything on the planet, but there was one thing amiss in the beauty of the moment. Her eyes held a look of sorrow, not on the surface, but very deep down like a cancer festering slowly that would eventually kill, years from now. The moment disappeared and the spell of the magical atmosphere vanished with it. Only her light brown eyes were left, with the soft sorrow hidden behind each eyelid.

"What's wrong?" Kel said, genuinely caring about her well being.

Her voice began to drop into a lower tone as their eyes met, "Kel, I've never felt this way before," Crystal began. "I just want you to know that this small amount of time that I've had with you was special to me." She stared at Kel a moment longer, then slowly, very slowly her eyes broke contact with his, and she gazed downward toward her abdomen. A few tears dropped from her cheeks and she continued speaking in sobs. "I'm only twenty one years old. I'm so scared and I need someone I know will stick with me when I need him the most. What I'm trying to say is, Kel, I'm pregnant. You're going to be a daddy."

Kel blinked in disbelief.

"A daddy?" Kel repeated the words absorbing all of the various implications, which came along with the term. "Are you sure? You said you were on the pill. I mean... we've only been together for a short amount of time." Kel sat up and reached for his pack of Black & Mild cigars and lit one nervously.

"I'm sure about the test results," Crystal said quietly, her voice no more than a whisper. "I only missed taking the pill one night. Yesterday, when I went to the doctor for a checkup he said I was a couple of weeks pregnant. I don't know what to do, but I don't want to have to kill my baby...I don't want to kill <u>our</u> baby." More tears fell from her eyes whenever she mentioned the word baby. Her tears choked her, getting stuck in her throat making her tremble. The emotion of the scene nearly brought Kel to tears, also.

Kel shook his head vigorously in disbelief of the facts. "I have to go. Everything is moving to fast for me right now." Kel took a few puffs of the cigar and put his shirt on quickly. "Sign me out downstairs. I can't deal with this right now. I'll give you a call later on tonight," Kel said rushing toward the elevator. He knew that he wouldn't call her that night or the week after. The realization that he was going to be a father was too much for him to handle. For the next month Kel successfully managed to avoid Crystal. It wasn't that he wasn't ready to be a father; it just seemed to him that everything was moving all too fast. For now he all he knew is that he would have to have time to himself.

CHAPTER 9

Homecoming

The air was filled with moisture and the sky was scattered with clumsy clouds, which managed to hide the beaming rays of the sun from time to time. The long awaited Homecoming Weekend had finally reached Blanding University. An unmistakable energy was in the atmosphere flooding the small southern town with a frenzy of energetic emotion. Homecoming weekend was the only two days of the school year when students past, present, and future would congregate in celebration of their mutual experiences at the historical black university. The majority of the Homecoming week festivities had been basically uneventful except for the nightly parties held in the gymnasium and the occasional cookout. Everyone knew that two things truly defined Homecoming Weekend at Blanding University: the Homecoming football game and Red's Homecoming House Party. Because of the recent death of Midget Moe, Red had declined to throw his own annual house party that week, leaving only the highly anticipated football game.

Lines of newly washed vehicles were packed bumper to bumper, stuck in traffic outside of the prestigious university's hollowed walls. Once inside the walls of the university, the traffic wasn't much better. Campus police had taken it upon themselves to set up several barricades and detours, which only helped foster the horrible traffic jams. Several cars were parked illegally on the sidewalks as well as midway in the street. Realizing that it would be far easier and faster on foot, hundreds of people, different ages, sizes, and colors could be seen marching toward the football stadium. A wonderful clash of different forms of music and aromas of several different foods emerged from the direction of the football stadium.

Cramped in Bobby's car the small group of friends slowly made their way through traffic toward the gigantic stadium on the far end of the campus. Bobby drove the car calmly with one hand on the steering wheel. JC sat partially in the passenger seat hanging out of the window bouncing slightly to the bass filled music coming from the car. Larenzo slouched in the back, his arm leaning against the glass, his traditional White Sox baseball cap tilted upward so he could clearly see the crowds of people steadily making their way toward the stadium from the halfway opened car window. Red sat beside the other backseat window, his eyes showed that he was completely unimpressed by the school's festivities. In between the figures of Red and Larenzo, sat Malik. His eyes were closed tight as though he were concentrating on something that was just outside of his mental reach. His breath reeked of alcohol, and the unmistakable stench of marijuana lingered on his clothes and hair.

Malik reached into his jacket and pulled out a small bottle of liquor, lithely taking a swallow of the liquid inside. It was obvious to everyone in the car that Malik was well on his way to becoming completely drunk. He had no desire of drinking in moderation. For Malik, the alcohol was a means of covering the painful memories of his past in a tornado of emotion, eventually causing nausea, disorientation, anger, and finally guilt. Yes. Ultimately it was guilt, guilt that he would bear all of his life, that he had not tried harder to make the relationship with Ebony work, that somewhere, deep in the very pit of his soul, he didn't allow himself to forgive her.

Everybody was present in the group except for John and Kel. Kel had been missing since his argument with Larenzo, but it was a rare occasion in deed when he would miss a school event as popular as the Homecoming Football Game. John, on the other hand, had decided to spend some time with his girlfriend instead of hanging with his new friends. It wasn't fully unexpected considering that he did love his girlfriend very much.

From a distance Bobby could see the university's enormous stadium. The off-white circular structure rose to the sky gracefully defying even the heavens themselves. Flags of the school's colors waved proudly in the air attached to poles at the top of the building. Created several decades before, Blanding University's football stadium stood as a testimony of what was possible through the hard work of the black community combined with the few government funds given stingily toward the state funded school every year.

As Bobby's car slowly drove around the packed parking lot, Larenzo could see the endless rows of people tailgating.

Eventually the carload of friends parked in the nearby dirt filled parking lot near the stadium. Moments later they quickly walked to the stadium becoming merrily engulfed into the mob of students and alumni alike. Like leaves caught in the wind, the group was gently pushed toward the stadium's outer gates. Eagerly, the game's spectators uncaringly pushed and shoved their way through the metal gates of the stadium. Once inside the tall metal gates vendors of all sorts of products stood proudly by their wooden tables. The vendors sold everything at their tables from poorly knitted clothing to bootleg CDs copied off of someone's personal computer. Homecoming for these vendors had become more than a day of celebration. It had become a major payday out of the year.

Once inside the stadium, the hordes of people broke into large clusters according to different group affiliations and classes. The different fraternities and sororities grouped together creating waves of colorful gold, green, crimson, and pink in the stands. Larenzo stood amazed at the sea of color that had unfolded before his eyes. The self-segregation of the different groups was completely routine and expected. Aside from the different masses of Greek organizations, the athletes usually sat together, as well as the older generations of alumni.

Legal segregation had ceased in the South decades earlier, yet the mobs of students and alumni seemed to naturally separate themselves. Greek from non-Greek, old from young, alumni from non-alumni, and student from non-student. Separation into different factions seemed to come completely naturally for the mass of African Americans whom had come to enjoy the annual celebration titled "Homecoming." Much like the rest of the student body, Larenzo, Red, Bobby, JC, and Malik also sat together in a small huddle on the cold, hard, metal benches. Larenzo checked his watch as they sat down in the section by Blanding University's band. The time was already 3:30 in the afternoon and game had just begun to start. Officially, Larenzo knew that they were twelve minutes late, but unofficially he knew that school sponsored events such as the long awaited Homecoming football game always ran on C.P. (colored people) time. It wasn't unusual for the game to start ten, even twenty minutes later than it was originally scheduled.

Shortly after most of the student body had crowded the long metal stands of the stadium an energetic voice came on the overhead loud speaker drowning out the roar of the ever increasing crowd, announcing Blanding Universities marching band and the start of the game: "Ladies and gentlemen, welcome to Blanding U's Homecoming! Would you please stand as your world famous marching band plays *Lift Every Voice and Sing* and the *National Anthem*! Blanding University put your hands together for the highly anticipated, often intimidated, never duplicated, World Famous Marching Band of Blanding University!"

The band began to play the first few cords of *Lift Every Voice* and a hush ran through the enormously crowded stadium. The endless stands of students, fans, and alumni simultaneously and solemnly stood up. The band's drums and trumpets section magnificently played the timeless instrumental perfectly. "Ladies and gentlemen would you please remain standing for the *National Anthem?*" the energetic voice spoke once again over the overhead loudspeaker. Everyone stayed standing except for one lone figure that plopped down very boldly when he heard the first few cords of the song. At once all of the people in that section of the stadium looked down at the young black man very crossly.

"I'm a black man, and that song don't mean shit to me!" Malik said very defiantly in defense of his actions. His voice began to become louder and louder as he continued to speak, almost as though he wanted the entire stadium to hear him over the deafening sound of the band. "That song represents four hundred plus years of the undemocratic racist control of one of the most evil Anglo-Saxon empires to ever dwell on this planet. It's just a shame that my young brothers and sisters don't see the hypocritical nature of the very civilization that you live in."

"Chill out," Red said quickly, cutting Malik's words off. "Don't no one want to hear that shit now."

"I'll be quiet for now, but only because these self righteous people aren't ready for the truth. They think this government is here to cater to their every whim, but the reality of it is that African Americans have been brain washed since the 1800's." Malik continued to ramble on, becoming louder and louder the more he was allowed to speak. Soon the marching band finished playing and only the yelling of Malik could be heard echoing through the still silent stadium. "The American society has even corrupted the minds of the black man's women. They defile they're own bodies in unnatural blasphemy!"

Finally a slightly overweight graduate student two rows directly above Malik put a finger to her lips and shushed the young black militant. "Who the fuck you think you're shushing, bitch?" Malik, now yelling at the top of his lungs, roared in reply. His words were harsh and to the point.

"Take it easy," Red said gently. "You don't know that girl and she don't know you. Just sit there and chill out."

Red's voice had a calming tone to it. His words were soothing, yet forceful, almost as though they were made with the exact pitch to ease Malik's troubled mind, almost as though Red knew the extreme torment that had haunted Malik for the last couple of weeks. With a look of a mixture of mental exhaustion and frustration Malik bit down on his lip preventing himself from speaking and folded his arms across his chest angrily.

Larenzo laughed politely at this, and then again made a silent chuckle. He shook his head. "You a wild boy, Malik. Just sit back and enjoy the game."

Malik didn't answer, but Larenzo saw his face fill with momentarily sadness. A sudden sense of grief arose in Malik's face and then he smiled fleetingly as though the smile itself hurt to maintain. Malik pulled out a miniature bottle of Crown Royal from his jacket pocket and swallowed a large gulp. His eyes began to become glazed and he made a ghastly face as the liquor worked down into the pit of his stomach, burning the entire way. Larenzo looked away from Malik, trying not to stare at the slightly intoxicated man anymore, allowing his eyes to roam the endless bleachers packed with fans.

Larenzo sat in amazement of the ecstatic aura that had enveloped around the football stadium. It was the end of the third quarter and the scoreboard read: Home 28 Guest 10. Everyone present realized that Blanding University was headed to yet another Homecoming victory. The entire stadium was filled with an electric energy, which coursed through everyone present. The band played victoriously and the crowds cheered louder than ever before. Then, almost by magic, Larenzo saw the one person present on the home side that wasn't ecstatic about the outcome of the game. Larenzo couldn't help but pay attention to the figure of the frowning man wearing a tight fitting pink golf shirt. It was not a huge surprise when Larenzo saw exactly who it was. He was the one person whom had attended the Homecoming game, and wasn't having the time of his life. It was John Spencer.

Larenzo wasn't sure whether it was the look of depression on his face or just pure coincidence that had caught the eye of Larenzo, but one thing was for sure, the woman sitting beside him was a very unhappy looking Janet Stub. With just one glimpse it was obvious that they had been having a lovers' quarrel. Expensive gold earrings dangled from Janet's earlobes. Her long jet-black hair was pulled back and tucked in a tight bun behind her head. Her full lips were covered with glossy lipstick. She possessed high cheekbones and a very soft feminine jaw line; one would never have guessed that she was actually a part-time stripper. Like always she was the vision of a beauty queen, except for the fact that she chewed angrily on a stick of gum and her faced was squinted up with the unmistakable look of annoyance.

From a distance Larenzo continued to spy on John Spencer and his girlfriend. John Spencer, like so many other times in the recent past, seemed to be completely uncomfortable. His fingers were folded in his lap, and he sat up on the metal bleachers properly, his back very straight. Larenzo could tell with one look that John wasn't enjoying himself, and by the look of loathing on Janet's face it was obvious that they had been arguing earlier. They had begun to despise each other's presence, and it was just a matter of time before they would get into another disagreement.

When the game was over, Blanding University's football team marched triumphantly back towards the locker room. Meanwhile the enormous crowd had begun to break up and slip away into the night for an evening full of campus partying and youthful delirium. Likewise, Larenzo, Bobby, Red, JC, and Malik also left the stadium Bobby's car.

After the football game was over and the crowds of fans had nearly disappeared. A few clusters of students lingered in one of the nearby parking lots. The night was filled with a chilling breeze as the group of friends walked towards Bobby's car. Malik wobbled a little, trying to steady himself. His walk was that of a concentrated pace that only expert drunks have the knowledge to experience. He dangled the empty bottle of liquor in his hands without shame.

Bobby opened the door to his car and the group of friends piled themselves inside in the same seats they'd been in earlier. Bobby put his key in the ignition and turned his radio up until the speakers rattled in his trunk, and the entire car vibrated from the bass filled Rap music. Everyone in the car simultaneously bobbed his or her heads to the music, when suddenly a bright blue light flashed in the rearview mirror.

"Damn!" Bobby cursed under his breath. Bobby knew what those lights meant as well as any young African American. His body froze at the sight of the flashing blue lights and the campus police that were sure to follow. Without any warning, two white police officers quickly ran up on both sides of the car. Their weapons were already drawn, and the light from a pair of flashlights roamed the interior of the car.

Seeing them approach from the rear of the car, Bobby let his window down slowly. The words flashed across his mind and sat on the tip of his tongue. *What the fuck do you want, pig?* He wanted to say those words but instead the statement came out as, "Can I help you officer?" Bobby's voice trembled a little as he spoke trying in vain to hide his fear. He couldn't help it. In his youth, he had obtained a strong phobia of cops ever since his father was gunned down. The death of his father had instilled a menacing fear in him, and his view of police officer had never been the same. Even the out of shape security guards of Blanding University made the hairs on the back of his neck stand up in fright.

"Put your hands up and get out of the car, now!" The white man's voice was filled with the authoritative tone that can only be found with the law enforcement. Bobby looked out of his window and realized that the police officer's handgun was already out and pointed directly at his temple. "I said put your hands up!" Bobby tried to react but his limbs were paralyzing his hands to the steering wheel with a numbing fear. No matter how much he tried he couldn't get rid of visions of his father dying at a routine police stop very similar to this one.

Instead of Bobby answering the cop, JC spoke up quickly in reply to the police officer's command. JC coolly put both of his hands in the air so the cop could see that they were empty and slowly placed one hand down toward the door to open it. He then stepped out of the vehicle very cockily and said, "We're willing to cooperate we just need to know what's the charge officers?"

When JC stepped out of the car, the police officer nearest to him let out a short laugh. "Hey, I know you, you're JC Reid. I've been following your games pretty closely since high school. You're the new starting point guard for Blanding U. Well, why don't you look at this. Johnson, we done apprehended ourselves an authentic basketball star. Aren't you suppose to be practicing or something? You shouldn't be riding around here with hooligans with open liquor bottles." The cop pushed him onto the hood of the car and began to pat him down searching for any other weapons or paraphernalia.

"What are you doing?" The second police officer asked harshly of his partner. "Let him go, O'Brian. The first basketball game of the season is coming up pretty soon and I'm not going to be the one to tell the chief that we're the reason the new basketball star for Blanding University spent the night in the pen. Blanding University is going to need all the help they can get against Grambling basketball team. The chief will have both of our hides if they lose. Leave him, we'll take the rest of them in for the open container."

"What open container?" JC asked quickly.

The officer nodded his head in the direction of the Bobby's backseat. Sitting in plain view, on Malik's lap, was a mostly empty bottle of Crown Royal. "We were watching as the suspect entered the vehicle with the open container in his possession. We have to arrest everybody in the car and tow it. Step aside Mr. Reid, we're just doing our job," the police officer stated plainly, reaching for his handcuffs.

At the sign of the silver handcuffs a sudden chill ran through Red's body, and up the side of his face. His eyes blazed with ruthless abandonment and his facial features became cold and merciless. With one look, Larenzo knew that Red was willing to shoot his way out of the car if necessary.

"I'm not going back to jail," Red whispered, his voice more heated than ever before. "I've been there and I'll be damn if some flashlight campus cop is going to take me back." He suddenly hunched his shoulders forward and reached for the .45 caliber handgun that was holstered behind his belt on his back.

Larenzo stretched over Malik to grab Red by the shoulder. "There's gotta be another way. Let JC talk with him first."

The police officer reached for the handle on the door, and foreboding panic ran through the occupants of the vehicle. Larenzo held his breath. He could tell by the change in his demeanor, that the look on Red's mug was filled with murderous desperation. Red's .45 was now in his hand. The weight of the weapon gave him no comfort as he prepared to fire upon the cop. His face was literally dripping from nervous sweat. Malik, sat in between Larenzo and Red, his eyes were closed tightly as though he was trying to wish away the cop. The police officer inched closer to the door handle, until a single brave voice rang out stopping his hand.

"No." The voice belonged to JC. Stepping forward, JC placed himself directly in the path of the officer and the car door. For what felt like an eternity, the white officer and JC stared at each other. The police officer was so close to JC, that JC could actually smell the jelly filled doughnut on the cop's rancid breath.

"What did you say, son?" The cop tilted his head as he spoke. He had heard the word very clearly the first time he just didn't believe his ears. "Didn't you hear what I said Mr. Basketball star. You're free. Get out of here!" His voice began to become louder with each word. The slight sound of aggravation was present.

"No." JC repeated, giving a deep sigh. "I said 'no.'"

The police officer stared at JC perplexed, his confusion intensifying. He had never seen anyone so righteous, so loyal to his friends in every way. The police officer examined the youthful man standing between himself and the car. His muscle toned arms flexed at his sides, fist clenched tightly. His sneaker-covered feet were planted squarely, defiantly, to the pavement. A flickering light from a nearby street lamp gleamed off of JC's face. The officer recognized instantly that no longer did JC possesses the half smile and smug attitude that had become so common with his basketball personality. His face was filled with an unspeakable determination.

"Where I go; my friends go. Listen, officer, I know that you're just doing your job. But Malik is the only one drinking, and I'd take it as a personal favor from you if you turn the other way this one time.

Truth to tell, it can be quite profitable for you as well. I know that security guards don't get paid much, so just consider this a small contribution from some of the students that you've been sworn to serve and protect. How about one hundred dollars each?" JC slowly reached into his pocket and pulled out a pair of one hundred dollar bills, holding out the money so both cops could clearly see the dark green paper.

JC knew that bribing cops wasn't a very risky business, in truth; most of them were more corrupt than the citizens that they locked up each day. Security guards for Blanding University were paid a little bit more than minimum wage and worked horrendously long hours. JC knew that a free hundred dollar bill for each of them was simply too much of a temptation for the cops to resist.

The officer squinted at him for a long moment, glancing from side to side; making sure that no else was viewing them. After a short period of contemplation, the cop took the hundred dollar bill folded it in half and placed it in his shirt pocket. Without saying another word, the second police officer did the same and then drove off in their squad car.

Moments later, JC slid back into the passenger side of Bobby's automobile. A long pause of relief swept through the friends. As the police car pulled off, Bobby could feel his body beginning to relax once again. Placing his face in the palm of his cold hand, Bobby began to shake himself from his self inflicted paralyzed state. Taking a deep breath he began to speak. His voice was cracked and his emotional state was still very visibly shaken, "Malik, throw the bottle out."

"It's almost empty," Malik responded quickly, "Let me finish it. Besides, that pig didn't have any reason to pull us over anyhow. I mean, I'm not even driving the damn car. It's just simple harassment because we're black and they know that they can get away with it. Those cops our simply power hungry. If we don't take a stand ourselves as a culture now they'll never stop this blatant racial profiling."

Bobby turned in his seat and glared at Malik with odium in his eyes. "I said throw the fucking bottle out! You weren't saying anything when the cop was trying to put us all in jail! Don't nobody want to hear that African pride shit now!" After a few moments Bobby manage to get his temper under control. "I gotta a daughter and I can't be going to jail or dying over some bullshit. Just throw the bottle out."

Larenzo sat back in the chair, hand resting peacefully on his chin, silently watching the argument as an impartial witness. Red had once again tucked his gun in its holster located by his back. His face was emotionless once again as though the cops had never pulled over the vehicle to begin with.

"Both of ya'll need to just chill out," JC groaned. "Ain't nobody going to jail or dying. This is homecoming. We're supposed to be enjoying ourselves, not arguing over some shit that could have happened. It didn't so forget about it. And anyway, I think everyone will agree that you've had enough to drink for one night."

Malik nodded his head slowly in agreement. Larenzo rolled down his window. Malik held the small bottle of Crown Royal, admiring the small corner of brown liquid that was still in its glass frame, and then mournfully threw it from the open car window.

CHAPTER 10

Consequences

It was late November on the small HBCU and the majority of the campus was silent. The cool winds blew through the leafless trees teasing the limbs. Yellow and red stained leaves were scattered across the landscape and the picturesque skyline was cloudless as the sunset shined beautiful rays of yellow and gold onto the horizon. The campus seemed dead, or at least hibernating in that unusually frigid atmosphere for South Carolina. The entirety of the HBCU wasn't as peaceful as that sunset though. No, there was life on the campus still. College basketball season had struck Blanding University and was spreading like wildfire through a dry field.

In the Mackey gym on the edge of campus the sounds of a whole university could be heard within the walls. Mackey gymnasium was filled with students cheering their side on to victory. Inside the gymnasium a vicious war was being battled. Not a war with guns and swords, but a war nevertheless, waged over a single small orange ball. In this war, JC was a legendary gladiator feared by the opposing force. With superb skill JC dribbled the ball between his legs bypassing two defenders as if they were standing still, and then dunked the ball pleasing the rowdy crowd. He was a force of nature, he was unstoppable whenever he stepped foot on the hardwood floor of the court. The crowd cheered and whistled whenever JC would touch the ball. They loved him, and he loved them in return. On the basketball court JC felt at home like no other time. He had quickly turned Blanding Universities' basketball games into a one-man highlight reel.

It was the fourth quarter and only a minute and a half left on the clock. The score was 68 to 53 and Blanding University was winning. JC contributed thirty-five of the sixty-eight points and he was well on his way to earning another triple double. JC confidently smiled at the opposition. The look of fear was present in their eyes as they dribbled the ball back up the court. The other team tried to keep the ball away from JC as much as possible but their efforts were futile. With stunning speed JC interrupted a pass and drove down the court. The other team reached for him, trying to foul, but it was too late. JC was too fast for them going behind his back, breaking away from defenders easily. On the opposite end of the court JC did a Michael Jordan double-clutch reverse slam. After the dunk, the crowd went crazy with delight cheering loudly. JC smiled when he looked into the sea of heads cheering and chanting his name.

It seemed like everyone that lived in the small town was present at the game. JC's friends were sitting in the crowd clapping happily for him. Red sat in the front benches, his arms crossed against his chest, watching the game unimpressed. Malik sat to the left of Red, his eyes still very bloodshot from the blunt he smoked earlier that night. Larenzo, sipping on a bottle of water, sat behind Malik. Sitting to the right of Larenzo was the new guy, John, watching the game in silence. Even Kel was present, standing away from the rest of the guys smoking on a Black & Mild cigar. Everyone knew that he was still a little angry with Larenzo.

One look at Kel and JC knew that he wasn't watching the game at all; his attention was occupied by someone else. Kel was too busy eyeing the cheerleading squad closely. Crystal Kerry was in full cheerleading uniform leading her squad on the floor. Kel's attention focused on Crystal Kerry's abdomen, a slight pouch was beginning to show. No one else suspected, but Kel knew that Crystal was beginning to show and that his greatest fears were becoming reality.

JC pointed at the crowd and smirked. The crowd cheered louder than ever before. JC was showing off, and he knew it. He was the youngest player to ever dominate for Blanding University. He learned how to play basketball on the cold streets of Brooklyn, New York. He was cocky, flashy, and his inevitable greatness was undeniable. JC loved to show off, but it wasn't the student body that he was trying to impress on that frigid November evening; it was NBA basketball recruiters. He knew that a recruiter for the NBA would be in the gymnasium watching him that night and he planned on giving him a show that they would never forget. Sure, some players would make it pro from other universities, but not many Division 1, black universities ever got the attention of a professional NBA team.

The other team called time out, and their coach put his second string team in to play. JC smiled contently. JC knew that the other team was substituting the good players for the students that didn't get a chance to play on a regular basis. The other team knew like everyone else in the building, that this game was over and JC had brought home another victory. Blanding University's coach wanted to sit JC down so he could catch a breath, but JC declined. "Keep me in coach. The recruiter for the Washington Wizards is in the stands. This is my chance to show everyone what I got," JC said proudly as he sipped on a cup of Gatorade. The coach nodded his head in agreement.

Soon the referee's whistle blew and the timeout was officially over. Both teams walked on to the court ready to finish the game. Many people in Mackey Gymnasium had already started celebrating Blanding University's glorious victory. JC scanned the pitiful eyes of the opposite team feeling no remorse. The other inexperienced team threw away the ball on a fast break and now Blanding University controlled the basketball. JC dribbled towards base line and crossed over one defender. Then JC backed up tentatively when he saw the other teams center standing underneath the rim.

The player that the other team had in the center position was a huge dark-skinned husky man. He stood at least six feet nine inches tall and weighed at least three hundred and seventy pound. His pig like eyes stared out from underneath rolls of fat awaiting JC to make his move. The huge man wet his blubberish lips when he saw JC beginning to advance toward the rim. The last ten seconds of the game were ticking away and JC had made it up in his mind to end the game with a dunk. JC knew that the opposing center was large, but the man was too slow to guard him and too overweight to out jump him. JC's eyes grew large with anticipation as he exploded to the basket with incredible speed. JC went baseline with tremendous momentum, his eyes fixed on the rim.

JC took off in a vertical leap from under the basket, his fingertips reaching above the basket, the dunk seemed inescapable. At the last second, the obese center stepped up, refusing to be embarrassed, plowing his gigantic body into JC hugging him on the way up to the rim. The impact of their bodies colliding in the air knocked the wind out of JC sending him to the hard floor. The overweight center, surprised at the fact that he wasn't dunked on, lost his balance in the air and pummeled down on top of JC.

When the overweight man landed on the much smaller guard for Blanding University the once rowdy boisterous crowd held their breath stunned at the collision. The loud sickening sound of crunching bones and cartilage ripping was the only noise heard echoing through the gymnasium. The spectators looked on in silence, wondering whether their hero, JC would walk away victorious from the clash.

After what seemed like an eternity, the first sign of activity could be seen on the basketball court. The corpulent center began to move slowly. At first he tried to stand straight up but his huge size prevented him from that activity. Instead, the center pushed off of the floor and rolled onto his side, crushing JC underneath him again. Once on his side, with the greatest amount of effort, the center got to his feet. JC on the other hand, was still lying on the floor motionless.

Blanding University's head coach and the rest of the bench ran to the aid of the fallen basketball player. One look at JC and everyone at Mackey Gymnasium knew that he was definitely injured. Tears of pain had begun to emerge on the sides of his eyes. JC blinked several times trying to prevent himself from weeping but the pain was too extreme, even for him. His chest heaved up and down with deep, erratic breaths. His face was wet with perspiration against his bronze skin. JC looked up at his coach standing above him and then reached for his leg in agonizing pain. JC's leg was completely limp and laid at a ninety-degree angle from the rest of his body. His fragile bone had ripped out of its joint, puncturing his skin, exposing itself for the whole gymnasium to see. JC couldn't see his own leg but he knew that the final result couldn't be good.

"Don't look at it son," the head couch said to JC carefully, calmly not to alarm him. "I want you to look up. Just look up at the ceiling and everything will be all right. The medics will be here soon."

JC didn't have to see his leg to know that the injury was serious. No matter how hard the coach tried to make his voice sound calm, JC knew that there was a panic in his words. Whenever the coach would glance down at his leg JC saw that panic present in his eyes also. When JC did stare up at the game clock on the ceiling he saw that the referees had let the time wind down by itself. A loud horn sounded signaling the end of the game...and maybe, the end of his career.

The spectators soon left the gymnasium filing out one behind the other gossiping about their chances of winning the MEAC that year. Many of their hearts and minds went to JC, their fallen hero. JC would have never thought that he would ever end up in this position. Right now he was supposed to be surrounded by beautiful young ladies fighting for his attention. Instead, he was in pain on the floor with his teammates gathered around him. The pain in JC's leg spread upward to his knee enclosing around his every thought. Never before had he felt this much physical pain. Beaten and battered, JC lay on the cold, hard floor of the bloody battlefield. The game was over and Blanding University had gained another victory, but this victory came with an immense price.

Someone from the university called an ambulance. Nearly twenty minutes later, the ambulance was just arriving at the gymnasium. It was what was expected for a Black University. Blanding University didn't have a medical facility on the campus that handled serious situations like sports injuries. The only hospital in the rather small town was several miles away, and whenever they heard that they were going to the Black University they never hurried. JC tried to muster up a smile when he saw the stretcher carried by two ambulance drivers. Men were lifting, putting him on a stretcher, and strapping him down, and his leg was filled with horrible pain. The pain became so excruciating that he could barely keep his eyes open. JC could feel his mind blacking out, pushing the unbearable pain from his reality. They picked him up and placed him on the stretcher making sure not move him too quickly. Moments later the ambulance took off with JC in the back of it.

"Malik and me are gonna drive behind the ambulance to the hospital," Larenzo said when he saw the paramedics place JC in the back of the ambulance. "He needs someone to reassure him that everything is going to be alright. I'll meet you guys back at Red's house later on tonight." Larenzo spoke quickly as he hurried toward Malik's newly repaired vehicle.

Red, John, Bobby, and Kel left Mackey Gymnasium with a sense of desperation in their hearts. One of their own had been hospitalized, critically injured playing a game for the amusement and financial stability of the university. The crowds in the gymnasium wouldn't remember the sacrifices that JC had made that evening. The crowds in the gymnasium might not even remember JC's name tomorrow. Blanding University didn't care about the well being of the individual at all. They only cared about the future of the team. JC forced his lips into a smile at the ironic situation. Just the idea that Blanding University was an institute dedicated to the well being of the students was hypocritical in its simpleness. He had played the game of basketball for them as much as for himself. Popularity was always fleeting for the sports stars of Blanding University. That was always the price of stardom for students that attended Blanding University. One day you're on top of the world, the next day your accomplishments have been forgotten. Blanding University made thousands of dollars off of each game, yet the players would never see a dime. One thing was clearly obvious; the athletic department wasn't developed for the betterment of the students.

After the basketball game was over a large crowd of people always jammed the front entrance of the gymnasium. Crowds seemed to hover in front of the entrance. Many of the students used the end of the game to say goodbye to one another, but many waited for their friends because they were afraid to walk home by themselves. Blanding University was filled with dangerous, everyday threats around each corner. It didn't matter whether you were walking or driving; there were numerous aspects that students had to beware of during the night. Police officers would harass young black motorists after the game, stopping them and checking for open alcoholic beverages in the vehicles. On the other hand, young muggers constantly preyed upon students that chose to walk back to their dorm rooms.

Bobby, John, Red, and Kel casually walked through the campus that night mostly in silence. The night air had a chill in it. Bobby had let his girlfriend drive his car to take the baby to her mother's house. John lived on campus and liked to park his car by his dorm on the other end of the campus. Without Malik or JC to drive, they would have to walk across campus to get to John's car. They didn't mind the walk at all. No one would dare bother them while Red was walking with them. Kel was acting more like his old self with every passing day, and talk about Crystal Kerry had become almost inexistent. As they walked on, the four men couldn't think of anything except JC's health.

"JC's career might actually be over," Bobby said recalling the implications of the evening's events. "I hope he gets better, but I don't know. His leg was really fucked up pretty badly."

"That fat ass center on the other team should have stepped his grilled-cheese- eating ass out the way if he didn't want to get dunk on." Kel cursed out loud full of anger, still unable to clear his mind of the recent tragedy, which had befallen his friend. "I mean, it just doesn't make sense for some fat loser ass prick to even have the nerve to waddle his mother fuckin', two-ton, cockroach looking ass on the basketball court anyhow."

"I also mourn for JC's loss, but I don't feel that it was entirely due to the opposite teams center," John said very properly with his nose high in the air. "The center was just doing his job. I don't see any reason at all to call him names. I think that it's completely unbecoming."

"Shut the fuck up!" Kel answered quickly. "For being so smart, John, you say some of the dumbest shit. That's not your friend riding to the hospital in the back of the ambulance."

"JC is my friend, also," John said quietly.

"He never even liked you," Kel's words struck John like a poison dart. "The only fucking reason why we even let you fucking hang around is because Larenzo likes you. Look, just shut the hell up."

"Excuse me?" John inquired curiously. "I don't understand why African American men feel that they are required to use profanity. I feel as if it shows a direct reflection of a lack of vocabulary and as a result it makes you sound ignorant. Studies prove that the excessive use of profanity will eventually become mundane, therefore giving less and less shock value to the meaning of the words. Eventually the uses of those harsh words will lose the initial potency that they once possessed. What will you do to communicate once those obscene words have lost their meaning?" John crossed his arms about his chess smugly, and patiently awaited Kel's answer.

"Well, Mr. John Spencer," Kel said imitating John's proper speech pattern perfectly. "When the obscene words 'shut the fuck up' stop becoming effective. I'm going to start taking lessons from the great mediator Ike Turner." Kel allowed his inner city Chicago accent to slowly return. "So if you know what's good for ya...you'll shut the <u>fuck</u> up!"

Traffic was always horrible after a basketball game, as a result many of the students decided to walk back to their dorm rooms. Most of the students walked in small clusters, huddled together safely, talking to each other. A very brave few, dared to walk down the unlit campus streets by themselves. One of these brave individuals went by the name Janet Stub. She had been missing for a few weeks after Homecoming. The shooting at Tony's and the constant arguments with her boyfriend had sent her into social hiding. Only now, had she decided to reemerge to watch the basketball game in peace. She walked with the collars of her coat around her ears hurrying toward her dorm. Not speaking to anyone, with her eyes straight ahead, making sure not to make eye contact with anyone. She smiled when she saw the lights from her dorm in the distance.

"Hey Créme!" a male voice yelled out behind her. Janet tried to ignore it, walking faster than before. Créme was her stage name when she used to strip at Tony's. "Créme it's me! You remember me? It's me, Corey, from the club." This time Janet turned her head slightly catching a glimpse of the guy following her. He was dressed in a black hooded sweatshirt, blue jeans, and black boots. He grinned from ear to ear, showing a large gap in his teeth, when he saw that he had her attention. She was sure of it now. He was the guy from the night of the strip club shooting; not the shooter but the guy that he was with him.

Corey ran up behind Janet quickly grabbing her by the hips and whispered in her ear, "Hey, my lap dance got interrupted by my friend. Why don't we pick up where we left off?" Janet dismisses Corey's heavy southern accent as he palmed her buttocks with his right hand. With his left hand, Corey unzipped his jeans and reached in for his genitals. "I been waiting to give you this for a long time."

Janet shoved Corey away from her, when she felt the imprint of his fingers on her rear. She looked at Corey straight in the eyes, put her hand on her hip and said, "Listen, you sick murdering bastard. I'm a stripper, not a whore! I'm not dancing tonight and even if I were, I wouldn't dance with you! All I'm trying to do is get to the dorm and not be harassed by some horny, little-dick, fucking loser." Janet spun around on her heels and continued to march toward her dorm, her head high in the air.

Without delay, before Janet could get to the sidewalk Corey gripped her by the back of her neck. Janet struggled but it was no use; Corey was much larger and stronger than she was. He threw her to the cold, muddy ground at his feet. His eyes were bitter and angry. "Bitch. You're gonna give me what I want!" he yelled, unfastening his belt and pants. "I'm going to show you how big I really am! I know you want this as much as I do." Janet screamed, cutting his words off, struggling with every fiber in her being. Corey grabbed at her kicking legs and spread her fertile thighs apart. Janet screamed again, this time clawing at his face franticly.

It was that kicking that got the attention of Bobby that night. The moonlight peeked through the night clouds revealing a couple struggling. The shadows gave way to the unyielding battle a block away. At first he thought that it was just a couple, making out in the dark, but upon closer inspection he saw the truth. The lady screamed out again. This time, Bobby heard the muffled screams of Janet Stub and he reacted.

Bobby started to run toward them. "Hey! Get off of her!" He yelled as he neared the struggling couple.

Corey looked up when he heard the bass filled voice of Bobby King rushing toward him. With just one glance Corey knew that he was in trouble. Bobby was big enough to give him a problem, but to make things worse, Kel, John, and Red were following close behind. Realizing that he couldn't fight off all four men by himself, Corey ran away, disappearing in the shadows of a dark alley.

Bobby stopped to check the woman in distress but Kel ran past her still closely following Corey's trail. Janet's shirt was torn and her face was dirtied with mud from where she was thrown to the ground. Janet looked up with a sense of relief when she saw the look of concern on Bobby's face. Bobby leaned down beside the battered woman and helped her to her feet. As Bobby's face drew closer to Janet she spoke. "Thanks for the help. That creep was trying to rape me. They act like just because you're a stripper they can treat you anyway they want. If you hadn't come along I don't know what I would have done." Janet flirtatiously stared at her knight in shining armor, Bobby.

"It's no problem," Bobby said smiling showing his dimple. "I'm always down for lending a helping hand to beautiful women in distress." Bobby King was naturally flirtatious and just his presence around her comforted Janet Stub. Bobby gently kissed Janet on the hand and helped her to her feet. Janet blushed and straightened her clothes, attempting to make herself appear presentable.

Before too much longer, Red and John walked over to Bobby and Janet as they ended their conversation with each other. Red was already holding one of his .45 caliber pistols in his hand. Red looked at Janet with a glance of indifference when he saw that she wasn't that badly harmed. John on the other hand, stared at Janet Stub with a look of uneasy bewilderment. John hadn't spoken to his girlfriend in days. Last time they spoke to each other she said that she couldn't accompany him to the basketball game this weekend because of a family emergency. John would have never believed it if he didn't see it with his own two eyes; Janet Stub, his girlfriend, had blatantly lied to him.

"Janet?" John said more confused than angry at her presence. "I thought you were going to see your grandmother this weekend? You told me that you weren't going to be in town tonight," John said very feebly as if he didn't want her to answer. Janet Stub looked for the right words to say to John but it was no use trying to lie. Just the guilty look in her eyes alone painted the truth for everyone to see.

Sobs were in Janet Stubs voice as she began to speak, "John...Oh my God. John, this man grabbed me and tried to rape me and all you can think about is why I'm here. I came back early and I tried to call you, but you were out with your friends. You're always out with your new friends. Sometimes I get the feeling that you don't trust me." She broke down and began to weep uncontrollably. Her sobs were deep, the kind of sobs that are usually done in private. Purely out of force of habit, John embraced Janet, holding her body close to his. Caringly, he kissed her on her on the forehead.

Red put one of his guns away and laughed sarcastically when he saw the couple embrace. "You got to be kidding me. It's obvious that the bitch is lying through her teeth. I used to watch her work at Tony's strip club on Thursday nights. I can't believe that this is the Janet that you've been whining over for the last couple of weeks. No wonder she's never home when you call her. Wake up, she's a damn stripper."

Before John could give his angry reply, Kel rushed back to the site of the incident. Beads of sweat ran down his Kel's brow and his chest heaved up and down because of loss of breath. "That guy got away. He ran through Allen Hall's parking lot and jumped the fence. How's she doing?"

John gave Red an unpleasant glance then said, "My girlfriend will be all right. She just needs some rest and relaxation. I'm going to take her back to the dorm. Thanks for your help." John put his arm around her shoulder and began to walk her back to her dormitory. No one spoke as John escorted Janet to the safety of the dorm, but something that Red had said definitely had the ring of truth in it. John never saw Janet on Thursday nights and he still couldn't explain the extra money that she would have. John tried to shake away the thoughts of his girlfriend dancing in front of strangers with her body exposed for the world to see. The idea alone was too much for his mind to handle.

When they reached Allen Hall, John gently kissed her goodnight on the lips. After John left Allen Hall, he drove Bobby and Red back to Red's house. The trip was filled with conversation about Janet dancing at Tony's strip bar, but John refused to listen to them. John never asked her if Red was telling the truth. In all honesty, after that night he didn't want to know. Seeing Janet in distress made John realize just how much he loved this woman and his feelings for her wouldn't change no matter what anyone said. The rumors about her stripping career didn't even seem to matter to John anymore. All John Spencer was sure of was in the fact that he loved Janet Stub, and she was his girlfriend. Everything else came second to his relationship.

Two nights later, JC showed up at Red's house. His leg was in a cast, and using a set of crutches he limped through the front door with difficulty. JC tried to force his lips into a smile when he entered the house. As usual, all of his friends were already inside, minus John Spencer who was spending more and more time with Janet. "What's up everybody? Did anyone catch that last dunk on videotape?" JC joked trying to grin and make the most out of his situation. "I guess you just can't dunk on everybody. I should have just shot a damn three pointer to end the game, huh?"

At once several people in the living room rushed over to JC and embraced him with handshakes and hugs. For the first time since the basketball game, JC felt at home again. Several women kissed JC on the cheeks, and many of his friends began to sign his cast. JC tried to be as cheerful as possible, but he couldn't help feeling a slight depression when he saw the signatures on his cast. He sighed and stared uncomfortably at the white plastered membrane on his limb. JC sniffled a little as he continued to speak, "That was a hell of a game. I kind of wished that fat mouthafucka had just stayed out of my way."

"Welcome back, JC," Bobby said happily when he saw the crippled figure walk through the doorway. Bobby could tell that JC was faking his happiness for his friends. His eyes had the look of a broken man to them. Bobby had seen that look in the eyes of prostitutes after they'd been beaten by their pimps and down on their luck. Bobby didn't know exactly how bad the damage was to JC's leg, but he knew it couldn't be good.

Slumped over on the couch, Malik barely managed to open his eyes when JC walked into the room. Still very much under the influence of marijuana, Malik only waved in the general direction of JC's voice. Nowadays, Malik was almost always high. It was actually odd not to see him under the influence of a drug or alcohol. His drug use had become so common that no one at Red's house ever mentioned his addiction.

"Well I'll be Goddamn!" Red exclaimed handing JC a can of beer. "It's good to have you back. The place has been too quiet without you. Anyway, how was the hospital food?"

"They didn't serve a nigga cafeteria food but I made it somehow," JC said jokingly. "I did have a sexy-ass nurse. You know, I was trying to get a sponge bath every night."

Kel rushed over and patted JC on the back glad to have him around. "So when are you going to get that ugly cast off your foot. I need you to get back to working out on the basketball court so I can win some more money off of the games," Kel said smiling very good-naturedly. "How long did the doctors give you?"

JC knew that someone would eventually ask it and deep down he dreaded that moment since he first left the hospital. JC clutched at his injured leg and gave a half-hearted laugh full of anger and pain. The laugh died quickly. "The doctors said that I suffered a torn MCL. Much of my calf tissue was torn in two parts and my leg was shattered from the fall, rupturing my skin." JC paused though he could remember the physical pain of the injury all over again. "Um...Kel, the doctors said that I'm never gonna play ball again. There was just too much damage done. On the lighter note they said that with a lot of hours in rehabilitation, I'd be able to walk by myself one day." JC voice had dropped down to almost a whisper as he finished. There were tears in his eyes but he didn't allow them to fall.

JC gave a large artificial smile, then wiped away the tears building in his eyes. JC smiled on the outside but everyone in the room knew that he was just hiding his pain. Larenzo walked over to the card table and pulled out a deck from his back pocket. "So how about you come over here and play a game of Spades? I got ten dollars on the table," Larenzo said trying to change the subject to a lighter topic.

"I can't," JC replied quietly. "I can't put any money on the card table like I used to. Blanding University was paying me under the table for playing on the basketball team. They were scared that I might transfer to a higher ranked ACC school. I had been offered opportunities to play for other schools, but my mom wanted me to attend an all black university like she did. You know, get the full black experience and all. They wouldn't exactly pay me a paycheck or nothing, but they would give me a certain amount of spending money each week. That's how I could afford the car I drove. That's why I could afford to bet away large amounts of money like that. Yesterday, after the injury, the coach said he wasn't allowed to give me any more money. The fuckin' school wouldn't even pay for my surgery or my hospital stay."

"It's okay," Red said calmly, taking a seat at the card table. "We'll play without money this time. Besides, I didn't feel like losing any cash tonight."

JC smiled and hobbled over the table slowly sat in a chair. Surrounded by his friends JC managed to forget about his problems. All of his hopelessness seemed to melt away during the card game. No longer was JC bothered by his broken leg, lost professional basketball career, or his new money problem. Life seemed much easier for JC after he began to play the card game. A game of Spades can do that... if you're around your friends. Since he was a child he had struggled through the mean streets of Brooklyn and survived each encounter. This leg injury was no different. Before the Spades game was over JC had decided to overcome this obstacle like every other obstacle that ever stood in his path. Deep down, JC knew that he was a survivor, and this was just another test that he had to overcome.

CHAPTER 11

Kel's Choice

It was no use, Kel finally decided. He turned on the miniature lamp beside his iron-framed bed, staring hopelessly at the alarm clock on his dresser. The alarm clock read 4:15, and Kel knew he couldn't sleep because of frightening nightmares of the wails of babies crying in his dreams. If it wasn't the horrifying wails of a child echoing in his dreams, then it was the annoying phone calls in the middle of the night from Crystal begging for money to see the doctor. He hadn't been able to sleep because of the slight pouch, which was beginning to show on her abdomen, and he had turned the ringer to his phone off weeks ago. Kel knew that it wouldn't be long before everyone in the school knew about his little secret. He knew that he would be up all night again, and the strain of staying up all night was beginning to wear down on his body and mind.

He could hear the morning's birds singing in the distance. Kel kicked the sheets off his body and sat up, distressed about the argument with his best friend and the future of his unborn child. Kel could go nights without sleep but this was going on his fourth night straight without any sleep at all. Any more sleepless nights and Kel was sure he would eventually be in the Guinness Book of World Records. When he wasn't able to sleep in his biology class, Kel knew there was a serious problem.

The first thing that the distressed young man did was reach for a brand new pack of Black & Mild cigars and lit one nervously. The smoke from the cigar helped ease Kel's mind, but he knew that it wouldn't be enough. Unable to think of anything else to do, Kel began to do push-ups and sit ups in his room until the sun eventually rose in his window. He didn't care that smoking while he was working out was counter productive; he just knew that it made him feel better.

When the first rays of the morning's dawn began to beam through his window, Kel's first thought was to reach for the telephone and wake Larenzo up early for breakfast. Then as if a bolt of lighting struck Kel, he reflected on the argument they had at the card table. He hadn't spoken to Larenzo in days. A cold shiver ran through his skinny body as the notion of losing his best friend flashed in his mind. For a moment he considered walking down the hallway and knocking on Larenzo's door, but his pride kept his feet planted. Kel knew that if he knocked on Larenzo's door it would declare to everyone, especially himself, that he was in the wrong arguing with his best friend over something as minor as a card game. But Kel knew that the argument wasn't truly over a card game. It was over a girl, but not just a girl. She was the future mother of his child.

Kel inhaled another deep puff of smoke from his cigar and walked over to the cafeteria for the early breakfast when most other students on the campus were still fast asleep. He merrily pranced from Monroe Hall to the cafeteria, thrilled to finally escape the dungeon, which the Blanding University called a male dormitory. Within minutes, Kel had reached the doorway of the cafeteria and the aroma of eggs and bacon in the air had thoroughly awoken his senses. Kel walked inside and glanced around casually. The cafeteria was mostly empty except for a few servers, female student joggers, and a small group of fraternity boys eating an early breakfast.

The three frat boys wore black t-shirts with the name of there fraternity outlined in gold italic lettering. The first of the threesome was a tall, lanky, dark-skinned man with a neatly trimmed beard. Sitting across the table from him was a shorter, younger light-skinned gentleman laughing loudly as he shoveled runny scrambled eggs into his mouth. Sitting directly between the fraternity brothers was the third member of the threesome. Much more muscular than the other two, he sat like a giant surrounded by his fraternity brethren. The fraternity boys sat around a circular table laughing wholesomely amongst each other. When Kel walked past the group they instantaneously became silent as they stared at him coldly. Dressed in a cut up white t-shirt with the words "F Da World" on it, Kel was used to attracting attention to himself.

The tallest of the fraternity boys frowned as his eyes quietly followed Kel to an empty table on the far end of the room. A look of rage filled his dark brown eyes at the sight of Kel. He leaned over and whispered in the ear of his muscular frat brother, "Yeah. That's the sonofvabitch. Come on House. I say we have a little talk with him." They turned and looked at their smallest member to see if everyone was in agreement.

Kel glanced up from his plate of bacon and eggs to see the threesome walking toward him. Just the sight of them brought a feeling of cautiousness to Kel. They approached uneasily with dim eyes like hunter's stalking prey in the wilderness. They paused about five feet from Kel, their stares as cold as icicles. Kel knew they would be trouble before they even reached his table. For a moment they only stood there, watching him, slowly plotting. The tallest one with the eyes filled with anger patted the muscular one named House (because of his humongous size) on the back, and, as expected, he walked up to the table first, his two fraternity brothers standing watch behind him. House approached the table removing his glasses, folded them and carefully placed them in his pants pocket.

Kel still sitting peacefully at the table looked up at the muscular giant of a man. He stood above Kel's table confidently, quietly watching his every move closely. He smelled of sweat and sophisticated cologne. When he breathed, his muscular chest flexed up and down. His large black nose was porous and shaped like that of a gorilla. The light of the cafeteria gleamed off of his bald head, and when he spoke his voice sounded like that of a professional wrestler, full of confidence and masculinity.

"Your name is Kel Jones?" It wasn't really a question, everybody on the campus knew who Kel was. House glanced behind his own shoulder quickly, making sure that he knew exactly where his friends were, then continued. "The brothers of Alpha Phi Alpha don't like the way you've been treating our sorority sista, Crystal Kerry. We would appreciate it if you show some responsibility and take care of your business. I don't like the way you've been treating her or the child she's holding in her womb. Little man, you need to handle your business."

The statement "little man" resonated in Kel's subconscious over and over again. He hated being referred to as little and even worse, the mention of someone else knowing that Crystal Kerry was pregnant with his child drove Kel to unspeakable limits of unbridled fury. Kel's arms numbed slightly at the thought of everyone involved in Crystal's sorority and their male fraternity counterparts knowing of his situation. Damn it, Kel thought to himself. His own mother didn't even know, yet some hulking steroid pumping stranger knew his most intimate secrets. Very calmly, Kel took his Black & Mild cigar from his mouth and stamped it out on the wooden cafeteria table.

Without the slightest bit of fear, Kel stood up from his chair, maintaining a cold stare with the bulky muscle bound man in front of him. With the top of his Afro only reaching to the House's chest. Kel resembled a mere child as he stood next to the much larger man. "Ha. Ha. Ha. What? You want to fight me!" House laughed at the absurdity of anyone so puny standing toe to toe with him. Never before had any man at Blanding University stood up to him before, and now with his fraternity brothers standing behind him, the class clown of all people, was standing his ground. House would have laughed again if not for the look in Kel Jones' eyes. His eyes were cold and dead like that of a man who had just lost everything he truly cared about. The frigid look in the smaller man eyes made the massive fraternity man take a tentative step backwards.

House hesitated for a minute. He didn't really want to fight Kel and it showed momentarily in his eyes when he hesitated. He just wanted to scare him a little bit, to make sure that he call and check in on Crystal. He never had to fight as a youth because of his extremely large size. When Kel stared at him with those dead eyes, it more than surprised him it also scared him.

Because of the hesitation on the fraternity boy's part, Kel was swift enough to throw a roundhouse right hand. The punch landed flush on his cheek shattering the other man's face and nose with a gruesome crunching noise. The punch was thrown without thought, without worry of consequences. Kel smiled like a mad man, showing all of his white teeth, when the fraternity boy's massive body crumbled to the floor with the first punch. "C'mon! Come on!!" Kel screamed at the top of his lungs with both of his hands up like a boxer. "You want some too! I'm sick of people telling me what the fuck I should do!"

The other two men simply stood in shock as they watched their fallen fraternity brother slumbering in his own blood. Their eyes bulged with disbelief as Kel stood before them, his fist still red from the impact of knocking out their friend. Bypassing House's unconscious body, Kel leaped across the cafeteria table and jumped directly in the face of the taller fraternity boy. The sight of his fraternity brother on the floor paralyzed him with fear.

Kel stood only inches from the taller frat boy now. He could smell the aroma of the school's breakfast on his breath and the manifestation of fear in his once angry eyes. "You want some, too? Huh?" Kel yelled in the face of the taller fraternity boy flinching occasionally as if he was going to hit him also. "You chumps run around this campus like you own it. I don't need a group to express who I am. I'm an individual! Dressing alike, talking alike, walking alike, staying in each other's business, you're all pale imitations of one corny-ass mold. You guys really make me sick! What Crystal and me do is our business. You should mine yours, or else you'll end up like your bro sleeping on the floor! Brotherhood, huh. You guys don't know the meaning of the word. You guys are just a bunch of fucking cowards who only feel secure approaching people to fight if you have your friends standing beside you. You guys ain't nothing by yourselves."

Completely disgusted at the taller frat boy's petrified posture, Kel took the palm of his hand and mashed it hard against the face of the frat boy pushing him back disgracefully. Again the man stood completely still, lost in the shock of the moment, unable to defend himself or put up the least little bit of resistance. "You ain't shit!" Kel growled as he walked past the couple, purposely bumping into the smaller frat boy to show he hadn't forgotten or forgiven his involvement either. "When you see me you better walk on the other side of the street," Kel stated ferociously as he walked away.

As Kel walked away he made a little frown, just a tiny perfectly symmetrical grimace. Belittling the group of fraternity brothers and even physically knocking one of them out didn't make Kel feel as good as he thought it would have. He could still feel a stinging sensation from where his hand connected with the fraternity boy's face. No, the small victory he had achieved was a hollow one. If the likes of these three knew of the baby, then that would mean Crystal had told all of her friends. Crystal was never any good when it came to secrets anyhow. Kel knew instantly that his situation couldn't be hidden any longer. It was just a matter of time.

CHAPTER 12

The Call

The next night Larenzo sat in the Pitt alone with only his thoughts of Joy to keep him company. The greasy restaurant was filled with students scrambling amidst each other, but their movements didn't concern Larenzo in the least. Larenzo was only predisposed with waiting impatiently for Joy to meet him for dinner. It had already been ten minutes since he sat in the Pitt, and with a quick glance at his watch Larenzo realized that his dinner partner was late. Larenzo's facial features throbbed with sensations of annoyance as he checked his cell phone for any messages that she might have left.

Coincidently, at that exact moment, Larenzo's cell phone lit up with a blue neon light. A call was coming through, and his heart leaped full of bliss at the notion that it might be Joy dialing on the other end. Larenzo quickly checked the cell phone and was disappointed to see Crystal's name appear on the caller ID screen. Tentatively, Larenzo opened his cell phone to speak with her. At first he contemplated not answering it on account that Crystal was officially Kel's girlfriend, and therefore off limits. But one possible questionable situation prevented Larenzo from ignoring her phone call like so many other females who called before that day: what if Kel was in trouble and needed his help? With the utmost hesitancy Larenzo answered his phone placing it gently to his ear.

"Hello," Larenzo answered his phone, his voice no more than whisper.

"Larenzo, it's me Crystal," she responded somberly. "I've been calling you all week but you haven't been answering your phone." There was sadness present in Crystal Kerry's voice that Larenzo had never heard come from her lips before.

"What'd you want?" Larenzo said ignoring her depressing voice. "I only answered the phone because I thought that Kel might have been calling me from your room. I'm waiting for Joy to meet me for dinner, so I can't talk for long." Larenzo stated meanly, inappropriately attempting to get an emotional fluster from her.

There was a long moment of silence, which seemed to last an eternity to Larenzo. At one point he even thought that he had successfully managed to goad her into hanging up on him, which was his initial purpose. He didn't despise Crystal; in fact Larenzo still cared for Crystal as much as he ever did before.

Crystal sat on the other end of the phone emotionally torn in several pieces at his words. Larenzo had deliberately tried to hurt her feelings by mentioning Joy Summers' name. Crystal had seen Larenzo and Joy together hugging and kissing in the library. She had watched them enviously as they happily played with each other outside of Allen Hall. Just the mention of her name revolted Crystal bringing her to painful memories of her and Larenzo's sexual encounters together. Crystal sat down completely shocked and pondered, or more or less, drew together her thoughts sobbing freely to herself. Never before had Larenzo so blatantly been so indifferent of her feelings. He seemed so uncaring and heartless.

Now fully crying loudly on the phone Crystal began to speak, breaking the uneasy silence. "Larenzo, I know that you're mad that I'm with your best friend. You got to believe me. We never planned on hurting you... I mean we never meant to hurt you. It's just one of those things that seemed to just happen. It's like..."

"Just seemed to happen!" Larenzo said crossly cutting off her flow of words in the middle of the sentence. "It just so happens to rain or you might just happen to trip down the stairs. People do not just happen to fuck each other. So what was it? I guess you just so happened to fall on his dick!"

"No! It's not like that," Crystal paused for a moment to sob. "I just happened to fall in love."

"Love!" Larenzo repeated the word aghast. "You have no idea what that word means. Love is a strong passionate connection between two people like Joy and I have. It's like being willing to give up your life for someone. It's like being willing to kill for someone. Love does not mean fucking two best friends." Larenzo sat silent for a moment.

Agitated at the flow of the conversation, Larenzo sighed in disgust. "Well is this why you been calling me? Do you want too apologize over all of the vile things that your love has caused me? Is that why you called me? Well don't worry about it because I got over it.

Thanks for thinking about me," Larenzo stated sarcastically ready to hang up the phone.

"No, Larenzo don't hang up," Crystal stated hysterically. The sounds of sobs and sniffling could be heard on the other end. "That's not why I called you. Larenzo... I'm pregnant."

Larenzo caught his breath at the statement. His heart pounding uncontrollably, as if it were going to leap from his chest. A chilling shiver ran through his body. Larenzo automatically broke out in a cold sweat and trembles. The phone dropped away from his head lightly as he went through a sort of shock. "I'm too young for a child. Please, God I'm just twenty years old," Larenzo thought to himself. His eyes roamed the Pitt wondering if only he was cursed with such horrible luck. A jukebox was playing in the corner, and the sizzling of food frying created an atmosphere of peace. Students bobbed back and forth gently to the rhythm and blues music. Other students greedily shoveled large portions of food into their mouths quickly, only chewing occasionally.

"Larenzo! Larenzo are you there?" The voice of Crystal Kerry's sniveling voice on the other end of the telephone brought Larenzo back from his panic induced shock.

Larenzo placed the phone to his head as though it were a loaded gun. He gulped down a wad of his own spit before he could finally speak again. "Yeah...I'm still here." All of his life he had dreaded this moment. Most of his cousins his age already had several children out of wedlock, but Larenzo always thought that he was better than them. He thought he was too lucky to ever get some girl he didn't love pregnant. Larenzo had seen too much baby-momma-drama in his life to know this wouldn't have a happy ending.

Larenzo shook his head in a negative gesture. With the utmost difficulty he formed words. "So what are you saying? I mean why are you telling me this? The child isn't mine! I'm not the daddy, Crystal," Larenzo said out right. His words were no longer angry or frustrated. There was a new emotion present in his voice that Crystal Kerry had never heard in him before. That new emotion was fear.

"You're not the father," Crystal whispered quietly.

Partially relieved Larenzo exhaled when he heard the statement. He hadn't realized that he was holding his breath as he waited for the answer. A gleeful happiness ran through his body followed suddenly followed by a small glimmer of doubt as he considered whether Crystal would lie to him about matters as important as this. "Are you sure...I'm not...you know?" Larenzo said stumbling over his words.

"I'm sure that you're not the father," Crystal repeated her answer, sounding more certain than before. This time her answer satisfied Larenzo bringing a more confident smile of relief to his face.

"That's good because I don't want to be on Ricki Lake or some other talk show taking a paternity test ten years from now," Larenzo joked happily at her expense. "You be calling me when the kid is ten years old talkin' bout you made a mistake. I'd have some rug rat knocking at my front door talkin' about 'You're my daddy.' HA!HA!HA!" Larenzo didn't want to laugh at Crystal's expense but he couldn't help himself. Laughter was the only way that he had of dealing with the fear that he once had.

Crystal tried to smile when she heard his joke but just the sound of his laughter made her nauseous. Her voice was dry and course as she spoke. "Please don't laugh at me," Crystal said pleadingly finding a pool of inner strength allowing her to stop crying. "I've been crying at night for two weeks straight. I told my mom and she threw my clothes out of my house. Larenzo, you know my father is a reverend. He won't even look at me now. I don't know what to do. The father stopped talking to me after I told him, and he hasn't even told any of his family yet." She paused wiping a few tears from her cheek and then continued. "He doesn't have a job, and he's so irresponsible. He won't return my phone calls even when I know he's there. I don't know what to do. After this semester is over, I won't even have anywhere to stay."

"Hold up. Who's the father?" Larenzo inquired seriously.

Disbelief spread across Crystal's face at the suggestion of what that question would imply. "What do you think, that I am some type of whore, or something? Larenzo, the father is Kel."

"Kel is the dad," Larenzo said flabbergasted at the statement.

"I thought that he might have at least told you," Crystal admitted, freely crying once again. "You two have been best friends since junior high school. I thought that he would have said something to you. Larenzo I think that he's ashamed of me and the baby."

"No, he never said anything. How long has he known?"

"Three months," Crystal said under her breath as if she were ashamed.

"Well, why don't you go get an abortion? One of my friends made his girl get an abortion last semester when he found out she was pregnant. I know where the place is...I drove them there myself."

"It's been three an a half months. The state of South Carolina won't allow me to have an abortion this late in the pregnancy." Crystal let out a depressed cry of tears and snot when she admitted her predicament. "Larenzo, what should I do?" Of course the question was completely rhetorical but Larenzo felt compelled to answer her anyhow.

Larenzo was speechless, completely in awe of the revelations revealed to him. Kel had never held anything secretive from him before. The whole idea of his best friend, his blood brother, being a father startled Larenzo shaking him to his bones. If his blood brother was a dad, did that make him an uncle? He had never pictured himself as a uncle before and the mere mention of the word sent a warm feeling rushing through his limbs. Larenzo grinned cheerfully and curled his hand underneath his chin. "I have no idea what you should do. I'm not some psychiatrist or nothing. I don't have a major in that sort of stuff."

"I don't know why I'm telling you this, except that I still trust you," Crystal confessed. Her heart yearned for an audience that wouldn't condemn her like her parents did. She needed someone who would just listen to her problems. There was no more hurt, trickery, or malice in her voice at all. It no longer held the contemptible tone of an ex-lover. She was just another person in search of someone to talk to, someone whom she could trust.

"I trust you, too," Larenzo stated plainly, partially lying. He didn't truly trust her, but it did sound convincing and quite poetic.

"Talk to Kel for me. I know that you guys are still friends. He'll listen to you."

"I'll see what I can do. He's not the easiest guy to reason with, even for me."

She giggled a little at Larenzo's comment. The sorrow in her voice subsided a little as it was quickly replaced by the sounds of mirth. Crystal knew that Kel was a stubborn man, and full of pride. It was one of a dozen reasons why she felt Kel was so irresistible to her. He had a moral complexity about him, which made him truly believe that every choice he ever made was the right one. In that small characteristic, Kel and Larenzo were very much alike, truly blood brothers. They were two rebels from the inner city streets of Chicago who answered to no one. If there were anyone with a minute chance in hell of giving Kel advice on anything, it would come from his best friend, Larenzo.

"All I'm asking for is that you try," Crystal laughed bitterly, relieved to finally have told someone else. "I'm glad to see that we can still be friends. Even after everything that has happened."

"Yeah. I guess we are friends."

"Thank you for doing this for me, Larenzo."

"No problem. I'll call you later and let you know how it went."

"Bye, Renzo." Crystal said pleased at her progress.

"Peace," Larenzo replied coolly.

Larenzo hung up his cell phone and leaned back in the dark blue cushioned chair, silently contemplating why Kel would keep something as important as a pregnancy secret from him. Joy Summer rushed through the doorway of the Pitt. In her hands were four rather large books piled up one on top of another. Her hair hung lightly across her face, a strand or two in front of her left eye. She was beautiful and her beauty allowed Larenzo to momentarily concentrate on the here and now. A glimmer of confusion spread across her face as she scanned the room, apparently searching for Larenzo.

"I'm over here, Joy!" Larenzo said more excitedly than he meant too.

Joy's princess-like, innocent face lit up with a smile as her eyes met with Larenzo's. She nearly dropped the pile of books in her arms as she hurried over to his table. She stared at Larenzo with her eyes filled with love. "I'm sorry I'm so late getting here. I was studying for Mr. Miller's class and I lost track of the time." Joy sat her books down on the table and gave Larenzo a compassionate hug. "Well, have you been waiting long for me?"

"All my life," Larenzo answered jokingly. "But seriously, I don't mind waiting for you."

"You're such a charmer. You probably tell all of the girls that," Joy said caressing his hand in hers. "What would I ever do without you?"

"You know I was just about to say the same thing. That reminds me..." Larenzo paused for a second, searching for the right words to explain his actions. "Joy, I can't study tonight with you. I'm gonna be at Red's house checking on Malik. His mom called me last night about him. Some girl pressed assault charges against him when he jumped on her a few months ago. His mother is worried about him. She hasn't seen him for days at a time. He's either way too drunk or high to walk into his mom's house. Shit, I'm worried about him, too. Lately, he just hasn't been acting the same. He's been sleeping mostly on Red's couch. I know this shit is all because of his old girlfriend. That bitch has him all fucked up inside. He doesn't even go to class anymore, and I'm really getting scared that he might hurt himself or something."

"Yeah, that's a shame," Joy added to the conversation. "Malik used to be so cute. He doesn't even sell candy anymore. You should go talk to your friend. I think that I'll make it just one night without you by my side." Joy reflected dreamy eyed.

CHAPTER 13

EXPERT ADVICE

Larenzo walked from the Pitt without a worry in the world. He reached for his cell phone and tried to call John Spencer but there was no answer on the other line. For a brief moment his bushy eyebrows came together as he frowned. Larenzo's brown eyes grew worried as he tried to remember the last time he spoke to the shy, light-skinned companion from Connecticut. "A week? Naw, two weeks," Larenzo said out loud trying to figure out how long it had been since they had last talked to each other. "First Malik, now John." A horrible vision of John lying dead on the side of a road quickly crossed Larenzo's mind, but he dismissed the image quickly as just a figment of an overactive imagination. He was sure that he would have heard news about another student's death at Blanding University. The press always made sure to publicize negative events concerning the historical black universities in the area.

Larenzo decided that John was ignoring the messages on his answer machine. It was simply the only answer that made sense. Larenzo's worry for John Spencer blew away in an instant when he saw Red's house in the distance. Just the sight of the home left Larenzo with a sense of reassurance that relaxed every muscle in his body. The building was a mental sedative of sorts for the exhausted college student. No matter what type of heartache fell Larenzo, he knew that he could always count on the small, dirty shack a few blocks away from campus to ease his frustrated mind.

The outside of the home looked deserted, but Bobby's four-door black Nissan was parked on the side of the house. Larenzo opened the door without knocking and moved a load of dirty clothes aside before plopping down on the couch nearest the door. The inside of the house was far quieter than usual. The home was mostly without noise except for the soft mellow sounds of R&B music playing in the background. Larenzo glanced around the room with vacant eyes, as if he were staring inward not bothered by his environment. Bobby sat on the couch nearest to Larenzo and a very attractive, chocolate-colored female was laying on his lap with her eyes closed, her long hair pillowing her head, seemingly asleep. She wore a skimpy little yellow dress barely covering her shapely figure. Around her wrist were delicate gold bracelets, and a petite gold chain draped around her ankles. Bobby smiled slyly when Larenzo sat down.

"Renzo, you should have walked through that door fifteen minutes ago," Bobby King said grinning from ear to ear as he zipped and buttoned the top of his slacks and grabbed for a small glass of brandy. "Yo, Stacy is no joke. I think she might be ready for the big times," Bobby said patting her gently on the head like a person would a common household pet.

"Where is everybody?" Larenzo said staring toward the back rooms for anyone else in the home.

Bobby gently massaged the neatly trimmed outline of his mustache before answering. "Red went to see JC in the hospital again. Kel came over but left really quickly. He said he had to pick Crystal up from the store or something. That bitch got him running around in circles. No one's seen Malik in at least a month. His mom keeps calling here looking for him late at night. Anyway, it's just Stacy and me here now. You know I don't get the chance to get out much because Terry been trying to keep a close watch on me, like I'm her ho or some shit."

"Whoever said pimping ain't easy, ain't never lied. It's hard damn work pleasing several beautiful women worshipped by average niggas," Bobby said smiling proudly about his profession. "You know what I mean Larenzo. You're with Joy right now, and I know she gets approached by average men all of the time. It's our duty to be more than an average man when it comes to our women."

Bobby lifted his glass in a small salute.

"The average female at Blanding University might get hit on by twenty guys a day. That's not even taking into account the amount of lesbians that will try their luck. It's like women our taught to turn average men down as a way of life." Bobby hesitated for a moment then added quickly, "It's only a select few amount of men whom are blessed with the gift. We have the gift. We should use it. In this world there are only two groups of men. On one side you have the customers and on the other side you have the players. I couldn't imagine being a client."

"Yeah," Larenzo added slowly staring out of the window absent-mindedly. "I'm supposed to study tomorrow night with Joy at the library and I know niggas is gonna be looking at her. You know finals are coming up, and the library is going to be packed tomorrow."

"Library?" Bobby roared with laughter at the mention of the word. "You acting real soft right now, Renzo. In two years, you ain't never even came close to the building and now some woman got you going to study sessions."

"Naw," Larenzo said smiling. "My mom will kill me if I fail any of my classes this semester. Besides, me and Joy have a different understanding than all of the other women that I used to fuck wit."

"Used to?" Bobby said inquisitively. "What the fuck is going on in the world? Goddamn, Renzo say it ain't so. Say it ain't so! Do I hear wedding bells in the future or what? Joy has got to have some excellent pussy to have Larenzo Baker giving up his womanizing ways."

Larenzo glanced at Bobby and smirked slightly dropping his head in shame. "Why niggas always have to bring up sex when it comes to how a man feels about a girl? If a man cares enough about the girl, sex shouldn't even be an issue." The words sprung from Larenzo's mouth before he truly contemplated what he was saying. It had been four months since Larenzo saw Joy sitting in the classroom next door to his, and he had not even considered rushing into sex with her. Since puberty Larenzo had never abstained from sex for that lengthy amount of time, and now that he had, he didn't mind the wait. Did he really mean what he said? The words echoed in his skull over and over again. If a man cares enough about a girl, sex didn't matter. Just the realization that his mouth could form the words made Larenzo turn red with embarrassment.

"Hold on now, Larenzo," Bobby quickly said becoming very serious. "You telling me that you haven't slept with Joy, yet? I know that you've been talking to her this whole semester, but you're not telling me that you haven't fucked her. What the hell are you waiting for? Ya'll need to stop bull shitting around and get it over with. This shit is more serious than you ever let on, too. You better watch yourself. It's beginning to sound like you're falling in love."

Bobby smiled lightly as he imagined himself becoming a complete monogamist one day with Terry. Bobby knew that it was only a pipe dream. Pimps could never completely settle down in a relationship. Never ever completely, it just wasn't in their nature. Even though some would try, the temptation was always too strong in the end. It was a curse, plain and simple, a horrible curse passed down by his father's bloodline, which he would have to deal with in his own time. "It could be worse. You could end up like your homeboy, John," Bobby said halfheartedly, smiling at the ludicrous suggestion.

"Well, what about John?" Larenzo questioned swiftly, wanting to change the drift of the conversation. "I haven't seen John in weeks. That nigga ain't returning my phone calls and shit. I mean, usually he would give me a ride over here, but lately I've been forced to walk all over this little mother-fucking town."

Bobby took a deep breath as he remembered the story in every detail. "Spencer isn't coming back to school. He dropped out of Blanding University over some broad."

He stopped for another sip of the Brandy.

"He dropped out over a girl?" Larenzo repeated Bobby's statement in disbelief.

"Ain't it always about a bitch?" Bobby said softly.

Larenzo leaned forward eager to hear the story that was sure to come next. Bobby paused for a moment to make sure that he had Larenzo's full attention before he began to narrate the events. Bobby simply loved to be the center of attention, and whenever he had the chance to tell a story about women, he embellished in every moment of it.

"About a week and a half ago I got a call from that girl that we stopped from being raped after the basketball game. She called me right at home like in the middle of the day when Terry and Sheena were out at the mall. It's a miracle that my woman and baby girl weren't home. She had gotten my home phone number from one of the girls that she used to work with. Well, the broad said that she wanted to thank me personally for scaring that rapist guy off of her. You know, she was really shaken up after the event and she thought that I really saved her life. Something about feeling a deep connection with me and all that other new age shit."

"Bobby, you didn't..." Larenzo voice trailed off before he could finish the question. But Bobby King realized that Larenzo already knew the answer without him having to verbalize it. Bobby decided to finish the story anyhow. He felt as though it would be better to hear the story from his own lips than to hear it later as a rumor.

Bobby took a deep breath as if each sentence burnt him with pain. "Yeah, yeah, yeah. I know it was wrong, but I went to her dormitory anyway," Bobby confessed. "She met me downstairs in the lobby, and shit you know. What can I say ... I'm a man." He laughed a small scornful laugh. "As soon I made it to her room she was clawing all over me like a bitch in heat. She was no virgin, this girl. Shit! She was definitely a professional looking for some good fucking." Bobby visualized the moment he held her back, merely to look at her, then kissed her back brutally, ripping off her clothes, relishing in the same amount of lust that she had shown him.

"Before I knew it, I was giving it to her standing up against the wall. She was screaming so loud from the moment that I was sure that someone was going to complain. I didn't know at the time, but at that very instant, John Spencer was walking down the hallway to check on his girlfriend. I'm sure he must have heard the screams and moans halfway down the hallway. As John reached the door, he could probably smell the aroma of sex in the air; the sounds of ecstasy shriek out of his girlfriend's vocal cords. Whatever it was, it wasn't a surprise when he started banging on the door, like he was the goddamn police trying to make a drug bust or something. He was screaming her name the whole time as he hammered on the door. 'Janet! Janet open the door!'

"When I heard him on the other side of the door my natural nigga instincts kicked in, and I tried to pull the girl off of me, like I was going to jump out the window or something. But by then, it was already too late. I could tell by the look in her eyes that she had no intentions of stopping so far into it." Bobby could still vividly recall the lustful, trance-like stare in Janet's eyes, and the feeling of the tender muscles of her shaved vaginal mouth fastening onto him, making him ride her even harder than before. The harder John banged on the door, the faster Bobby pumped into her, filling her body with each thrust. The result couldn't be helped; the outcome was never truly in doubt.

Bobby could hear John on the other side of the doorway screaming in agony. All of a sudden the screams suddenly became silent. He didn't have to open the door. Bobby and Janet could hear the sobs on the other end of the door and knew where the tears were coming from. Soon a crowd of students had gathered outside of the door because of all of the ruckus that he had caused. For a deafening moment, Janet and Bobby stood still, simply listening to the choked sobs from John on the other end. It was sickening.

Bobby took a deep breath as he finished the story. "I knew then that John Spencer wouldn't be returning to Blanding University. Not many men can be witnessed weeping in front of their girlfriend's bedroom door and come back to class the next day. It's just too embarrassing for anyone."

"How did you get out of the room without fighting him?" Larenzo asked quietly.

"Janet called the campus police and asked that they escort John out of the building. That's one cold bitch! When she picked up the phone and dialed I kind of felt bad for him. I could hear the security talking to him and eventually escorted him out of the building. After the shit was all over with, I was scared that John might have committed suicide or something, but rumor has it on the campus that he moved back to Connecticut to be around his mom and dad. I hope he's doing better up there than he was at Blanding. I mean, she could have at least opened up the door and told him she didn't want to be with him any more. But hey, what do you expect from one of these bitches?"

"Hey! All women aren't bitches." Larenzo said quickly correcting Bobby.

"Oh!" Bobby exclaimed looking at Larenzo in surprise. "Correction – all women aren't bitches, but all women have a little bit of a bitch in them. Remember that shit. You'll see... even your little future wifey, Joy, has a tail hidden underneath that dress." Bobby let out a big laugh at Larenzo's earlier confession of abstinence. "You just ain't seen her tail yet."

"Yeah, yeah. Laugh it up," Larenzo said a little embarrassed. "Hopefully, I can solve that little dilemma tomorrow night when I meet up with Joy at the library."

"Good luck. You're going to need it. If she ain't gave you no ass in two years what makes you think that tomorrow is going to be any different."

Larenzo shrugged his shoulders at the suggestion. "Guess I'll keep trying 'til I get it right."

CHAPTER 14

BAMBOOZLED

The alarm clock went off slowly dragging Malik Brown out of his intoxicated slumber on Red's couch. Without even opening his eyes, Malik reached toward a nearby ashtray searching for a piece of the blunt that he had left over from the night before. Malik's hand felt around the edges of the ashtray to no avail. "Shit!" he yelled out frustrated when he remembered that he had already finished smoking the rest of the blunt the night prior. His memory wasn't the same as it used to be, no doubt a side effect of the large daily quantity of marijuana use.

With just one look around the interior of the small home, Malik realized that he was the only one there. He wasn't used to Red's house being so quiet. The television was turned off, and an eerie silence ran through the home. Malik let out a deep sigh and closed his eyes tight trying to picture the exquisite peace that only exists in the whirlwind of intoxication. His head swam with dizziness, but something was missing from his high. For the first time since his break up with Ebony, Malik couldn't visualize the swirling colors of light. Malik shook his head "no" in defiance. Without the beautiful swirling colors he couldn't go back to sleep. Without the colors he couldn't make it to class or even begin to partially function like a regular person. Without the swirling of the colors he would have to think of how Ebony had betrayed their relationship. Without the swirling colors her face would emerge whenever he closed his eyes. Realizing that sleep was impossible now, Malik stood up leaning slightly against the wall for support. The compelling desire for the swirling colors drove Malik to stand up and begin his day.

Now fully standing up, Malik stared at the alarm clock in disgust. It was already 11:20 a.m. and his Psychology class would be starting in ten minutes. Malik quickly dismissed the idea of attending class. It was already near the end of the school year and he had missed more than enough days to fail the class. For the moment he actually contemplated explaining his situation to his teacher or even asking the instructor for some extra credit, but Malik knew that he wouldn't do either one. He had made up in his mind that he was going to fail that class and there was nothing else to it. Tired and depressed Malik checked his pockets for some extra money. "Only twenty dollars," Malik thought to himself as he straightened up his Malcolm X t-shirt on his frail body.

Discouraged and low on money, Malik staggered to the bathroom to wash up. Once in Red's bathroom, Malik splashed cold water on his face and over his head. He took his time soaking his face underneath the soothing cool water of the sink. Malik lifted his head and dried his wet braids and face with a towel. He peered into the mirror examining himself thoroughly. At first sight Malik didn't even recognize the features of his own face staring back. His eyes were bloodshot and slanted. His pupils were as small as pinpoints. His face had become sunken in and reminded him of a skeleton with flesh. His once pink lips had completely changed colors into a much darker tone, and his fingertips had burns on them from where blunts had scorched his hand.

Disgusted at his own reflection, with only twenty dollars left to his name, Malik left Red's home in search of some more marijuana. He could feel the absence of the drug in his body, and he hated it. Malik hated mornings like this more than anything. Without the drug in his system it seemed as though accomplishing regular everyday tasks became harder and harder. He closed his eyes again in an attempt to see the comforting colors that had soothed his mind in the past; but he couldn't picture them without the drug. His stomach seemed to be twisting in knots, and the only thing that he knew that would satisfy this feeling was the intoxicating aroma of marijuana.

With only the thought of stopping the nauseating pain in his gut, Malik drove his mother's newly fixed Cadillac toward the African House store on the corner. Within a few minutes Malik pulled up outside the entrance of the brightly colored store. The exterior of the building was painted green, red, and yellow. The large front window of the store was tinted black, so that there was no chance of any nosey people staring in from outside. A pair of homeless men sat in front of the store on the sidewalk huddled together around a bottle of wine. They were regulars that would hang around the African House about this hour of the day. The two homeless men were only around their mid-forties, but hard living made them look a whole lot older. Their clothes were ragged and stained with dirt. One of the homeless men nodded his wrinkled head in Malik's direction when he saw the youth walk toward the entrance.

"Hey kid, can I borrow a dollar? I'm good for it. Really I am," The man half-heartedly begged Malik. "I ain't eat nothing all day today. C'mon and help an old man out. Just let me get one dollar."

Usually, Malik would give what little bit of change he could to the two homeless men, but today Malik's only concern was obtaining some more drugs. "Man I'm hurting for money right now," Malik replied to the first homeless man. "I'm hurting real bad and I need to talk to Shabazz."

"Oh, I understand ya kid," the other homeless man stated shaking a cheap bottle of liquor at Malik. "You got to get that damn monkey off your back, huh? All you needs is a little bit of stuff to git you through the day. I knows all about it, youngster. Us junkies needs to stick together."

Malik began to shake his head in agreement with the homeless man's statement, and then he realized what he was truly saying. "You crazy old fool! I'm not a junky. All I do is a little bit of weed. That shit ain't addictive, it can't kill you or nothing," Malik stated angrily. The nerves of that bum to actually think that Malik Brown was like him at all. He wasn't addicted; he was far too strong for that. The only people who got hooked were weak, and Malik knew in his heart that he was too strong to ever get hooked.

With that thought in Malik's mind, he quickly dismissed the homeless man's statement as the preposterous ranting of a crazy, old man. Malik walked through the front door of the African House still upset. The strong smell of incense flowed from the entrance when he opened the door. The inside of the store was filled with figurine statues of African warriors and Kings. An "authentic" African drum sat undisturbed in the corner with a $400 price tag on it. A table full of bootleg mixed CD's was by the opposite wall. The mellow sounds of Caribbean music played in the background. Standing directly in front of Malik was the cash register and the smiling face of Shabazz Jacob, the owner of the store.

Shabazz was a Rastafarian originally from Jamaica. Shabazz was a medium-built dark complexioned man. His hair was done in long unkempt dreadlocks and had a tinge of orange color to them. A heavy black, bushy mustache connected with his nappy sideburns to create a beard which he would scratch whenever deep in thought. His dark brown eyes glistened when he saw Malik walk into his store. Malik was always one of his best customers, and just the sight of the young, black militant walking through his door brought him happiness.

"My black brother, Malik, what wrong wit you dere," Shabazz said good-naturedly. "Me tink you need some good fixing to get you back on track? I got some new cocaine coming in from Miami. This shit is way better than dat other stuff you had," Shabazz said in a strong Jamaican accent.

"I don't do that shit," Malik said repulsed at the notion that Shabazz would offer him cocaine. "Rasta man, you got the wrong brother." Malik paused, then continued angrily. "All I dabble in is with the herbals. I would never use no cocaine. You know that that shit is the white man's drug. That's just another way for the man to bring our people down. The original man has no right using that shit. It's just slow death. Look, I just need two-dime bags of weed."

Shabazz stared at Malik's statement perplexed for a moment, then he laughed out loud. "My brother Malik, that last ounce you bought was called Green Haze. It's a mixture of marijuana and cocaine. Me tink to myself, 'Dat man dere going tru some serious trouble.' So I gave you someting a little bit stronger than your usual weed since you broke up wit your girlfriend. I know how losing a love one can hurt a man. Don't sweat it. That little white powder is some good stuff, huh? I knew it would be exactly what you needed to get you tru your little tragedy. Now look at you, no worries about your girlfriend at all." Shabazz laughed again, this time patting Malik gently on the shoulder.

Malik just stared at the Rastafarian in disbelief. Shabazz smiled broadly at Malik as he lit another incant stick. "So, you're saying you been mixing cocaine with my weed and never told me?" Malik asked trying to control his anger. His fists were clenched so tight that his knuckles had turned white. "You didn't think that it was important for me to know that you put cocaine in my weed. That's why my stomach hurts so badly and I haven't been able to get my mind off that shit in the last couple of days. You fuckin' turned me into a crack head!"

"No little brother, not crack head," Shabazz said cutting off Malik's flow of angry words. "It is just a little cocaine, nothing as serious as crack. Ya just feel a little withdrawal down dere in ya belly. Regular weed won't help you anymore. Deep down ya body is cravin' for de powder now. Only two ways me see get rid of dat feeling: use some more cocaine or ya let it run out your body naturally in a couple of days. Do the reasonable ting, smoke more, ya pain soon go away. If you go cold turkey, it will take days, maybe even weeks. Ya choice," Shabazz shrugged indifferently as he took out a small package wrapped in plastic and opened it. The white dust lay on the counter, like a small mountain of flour.

Malik stared at the large pile of cocaine ominously. For a moment Malik considered walking away from Shabazz and telling him where he could shove that white drug, but then the stinging sensation in his stomach came to him again. Malik reached for his stomach and nearly doubled over from the pain. Just the idea of having that pain for another second was too much for him. "Alright, you win. Just give me the shit." Malik groaned still clutching his belly.

Shabazz glanced at Malik and smiled. "Me figured ya make da right choice. Look dat tis twenty dollars worth of stuff plus me tru in a little something extra to keep ya happy on those long cold nights."

Malik's hand shook as he reached for the bundle. He wrapped up the package and tucked it under his arm quickly. As Malik left the store his mind was set on nothing else except an end to the sickening pain developing in his stomach. Moments later he had driven back to his mother's home and hurried to his room in the back. He locked the door to his room just in case his mother came home early for her lunch break. Malik sat back comfortably in his chair and spread the drug out across his bedroom dresser. At first he separated a small amount of the cocaine from the larger pile then he made a small line out of the white powder. In a few moments he had snorted the line of coke, and then another line. The cocaine felt like razor blades had been shoved up each of his nasal passages.

Within a few minutes he had inhaled half the drug away without even knowing it. After two or three deep snorts of the powder Malik's head swam with feelings of empyrean. Completely satisfied with his high, Malik closed his eyes and his beloved swirls of colorful lights appeared once again behind his eyelids. His head would fall forward for a while, and then he would wake himself up. Finally, unable to keep his head up any longer, Malik allowed his head to nod off against his chest.

Suddenly Malik was awoken from his intoxicated slumber by a loud noise. "Malik are you in there?" a female voice bellowed from the other side of his locked bedroom door. "Open up the door. I need my keys."

"Mom, I'll be right there," Malik said nervously as he looked around his bedroom. Still in his lap were the remains of the white drug. "Give me a second. I had fallen asleep," Malik said trying not to sound too suspicious. He swiftly gathered the package of white powder and quickly hid it in the top shelf of his dresser beside his socks and underwear. He wiped a few smudges of the drug off of his nose and then unlocked the door.

Malik's mother walked into the room and stared at her son with concern in her eyes. "Malik is everything all right? You've been acting weird lately. You're not getting sick or anything, are you?"

Malik's hand shook a little when he heard her ask the question. He lifted his head slowly and his eyes met hers. "Mom, I'm okay. I just been tired lately that's all. You know. I guess taking classes and dealing with Ebony has got me a little stressed out, that's all. Give me a couple of more hours sleep and I'll be ready for dinner."

"Son, it's ten o'clock at night. I ate dinner with a few co-workers hours ago," Mrs. Brown said with a strange look on her face. "You haven't eaten yet? That's not like you Malik." Her voice was filled with compassion and sympathy as she continued. "Malik, if there was something going on you would tell me, right? You're so thin; you know that I worry about you. I'll understand, no matter what it is."

Once again, she looked at Malik with sly eyes.

Malik glanced out the window and realized that his mother was correct. The smell of the cooler, damp, night air extended from the open window, bringing truth to her words. The moon had already risen high in the air and the stars twinkled brightly against the dark-blue night skyline. Crickets could be heard chirping in the grass outside of his home. It was true Malik had slept through the entire day.

"Mom, you worry too much. Your keys are on the desk, I'm going back to sleep."

Before the words had fully left Malik's mouth, he had already begun to slip into a deep sleep. He fluffed his pillow and laid back in his bed only thinking about the small hill of cocaine stashed away in his dresser. As his body rested his mind still danced with the numbing sensation of the pure white cocaine flowing through his bloodstream. No longer did he have that horrible pain in his stomach and more than anything else he finally recaptured the beautiful lights, which had escaped him for so long. Now, when he closed his eyes the reassuring lights danced in front of him and even his dreams were filled with the swirling bright colors.

The next morning Malik woke up at five o'clock in a cold sweat. The sun was just rising and blinded Malik for a moment. In that grayish hour of the day, no one else is awake and a man is left alone with only his thoughts to keep him company. His guilt. Malik sat in his bed, his hands trembling slightly as he reminisced about the mistakes he made in the last couple of weeks. He tried to close his eyes to meditate, but he couldn't concentrate. The lights were dimming and the vision of Ebony began to appear. Her soft dark skin, the smell of her hair, even the tantalizing deepness of her eyes tormented Malik's inner soul.

Depressed from the vision of his lost love, Malik sighed and ground his teeth in silence. Only the idea of the cocaine sitting in his dresser dragged Malik kicking and screaming out of his induced depression. His stomach rumbled with the idea of satisfying his pain with some coke. What was it about that innocent pile of white powder that held so much power over him? Malik had seen skinny, shaking addicts on the streets. Never had he ever thought that he would join their ranks. He thought that in time he would be able to beat this yearning for the numbing of pain in his heart. He thought that he was too strong of a black man to fall prey to the white poison. Once he had possessed everything that he would ever want and now, because of drugs and a girl, he was a broken shell of the man he once was.

"This is the last time," Malik thought trying to convince himself that after this one last time he would stop using for good. Malik Brown could verbally lie to himself as much as he wanted, but deep down he knew the truth. The idea of taking just one more snort of cocaine had become all-consuming. He had become a statistic like so many other young black men before him. Unable to control the urge anymore, Malik stood up reluctantly and made his way to the dresser. Salty tears fell from his eyes as he approached the small package lying in his dresser. Malik's palms shook nervously as he took the drug in his hand and hesitantly placed it on his bed.

Malik hesitated at first, but the outcome was never truly in doubt, he shoved the powder into his nose at a frightening rate. He frowned as the bitter drug dripped down his nasal passages and dispensed itself into his bloodstream. The pure cocaine swiftly invaded his mind, causing Malik Brown to fall headlong into an eternal darkness of pain and regret. At that moment Malik stopped caring about going to class, grieving over Ebony, or even the feelings he had regarding his friends and mother. Malik's mind was trapped in the slow death that is drugs.

That evening was similar to many of the evenings before it. A crowd of students customarily gathered at Red's home. The small stereo pumped loud Rap music through the hallowed hallways of the little two-bedroom house, located in the slums. One group of students played the game of Twister happily spinning an arrow climbing over each other. Another set of students sat at the card table playing Spades, arguing amongst each other. An array of smiles and laughter spread through Red's house infecting everyone present except for Malik Brown.

Malik sat quietly on Red's couch undisturbed by the frenzy of youthful students pleasantly engaging in the recreational events about him. His face was void of all happiness as he witnessed his peers frolicking before him. His facial features were pale. Malik blankly stared into the crowd of students. His body was frail and bony from lack of food. His eyes were glassy and his pupils dilated to the size of pin needles. Ungroomed strands of nappy brownish red hair had sprung loose from his once tight braids. Malik shivered a little when he thought no one was looking at him. But someone was looking at

Malik. Red stared at him suspiciously, silently evaluating his friend's every movement on the couch.

Malik continued to stare indifferently at the energetic students. His face seemed so solemn, almost peaceful. His head dropped down across his chest, and he began to nod in and out of sleep. With just one look everyone present realized that he was obviously high. It was no big secret that Malik was a heavy marijuana user, but on this occasion there was something odd about his appearance. It wasn't his thin skeletal figure or the large dark bags growing underneath his eyes. No, the oddity arose with his aroma. Usually, the familiar smell of marijuana smoke lingered in his clothes. This time Red noticed the absence of the strong scent.

"Yo, Malik!" Red yelled, trying unsuccessfully to get Malik's attention. "Malik, let me have a word with you." Red walked over to the couch and gently nudged Malik on the shoulder breaking him from his frigid meditative stillness. Malik looked up Red barely able to keep his head up. In a dreamlike reality, Malik strolled quietly behind Red following him in the back of the house towards his bedroom.

Red's bedroom was more lavish than the rest of his poorly maintained home. A giant king-sized bed was in the middle of the floor with lavender sheets spread on it. A small nightstand sat beside his bed and its twin on the other side. A large 42' inch flat screen television lay on the right side of the floor beside the bed. The interior of the bedroom was dimly lit detailing the room with shadows. Heavy black drapes hung over the windows keeping the room as dark as possible throughout the entire day. Two of the walls of the bedroom were decorated with two large posters of *Scarface*.

Malik stood in the pathway of Red's bedroom door. His mind raced with apprehension of what Red would say to him. Malik quickly decided that whatever it was, it couldn't be good. His figure was awkward and gawky in its plainness. He could barely keep his eyes open. His hands trembled a little, and his stomach twisted from a combination of nervousness and the heavy portion of cocaine still running through his blood. Worst of all, his heartbeat pounded so hard in his chest that he felt for sure it would burst.

Dressed in all baggy red clothing, Red was the accepted vision of a young black gangster. Oddly enough, Red stood motionless at the

foot of his king-sized bed with the unmistakable look of immeasurable patience upon his face. His posture was casual as he simply
stared at Malik for a long period of time in silence. Red smiled at the
nervousness in Malik's posture, making quiet silent to himself of
everything he saw.

"I know what you're going through," Red said finally breaking the
silence of his stare. "I've seen it happen to niggas back home a lot,
but I never thought that it would ever happen to one of my peoples."
Red paused shaking his head regretfully as he analyzed Malik from
head to toe. "You need help and if we don't get you some, I'm afraid
you might get yourself killed. You my nigga, and I got love for you,
but you got to know your limitations. You can't be snorting up coke
like you're Tony Montana or no crazy shit like that. That's why I want
you to go to this rehabilitation center. It's the only way to survive this
shit."

Red's words came to Malik as though out of a dense fog. Malik's
stomach twisted with queasiness as he heard the accusation from
Red's lips. Just the idea that Red knew about his habit made Malik's
stomach even more nauseous than before. A flash of shock featured
across Malik's face as he tried to feign ignorance. "I don't know what
you're talking about. I'm just a little sick. My stomach has been hurting for the last two days. I don't need to go to no damn drug clinic.
I'm a strong black man and I don't have any limitations..."

Red stared at Malik with indifference over his last comment, ignoring Malik's pleas of innocence. "You don't have to lie to me, I
know the truth. It's all in your half- closed eyes. You're high as hell,
and I'm not talking about off some damn local dirt weed. For four
years, I used to sell that shit to junkies on the block. I know what to
look for in a coke fiend, and I'm not going to let you throw away
your life like that. You got too much potential to just waste your life
over some dumb bitch that broke your heart months ago. I'm telling you as a friend that drugs ain't the solution for your problems.
That shit is just getting someone else rich off of your weakness."

The word "weak" left a shiver down Malik's spine. It was an insult
to his black man pride that he cherished so very much. "I'm not
weak!" Malik said interrupting Red's speech abruptly. "I can handle
anything I do. I'm a man. I'm a black man. That shit means I'm a
sun. I don't need your help, and I damn well don't need the help of

no goddamn rehab clinic," Malik said, irritated by the slight tremor in his voice. He managed to fight down a shiver of horror as he returned Red's piercing stare. A few nervous strands of sweat began to emerge on his forehead. Just the notion that Red knew of his cocaine habit drove him to immeasurable amounts of panic. There was no way for him to conceal his addiction anymore, and his stomach twisted with revulsion at the thought of a rehabilitation clinic. Malik swallowed, fighting against the urge to throw up.

"You're a junkie, and you need help," Red said coldly as he stared down at Malik.

Malik opened his mouth as if he were going to yell out aggressively in rebellion to Red's statement but no sound came out. Malik's light hazel eyes teared up, and he doubled over from the excruciating pain in his stomach. He fell to his knees unable to bear the pain anymore, and then he threw up at Red's feet. Mostly embarrassed, Malik attempted to stand up, but fell to his knees once again. This time he landed face first on Red's wood-grained floor. His body shook violently, his legs kicking and his arms shivering uncontrollably. Malik's tongue hung from the side of his mouth and his eyes rolled to the back of his head.

"Malik needs some help in here!" Red yelled out alarmed. Red bent down gently cupping Malik's head in his arms. "I need to take Malik to the hospital!" Red knew that it was a seizure caused by an overdose. Red saw the signs coming a long time ago. He had seen drug overdoses several times in the past, and he'd seen several people die in the very same fashion. A sense of urgency arose in Red when he saw his friend collapse at his feet. "I need help now!" Red yelled from his room once more.

"Call 911," Red ordered loudly. "We're going to have to take him to the hospital ourselves. If we wait on an ambulance to get here, he'll die." Red realized that ambulances were never in a hurry to pick someone up in his neighborhood. Even the police were hesitant to drive through that section of town at night.

Immediately a group of Malik's friends rushed to his aid. Bobby and Kel were two of the first to burst onto the horrid scene. Their faces were aghast with what they discovered when they came into Red's room. Assessing the situation quickly, Kel helped Red quickly lift Malik off of the ground and hurried his body to Bobby's car.

They carefully placed Malik in the back seat of the automobile. Malik shoved the baby seat to the floor as he convulsed in Bobby's car uncontrollably. His legs were still kicking violently making it impossible for anyone else to sit in the backseat with him. Red jumped into the passenger side seat, leaning over, checking on Malik. Bobby slid into the driver's side of the vehicle and started up the engine.

The vehicle soon accelerated down the road at tremendous speed toward the local hospital. Bobby's hand tightened around the steering wheel as they raced through town running both red lights and stop signs. Malik's condition was steadily growing worse and there was no time to obey all of the traffic laws of the land. Malik's body shuddered a little while longer. Than all at once, he became deathly still.

"Oh my god I think that he's dead!" Bobby yelled out hysterically. He put his hand to his head concentrating on his next move if Malik was truly dead. Bobby became overwhelmed with the very possible idea that another of his close friends had died. He was miserable in his morbid pain. Bobby tightened his fingers around the steering wheel and closed his eyes shut. Lost in his despair, Bobby momentarily lost control of the steering wheel sideswiping a parked car.

"Fuck," Red roared, "just drive the motherfuckin' car. I'll take care of Malik." Red reached over placing two fingers on the side of Malik's neck. "I feel a pulse but I'm not sure if he's breathing. It's faint but he's still alive. I just need for you to get us to the hospital in one piece. He's going to make it. I know he is!" Red said very confidently. Bobby quickly got a hold of himself, now controlling the car expertly.

"Just hold on man," Red stated as he leaned down and spoke softly in Malik's ear. "You're gonna make it because you're a strong black man. You can't let this white man's drug beat you. Do you hear me? I said that you're stronger than this shit!" Malik laid motionless in response and for the first time that night, a flash of doubt ran through Red's mind as to whether or not Malik was going to live through the night.

Moments later, the automobile pulled up to the emergency entrance of the hospital. Red opened up his door and rushed over opening the backdoor to the car. Bobby sat paralyzed in the driver's seat. Two nurses rushed over to Red as he tried to hoist Malik's lifeless body by himself. The two nurses quickly rolled a stretcher down the ramp to the car. After placing Malik on the stretcher, one of the nurses pushed the stretcher up the ramp. The other nurse began to speak to Red. "We got the 911 call a few minutes ago saying you were on the way. We have already prepared a room for him. We're going to need some personal information on the patient." The nurse stated flatly. "Do you know what type of drugs caused the overdose? What type of insurance does he have?"

"No, I'm not sure but I think that it might be crack." Red said looking at Malik lying on the stretcher helpless. "Who gives a fuck what type of insurance he has? Just make sure that he lives. Damn it, do you hear me? You make sure that he fucking lives!"

"His life signs are faint, but I'm sure he'll be okay," the orderly said indifferently. "The doctors will take good care of him, but I'm going to need for you to come inside and fill out some forms for us." The orderly handed Red a clipboard with a few papers on top of it. "Fill out these papers and bring them back to me when you're done. I'm sure that the doctors will get to him as soon as possible. We'll have to notify his parents and a police officer will come down to ask you some questions. You'll just have to trust in the doctors."

It was obvious that the orderly didn't care about the well being of Malik in the least. Malik was just another crack fiend dying of an overdose. The nurse calmly walked back toward the front desk and relaxed in his chair sipping on a steaming hot cup of coffee. He patted his mouth smugly with some tissue as he opened up a copy of the newspaper leaning back in his chair with his feet on his desk. The nurse had seen so many young black men die from drug over-doses, that the scene no longer bothered him. A tragedy in one man's life had become the regular routine for the nurse.

The mention of the word police worried Red. He knew what that word implied when it came to the racist redneck cops of the south...questions. They were questions that Red wouldn't be able to answer. It was obvious that Malik had become a victim of an over-dose, and if he did die, the police would have to investigate where the incident occurred and the residents of the house. Red was in-volved in so much illegal activity that it would be devastating for the police to search his premises. Even worse, the nurse said that he was going to notify Malik's mother, and no one wanted to be around whenever she would find out. On the other hand, Bobby had side-swiped a car on the way to the hospital and drove away from the scene. Within mere seconds Red had completely made up his mind to leave. Staying at the hospital and giving the orderly information about himself and the evening would only cause more problems. There was too much at stake to lose and not enough to gain from staying at the hospital. Sure he could stay at the hospital to see if Malik pulled through, but the orderly was right, Malik's fate was in the hands of the doctors. Other than driving Malik to the hospital, there was nothing else he could do to help.

Red rushed out of the hospital toward Bobby's waiting automobile in the front of the emergency entrance, still holding the clipboard in his hand. Bobby was still sitting on the driver's side of the running car, staring at the windshield. His face was concentrated in like a frightening hypnotic stare in front of him. His fingers were glued to the steering wheel. Red slid into the open passenger's side door and quickly slammed it shut. He could see through the side of his eye that the nurse was slowly chasing after him. He held a walkie-talkie to his mouth and limped slightly as he ran.

"Wake up and drive the fucking car!" Red ordered sharply as he saw the nurse steadily approaching.

The yell abruptly awoke Bobby from his self-induced hypnotic stare, causing him to accelerate quickly as he peeled out of the hospital parking lot. Red glanced over his shoulder through the rear window as the vehicle quickly sped away from the hospital. The nurse was standing in front of the emergency entrance screaming into his walkie-talkie. Red was sure that they were too far from the hospital for the nurse to have seen the license plate on Bobby's car. Now completely satisfied, Red slouched back into the seat relaxing comfortably.

"Why are we running away from the hospital?" Bobby said very agitatedly, his voice beginning to rise. "I can't believe we're just leaving Malik like this! He wouldn't leave us in some hospital by ourselves fighting for our lives on an operating table. It just isn't right. You hear me? It just ain't right!"

Red sighed when he heard the argument as if explaining his actions would drive him to scream. But then he was calm and collected again as he began to speak. His voice had become polite and almost humble. "We're doing what we have to do," Red began to explain. He wiped a small amount of nervous sweat from his brow as he continued. "You ran into that car on the way over here, right? That shit is recorded as a hit and run. Do you want to try to explain that one to the cops? I got a criminal record longer than my arm and if Malik dies in that hospital bed they are gonna want to blame his death on somebody. The cops are going to access the 911 call that was made from my house earlier and they're gonna ask questions. I got to get home and make sure they can't pin anything on me when they finally get there. I've already run this situation through my mind a hundred times. This is the only way out of here without causing anymore trouble."

"Yeah, I guess that you are right," Bobby answered somberly and full of pain. The rest of the trip was spent in silence between the two men. Bobby wanted to say something more, but in his heart he knew that Red had made the right choice. It was better for everyone involved that they didn't stick around.

Meanwhile, in the hospital bed, Malik fought for his life as the doctors operated on him in the intensive care unit. Several of the doctors doubted if they would be able to save the young black man's life. He had stopped breathing and the doctors performed an emergency resuscitation on him. The doctors pumped his stomach, withdrawing the deadly poisonous drug from his body. Within two hours, Malik Brown was in critical but stable condition. The doctors smiled happily congratulating each other, patting one another on the back. They had successfully saved the drug-shattered life of the young man. Finally in complete exhaustion, Malik's body lost consciousness in the cool white sheets of the hospital bed and pillows. The sleep was a dreamless slumber filled with cold sweats and chills as the powerful drug slowly withdrew from his frail body.

CHAPTER 15

Resolutions

The two days after the night Malik went to the hospital were the most strenuous days of confusion that the group of friends had ever had to endure. Very little word came from the hospital, but Bobby was sure that Malik would pull through. On the morning of the third day, word of Malik's recovery had reached the small group of friends. That evening was filled with justified relief for Red and several other friends of Malik Brown. They had recently received word of Malik's survival, but Red was entirely relieved that he lived for another reason. Red knew that as long as Malik survived the seizure, no investigative officers would be notified, too much paper work. Without the intervention of possible police interruptions Red wouldn't have to worry about cops running his records and discovering the various charges he had earned in other states over the years.

On the evening of the third day, word of Malik's drug addiction and miraculous survival had spread through the small southern town quickly. Widespread juicy gossip had become the norm for several southern cities. In the south your personal business is never really just **your** business, and no matter what anyone says it's never personal. Rumors through word of mouth quickly spread, infiltrating every aspect of the small community. The southern half of the United States of America had become a festering pot of swirling half-true vicious rumors. It wasn't long before his instructors at Blanding University found out about Malik's drug addiction. The results were never really unexpected. Since Malik was inducted in the hospital at the end of the school semester he would be forced to miss his finals. Of course, the University withdrew Malik from his classes forcing him to repeat the classes the following semester, if he chose to return.

Malik lay wrapped up in his white hospital bed, with his knees curled to his chest. His lips were pale and chapped. The room was dark, except for a single ray of sunlight that pierced through the open hospital window falling gently on the Malik Brown's forehead. Malik shuddered under the warmth of the light. He pulled his bed sheets over his face attempting to hide it from the intensity of the sun outside. The only concern on Malik's mind was trying to allow his mind and body to rest from the painful thought of his mother crying at his hospital bed the night before. The pain from the realization that he had almost died and the realization that all of his friends knew that he was an addict was horrible.

Sleep would help erase the painful memories that he had of the last few nights in the hospital as his throbbing body forced out the urge for the white powder. Sleep would help for now, but it wouldn't solely do the job. It would take several weeks of mental self-control to allow his body to once again become comfortable with the idea of living without the drug. For Malik, it was just the beginning of a lengthy hard-fought battle against the addiction of the drug that he was determined not to lose. But for now, his only pleasure would come from allowing his body to rest, sweet sober rest that had evaded his sub-consciousness for months. A rest that came with the absence of the swirling colors, which had brought him so much relief in the past.

He closed his eyes trying to concentrate on the future. Malik knew that he had disgraced his mother's trust in him. He realized that he had been ejected from Blanding University. He didn't really care; his grades weren't that great anyhow. He knew that he would never be able to graduate from that university. He would forever be remembered as the guy who overdosed on drugs. His reputation was over at Blanding University. How could Malik possibly bring himself to look his instructors in the face day after day, to attend class like the incident never even occurred? How could he deal with the whispers of his fellow classmates laughing at him behind his back? The whole experience was too much for him to take in at one time.

Realizing that he was shaking violently, Malik gripped the sides of his small hospital bed. He loathed the idea that he no longer even had the power to control his own body. Never before had he had so little control of himself physically, or mentally. The whole experience repulsed him. Spiritually broken, Malik Brown rolled over on his stomach, and the first time in his adult life, Malik Brown began to weep. Long streams of salty tears rolled down his cheeks soaking his pillow and sheets. The teardrops falling from his eyes were foreign objects. The tears fell freely from his eyelids, as a newborn child would weep as it took its very first breath. It was a cleansing sob, the sort of tears that would leave a person rejuvenated. Fearful of the future, and weeping at his unknown destiny, a Black man was reborn.

With the exception of Malik Brown the rest of the student body was preoccupied with passing their finals. The three-floor library on campus was filled with several students cramming for finals at the last second. Two of those several were Larenzo Baker and Joy Summer. The couple had been studying for three hours straight. The combination of extensive hours of studying and lack of sleep had exhausted Larenzo and Joy. Joy sat to Larenzo's right side, her head comfortably nestled under his arm, her attention centered on studying for her rapidly approaching final. In her hands was an open book on early childhood development. Her elegant intelligence and innocence delighted Larenzo as he sighed happily to himself.

The library held the faint aroma of moldy, unused books gathering dust on the endless shelves. The floors were polished to a mirror finish, a direct byproduct of the lack of use. Hushed whispers from other students could be heard murmuring in the background, as they quietly read to themselves. The florescent lights of the library were bright and dizzying, lulling the students to sleep with an artificial glow. Larenzo hated the idea of going to the library to actually study. In some small way, the whole notion of gathering thousands of books in an extremely large building seemed completely counterproductive and wasteful. For Larenzo, the idea of studying for examinations using paper books had become outdated. Most students used computers now, making school libraries like this one obsolete, and simply a meeting place used to congregate socially.

Larenzo sat back lazily on a small studying couch built for two. His Timberland boot covered feet rested comfortably on an end table directly in front of him. His fingers tapped impatiently on the spine of a humongous book of Shakespeare's works. His eyes scanned the stiff age worn pages of the book, but deep down in his subconscious, Larenzo knew that he wouldn't be able to get any studying done.

His mind was too distracted to concentrate on anything other than the youthful beauty nestled beside him.

When Larenzo listened very carefully he imagined that he could hear Joy's heart beating in tune to his own. He could feel the silky texture of her hair beginning to rub softly against his chin. The soft fragrance of her Vanilla Fields perfume emanated from her clothing driving Larenzo to insatiable frenzies of lust. Larenzo gently blew into her ear, soothingly placing his cheek beside hers. He could feel Joy's delicate hand on his arm, pressing on the fabric of his shirt searching for the fleshy warmth underneath. Her actions seemed flirtatious in a sort of playful youthfulness manner.

"Let's get out of here," Larenzo softly whispered into her ear. "I can't concentrate with you looking and smelling so damn good. Let's continue this in my room where we can get a little more privacy. I know that you want us to wait until the time is right, but I think that that time is finally here. If not, I don't know when. I've never wanted anyone more than I want you right now." Larenzo spoke honestly, unable to withstand the temptation of her seductive presence any longer. He knew that coming straight out and admitting his future intimate plans for her was a risk, but nevertheless, a risk well worth taking.

Joy contemplated the invitation in silence. In the past, she had always turned down Larenzo's offer for a nightcap. But something was different this night. This was the first time that Larenzo had asked her to come to his room since they broke up the semester prior. He had been a total gentleman, accepting her choice to wait until the time was right. Any other day she would have simply gave him the usual answer, but this evening was different somehow. Larenzo stared deeply into her eyes with self-confidence. Joy had never experienced a man like Larenzo before. He had waited months since the beginning of the new semester, and not once did he ever mention sex. He had given up all other women and now it seemed as though the time was finally right. To Joy, Larenzo seemed complex, unpredictable, and elusive. These complexities simply made her love him more.

"Let's leave," Joy said in a low voice closing her book.

The words caught Larenzo by surprise. In all honesty he was waiting for her to turn him down like she had several times in the past.

Her answer left Larenzo totally speechless. His jaw dropped slightly when he heard her response. After the initial shock, Larenzo, still in disbelief, began to gather his books and led the way out of the library.

Larenzo took Joy by the hand and walked from the library quickly, quietly as not to be noticed by other students. She followed slightly behind him struggling to keep up with Larenzo's wide-legged stride. In mere moments, Larenzo and Joy had walked across the campus arriving at their destination. Joy paused for a moment as she reached the outer steps of Monroe Hall. She had never dared to enter Monroe Hall before in the past, and a small shimmer of doubt ran through her body when she saw the menacing appearance of the three-story, brick-layered dormitory.

"You don't have to..." Larenzo began to say, seeing the uncertainty in Joy's face. "No," Joy said interrupting Larenzo in mid-sentence. "I want to. You're right, this is the right time for us to take this relationship to the next level. I just want this to be perfect for both of us."

"A relationship is built off of trust," Larenzo said understandingly. "I know that you're scared, but I don't want you to do anything that you don't want to. This is a big step for us and you should only go upstairs if you truly trust me. I know that I have hurt you in the past but you have to trust me. I would never do anything to hurt you again. Do you trust me, Joy?"

"Yeah," Joy replied shaking her head tentatively. "I trust you more than any other man I have ever known." Joy's massive urbanity was unimpaired as she spoke with a definite undertone of stylish seduction.

Reassured of their mutual attraction, Larenzo kissed Joy on the cheek lovingly, and led her into the dormitory through a side entrance avoiding the whispers and silent stares of other students who also lived in the building. Monroe Hall didn't have visitation but the few students watching were used to Larenzo sneaking young women upstairs into his room. With the utmost stealth and speed, Larenzo and Joy ran up the stone staircase to the second floor. The second floor of Monroe Hall was filthy as usual. The overhead lights in the dorm blinked on and off sporadically. A stale odor lingered in the air by Larenzo's room because of its close proximity to the toilets. Joy wrinkled her nose at the smell. Large holes, the size of men's fists, were scattered all across the ceiling. Long, black wires hung from the holes, making the dorm appear more like a dungeon than a housing area for the future black leaders of the country. She smiled nervously at the hallway, wondering how anyone could learn anything in this sort of living environment.

Larenzo searched through his large assortment of keys, for the correct one to fit into the lock on the door. His usual confident demeanor began to fade as he fumbled with his keys in his hands finally, finding the right one. Larenzo turned the key, holding the door, very gentleman-like, as Joy walked in.

Joy scanned the space thoroughly imprinting every single aspect of the small plain looking room to her memory. A 25-inch television sat on the counter. Several piles of paperback books were sloppily assorted on the bookcase in no particular order. The tile on the floor was textured and cheap. The walls were plastered with pictures and posters of various sports and music entertainers, as is the norm. The windowsill was completely bare allowing light from the full moon to pour undisturbed beams of light through it giving the room a romantic atmosphere. The bed lay in the right corner of the room. The sheets and covers were made up neatly, masking its true sexual nature with a shade of innocence.

Joy licked her lips when she saw the small iron-framed bed. Larenzo put his right arm around her protectively pulling her close to him. He slowly bent his neck downward to kiss Joy, but she pulled away at the last moment and gently placed her index and middle fingers on Larenzo's lips preventing him from speaking. She shoved him back onto his rickety bed making sure he landed comfortably. She paused staring at him for a moment in recollection. Fully satisfied, Joy turned from his baffled stare elegantly walking toward the window, but it seemed impersonal. Larenzo realized that she needed a momentary pause, an opportunity to memorialize this long anticipated moment in her memory. Her back was straight and her voluptuous hips moved from left to right. Joy's movements were graceful like that of a princess finally being crowned queen. Larenzo laid on his bed watching in complete awe as she poised confidently in front of the open window.

"I want this to be perfect," Joy said with her back still to Larenzo. "I want to remember this moment forever."

Before Larenzo could comment, Joy unbuckled her belt and dropped it to the floor at her feet. Next, she unzipped her tight fitting jeans, and slid them off, leaving them crumbled by her belt. Then, she carefully lifted her t-shirt over her head allowing her hair to fall once again down her back. Lastly, she undid her dark blue bra and let it also drop to the floor. Her perky breasts were unveiled in front of the window for anyone lucky enough to walk by at that second to catch a glimpse. Finally, she turned to face Larenzo. The moon shone brightly behind her, accenting her natural beauty, making her appear mystical in the light.

She smiled bashfully at the openness of her own actions. Joy's hands fell to her side unashamed at her nudity. Her nipples began to become erect from the enormous lust swelling within her bosom. Never before had she felt so comfortable around a man before actually be able to undress in front of him. Now her body stood exposed for Larenzo to examine at his leisure. Only her panties remained on her hourglass figure.

Larenzo sat in silence, unable to comment, still partially in shock over Joy's straightforward approach.

She came in closer and looked down at him sitting on the squeaky bed. Larenzo caught the scent of her perfume as she slowly neared him. He could see her every feature distinctly with the illumination of the moonlight in the blindless window behind her. At that moment, Larenzo could only think of one word to describe her, "perfect." Her face was gorgeous, the complete utter absence of all hair like a smooth stone statue. Her lips were full and wet, parting slightly in a devilish smile. A few loose strands of hair hung in front of her face accenting her true Ethiopian ancestry. He could see her curling black eyelashes underneath her naturally arched eyebrows. Her body stood in front of the window, a splendid example of genetic perfection. Her small but well-shaped breasts bounced with every step she took. The fragileness of her collarbone lay bare beneath her soft, yet firm, chin. Her waist was small and slender accenting her large hips and buttocks. Alluring in its bare simplicity, a single trail of light brown hair starting at her navel led downward to the laced sanctuary of her royal blue silk panties.

Never before had Larenzo wanted to sleep with a woman so much. Never before had a woman made him wait so long. Just the sight of her, gracefully walking toward him with the moon shining on her from behind, made goose pimples emerge on his arms.

She turned seductively, noticing that Larenzo was studying her every move. Joy stared down into Larenzo's eyes. Then, she slowly bent forward, her half-closed, light brown bedroom eyes glistened with delight. Her moist lips puckered. Her mouth gently and tentatively caressed his as their lust built to immaculate proportions. Unable to control his sexual urges any longer, Larenzo stood up and took her in his arms. At first they kissed slowly, sensually. Then when Larenzo felt her delicate fingers moving up and down his broad back, he kissed her more aggressively. Larenzo could feel her legs spread as they kissed, pressing against his body so she could fully feel his erection. Joy's slight moaning only aroused him more as his hands easily ran through her hair.

For Joy this was the moment that she had waited for the whole semester. It was the end result of a full year of nightly fantasies finally becoming reality. She temporarily pulled away from Larenzo's deep kisses grinning at him. Her eyes seemed to become smoky as she stared seductively into his. "Larenzo, I'm in love with you. We were made for each other," Joy whispered gently into his ear. "Tell me you love me."

The command hit Larenzo like a sledgehammer. He looked into her eyes searching for the right words to explain his emotions. He had never thought of whether he <u>truly</u> loved Joy. Without question she was the most beautiful woman he had ever seen in his life. And now, with her semi-nude body standing before him, embracing his, he honestly considered the question. He was sure that he loved her, but not sure if he shared the same sort of intensity, which she had. He loved her as someone who cherishes a beautiful dawn, exceptional in every way possible, but not enough to give one's life for. Not enough to kill another for. Not enough to die without her.

He wasn't sure if he was "in love" with her. Well, at least not in the traditional sense of the phrase, not in the traditional Shakespearean sense of the phrase. He wouldn't betray his parents' wishes for her. He wouldn't give up his life for her like Romeo and Juliet, the sort of love that people lived all of their lives for and were never given the opportunity to experience. No, he was sure of at least that much. When it came to his feelings he had never experienced that kind of

172 • Ron Baxter

love. Or maybe William Shakespeare's conception about love was all wrong when he described the obscure emotion in his plays. Maybe, just maybe, there was no such thing as true love and Larenzo was just chasing a figment of his imagination. A pipedream created for poets and fools to throw their money away on Valentine's Day.

If there was no such creature as true love, did that make the rest of the world hypocrites? Were they all simply liars or did they really believe that they were in love?

"Larenzo...?" Her words awoke Larenzo from his deep thoughts.

"Huh?"

"I said, 'I love you,'" Joy repeated. Her eyes pierced into his and through him into his very soul. "Aren't you in love with me?"

Larenzo hesitated when he heard her repeat the question.

"No," Larenzo said slowly, regretting instantly that he had allowed the truth to be whispered from his lips. Stress induced a light perspiration on his brow. "I'm not in love with you..." Larenzo continued, his voice quivering from fear breaking his usual self-confident demeanor.

She withdrew from his embrace, frigidly. Her arms wrapped around her chest, covering her breasts as if she were cold. Joy was aghast. Her emotions were shattered, spread to the far winds by his words. Never before had any man rejected her, much less the man she had decided she was in love with. Her eyes grew dim with rejection, and tears begun to build on the sides of them.

"Joy, I do love you... but I'm not sure that I am in love with," Larenzo said quickly trying to explain only making her despair worst. "I'm in love with the thought of being in love with you."

Long streams of salty tears fell from her eyes.

"How could you...?" She began to speak, her voice disappearing faintly due to the emotion. She inhaled deeply, trying to calm herself enough to speak. "You know I love you, Larenzo. How could you care so little for me? We were supposed to be forever!"

"Joy let me explain," Larenzo said reaching out to touch her on the side of her exposed hip. "I've never felt this way about any woman before. You're special to me but I'm not in love with you." Larenzo spoke quickly trying to explain, only making the situation worst.

"Don't touch me!" Joy exclaimed angrily ripping away from Larenzo's grasp before he could make contact. The very touch of his smooth palm against her skin both aroused and sickened her. Joy's body still yearned for physical contact, yet her mind rejected the idea of giving herself to someone whom didn't love her. "You said that you would never hurt me! You remember that? Well, you lied!" Her tears were falling uncontrollably now as she continued. "I can't be with someone who isn't in love me...." Joy's voice began to fade faintly again. She inhaled a deep breath of air, trying to calm herself. "I can't believe this! I can't believe you, Larenzo. We're supposed to be together!"

Quickly, Joy began to dress herself. Joy's tight fitting jeans clung onto her hips as she dressed. With the zipper and top button still undone, she slid her arms into her shirt covering her still exposed breasts. Not allowing enough time to properly dress, Joy held in her right fist her royal blue bra.

Within mere seconds, Joy burst from Larenzo's room, her heart pounding within her chest as though it would rupture. Her sobs were that of one who is heartbroken. Her tears became stuck in her throat making her sobs of misery muffled, choking her. Her teardrops fell like rain trailing behind her. Her legs burned with fatigue, and her stomach knotted up, but she knew that she wouldn't stop running until she finally reached the serenity of her dormitory, on the other side of the large campus.

Larenzo chased Joy until she reached the stairwell. He stalled at the very top of the staircase, and observed Joy reaching the bottom of the staircase escaping through the side door, running for her dormitory. He knew that it was futile to follow her. Larenzo knew that verbal protest was useless now. He wouldn't be able to take back what he said, even if he wanted to. The pain he felt was crushing. Larenzo had broken a sacred trust between himself and Joy, and no amount of fast-talking would be able to mend their relationship now. He had made an oath to her that he would never hurt her again, and Larenzo had broken that promise...by simply telling the truth.

"Fuckin' women," Larenzo whispered to himself as he watched Joy's distant sprinting figure disappearing into the darkness. "Can't live wit them...can't live without them. Huh...maybe it was love? Well, Renzo, guess you may never know." A horrible desolate feeling descended upon him.

Withdrawing from the stairway entrance, Larenzo slowly shuffled back towards the unbearable emptiness of his small dormitory room. Once inside his room, he plopped down in his bed making it squeak slightly from his weight. His hat covered his eyes as he slowly allowed himself to fall asleep. Vivid images flooded his brain, creating a dream world afloat with mind-numbing questions of whether he did the correct thing. Larenzo knew that no other man, with Joy Summers' partially nude body glistening in the moonlight, would have told her the truth at that moment. Why couldn't he just have told her he loved her?

The next day was dreary. The skyline above Blanding University was colored by grayish smog not usually seen in South Carolina. A humid heat surrounded the campus in an almost swamp-like climate. Everyone who attended Blanding University knew that a thunderstorm was coming. Steam could visibly be seen ebbing from the black pavement of the tar-lined streets. A desperate feeling of worry passed through the student body as everyone prepared for final examinations in their own way. Larenzo walked slowly through the campus on his way to Red's house with his head down. His fitted White Sox's baseball cap covered his eyes casting a shadow over his face. His mind was tormented by mixed feelings of bliss and torment. He had lost the only woman that he had possibly loved, all because of the truth.

At least, thought Larenzo, Red's house would be a little livelier surrounded by his close friends. "Yeah, they don't care if I lie," Larenzo said to himself jokingly. Within minutes Larenzo had walked across Blanding Universities' campus and reached Red's house.

When Larenzo reached the front door of the house, he could hear the loud static background sound of a television program playing from the other side. Larenzo walked inside without knocking on the door. He strolled with a stride in his step, with his head high in the sky, as though he had no worries in the world, hiding the pain of his encounter with Joy, but he knew that the pain of her lost was still present in his face. That type of pain would be impossible to hide forever.

Red's home was once again alive with the pleasure of youthfulness. Several of Larenzo's closest friends were gathered around the small couches in the living room watching morning talk shows on the small television. JC sat on the couch nearest the television, flipping through channels on the television, with his crutches lying at his feet. His right leg was still plastered together, holding the fragile tendons together as they tried to heal. Red sat by alone at the dining room table where they used to play cards, in his hands; he shuffled a deck of cards. Bobby sat on a smaller couch, in his usual pimp posture, with a petite woman on his arm. In his hand was a small glass of liquor that he sipped every now and then. He glanced up as Larenzo began to walk toward him. "My nigga, Larenzo," Bobby said smiling from ear to ear. "So what happened with your little study session last night in the library with woman of your dreams. Did you finally get some ass last night? I know you got some. Man, you better tell me every detail."

Larenzo grinned at the comment, shrugging his shoulders. "Bobby, you wouldn't believe me if I told you. Shit, I don't believe what happened, and I saw it with my own eyes."

Bobby glared at Larenzo inquisitively trying to read his facial expression. Larenzo was smiling, but not in the usual devilish manner that he uses after he sleeps with a woman. His bushy eyebrows were relaxed and calm. His arms waved calmly at his sides from left to right. Larenzo's whole demeanor seemed to be of a man relieved.

"Renzo, take a seat and tell me the story. Jasmine, move out the way so Larenzo can tell the story. Refill my cup for me while your up, and don't forget the ice cubes," Bobby said giving the young lady the glass and gently pushing her off the couch. The slender woman stood up slowly and walked into the kitchen.

Larenzo sat beside Bobby and began to tell his "love" story from the night before. He left in every single detail making sure not to exaggerate or delete anything from the story. At the conclusion of his tale, Bobby shook his head impressed at Larenzo truthfulness. "Larenzo, have you ever been in love before?" Bobby asked very smoothly.

"No."

"I've been inside more women than Wilt Chamberlain, and I've come to the conclusion, that God allows a man to have just one true soul mate," Bobby said very seriously. "For pimps they're called bottom whores. Larenzo, Joy's your bottom whore! Every pimp should have a bottom whore in their stable. She's the woman you wouldn't mind someday marrying and producing some kids with. You just have to recognize her when she crosses your path and when she does you won't even want the other women. They become strictly sources of income. I found my soul mate the first time I laid eyes on Terry. I mean when I saw her I knew that I would eventually marry her. I still pimp because it's in my bloodline, but I don't let my money interfere with my family. I've heard the way that you talk about Joy and I've never seen you talk about any other woman before like you do this one. Well, what I'm trying to say is that...what if you just let your soul mate run out of your bedroom because you couldn't tell her how you really felt about her?"

Larenzo nodded, overcame with doubt, and unable to fully answer Bobby's question. Larenzo wanted the question to simply disappear, but he knew that it wouldn't. Larenzo wrinkled his nose at the thought of Joy running out of his room. "It's too late now," Larenzo, said out loud as much to himself as too Bobby. "She'll never come back. I know that for certain." Larenzo took a deep breath and tried to steady his nerves. "Well, I know what..." Larenzo began but his words and attention were stripped from him by the sounds of a car engine pulling up in the front yard of Red's home. Larenzo saw Bobby's eyes shift, and followed them toward the window facing the front yard.

A few moments later, Red's door opened and the entire room fell silent to the figure that walked through the doorway. Everyone in the house stared in disbelief as the well dressed gentleman walked into the living room. His sleek, black slacks hung loosely over his newly polished black shoes as he carefully crossed the threshold of the home. His white dress shirt was ironed and a black tie hung to his navel. His hair was neatly cut in a low fade and shaped around the edges. Only his gleeful smile indicated a glimmer of his old personality. Red spoke first when he saw the neatly attired man standing in his living room, "I like the new style, Kel. You looking like a mobster."

Kel's light brown eyes scanned the room evaluating everyone's facial expression over his new look. Larenzo couldn't form words when he saw Kel. He had been a friend with the man standing in front of him since the seventh grade and never before had he seen

Kel dressed in this manner. Likewise, Bobby's mouth gaped open when he saw the figure of his friend. "A tie?" Bobby said aghast. "I can't believe that you cut your hair. I've never seen you with a haircut before!"

JC giggled slightly at the odd appearance of his friend shaking his head slightly. "What is this, like invasion of the fuckin' body snatchers or what? Where have you taken our friend?" JC said jokingly.

"Well, it was time for a change of pace. You really like it?" Kel said holding his arms out turning around slowly, to model off his expensive garments. "I just picked up the new threads. I'm going on a job interview later on today and I need to look my best." Kel reached into his right pocket and pulled out an unopened box of Black & Mild cigars and tentatively handed them to Red, Larenzo, and JC. "My brothers...it's celebration time! In approximately five months you will all be uncles. Crystal's pregnant. I'm gonna be a daddy!" Kel's smile broadened even wider with word of the good news, but the tone in his words held a sense of uncertainty, a hidden sense of sadness.

JC shook his head. "I can't believe that you're going to be someone's father. Isn't there a law or something to prevent shit like this from happening?"

The crowd of students wanted to laugh at JC's joke, but the immense shock of the situation hushed the crowd. Never before had Red's home been so quiet that only the echo of the faint static sound in the older model television set broke the silence. Everyone but Larenzo was still in shock over the recent revelation. He stood up, placed his cigar in his mouth and lit the end with a lighter, from his pocket. Larenzo coolly took two pulls of the cigar allowing the smoke to gather around his head before he began to speak, "Congratulations, my nigga." Larenzo blew the smoke out of his mouth and nostrils before he spoke again. "It's about time you told me about your upcoming seed."

Kel studied Larenzo for a long moment, trying to draw upon whether Larenzo had already known of the pregnancy, which he had tried to keep secret for so long. Larenzo smiled slyly. The validity of his statement was written in that smug grin. Kel knew automatically without even asking, that Larenzo had spoken the truth. "When did you find out?" Kel said staring Larenzo coldly in the eyes. "I wanted to be the one to tell you."

"Crystal called me and told me the news," Larenzo said taking another pull from the cigar. "That was like two months ago, and you ain't never even tried to tell me. We haven't really spoken in weeks. I was beginning to wonder if we were still friends."

"Always," Kel answered with a little soft, halfhearted sigh. Kel seemed to want to say more at this critical moment, but he couldn't put his feelings into words. Kel's cheeks relaxed and a bright smile once again returned to his face. He lifted his right fist, and teasingly struck Larenzo hard in the chest. Larenzo realized that it was a gesture of brotherly love. No matter how long two men shared a friendship, Larenzo and Kel knew that two men could never embrace each other the way women do after an argument. It just would have just been completely unacceptable in the masculine, male chauvinist environment of Red's house.

Kel was smaller than Larenzo physically, but he was one of the hardest punching men that Larenzo knew. With that punch to the chest, Larenzo knew that everything was forgiven. Larenzo smiled. Neither one of them would speak of the past now, and deep down they knew that the past belonged exactly where it was. Kel pulled another cigar from the pack and lit it with the lighter that was already in Larenzo's hand, offering it to Bobby.

Bobby declined, shaking his hand in front of him slowly. "I'll pass. You know I got asthma. Besides, smoking will kill you quicker than fucking Orangeburg hookers without a condom."

JC laughed outright at the comment, pleased to see that the atmosphere in the room had finally livened up to the point where humor didn't fall on deaf ears. JC hesitantly lit his cigar as he chuckled out loud like a man much older than his true age. JC stood up using the leverage of his wooden crutches to steady his injured body. "Do you know if it's going to be a boy or girl yet? Yo Kel, I ain't playing, if it's a boy I'm gonna teach the little nigga how to dunk by the time he's in the fourth grade. I'm talking NBA on NBC for the little man. And no matter what he says, he can't play ball for no corrupt ass black colleges. We'll get him accepted to some high class white universities up north or in California."

Everyone in the room laughed except for Red. He continued to shuffle the deck of playing cards in silence at the table with an ice-cold glare in his eyes. Then, very slow and deliberately, Red stood up from the table with the cards comfortably sitting in his left palm. He stared at Kel. His eyes lingered slowly allowing them to finally lock in eye contact. "So you gonna be a father, huh?" Red said a little disdainfully. "I hope you know what you're doing. Black men are always in a hurry to produce some seeds but don't nobody want to take care of them. I just hope that you're up for the task."

"I'm a man, and I'm going to take care of my responsibilities," Kel answered slowly making sure to word his statements perfectly. "I'm taking the job at the local factory and I'm taking a semester off to save up some extra funds. I mean... there comes a time in every man's life when he has to stand up for something. I've made a choice to do the right thing for my future family. Shit! My grades ain't that good anyhow. If dropping out of school is what I got to do...then I'm just gonna have to do it."

Red didn't verbally converse, but Kel saw the response in Red's eyes. *An education is the best thing to have for your future child,* his eyes said. *You already made one mistake. Don't fuck your situation up any more by making another. Stay in school and finish up your education.* Red finally blinked and the mental connection was severed. Red sat back down frustrated, as if he could say no more. "A man makes his own decisions," Red finally said as he lit his Black & Mild cigar and took a long pull. "The best of luck to you, no matter what."

CHAPTER 16

FINALS

Three days before the final day of the school year had arrived and the campus thrived with youthful energy as the concluding days of the semester steadily approached. The echoing boom of loud Hip Hop music carried quickly through the southern college university. The entire campus was a roar, as teachers and students had congregated in front of the Pitt to celebrate the annual end of the school year barbeque block party. The smell of roasting beef and pork helped to intensify the joyful laughter, smiles, and conversation of everyone present.

With his closest college friends walking beside him, Larenzo merrily treaded through several large gatherings of students on his way towards a large barbequing grill. Larenzo glanced at each of his friends, and his smile grew warmer when he looked over their faces, and a thoughtful look came to his eyes. Everyone but Malik was present. Larenzo knew that the doctors would hold Malik for at least another three months of rehabilitation before he could celebrate with the rest of the group.

Bobby King stood to Larenzo's left hand side; the unmistakable look of boredom was present as he ignored the beautiful freshman girl clinging to his arm. JC limped slowly behind Bobby, his crutches keeping him from catching up with the rest of his friends. Kel stood to Larenzo's right. Except for a Black & Mild cigar clenched in between his teeth, Kel looked the part of a dignified businessman complete with a three-piece suit and a neatly lined-up haircut. His face seemed relieved and relaxed. The stress caused by the last few months had disappeared from his demeanor subtly like the changing of the seasons. Finally, Red stood slightly behind the rest of the group. A definite uneasiness ran through him as he cautiously weaved through the massive crowd.

Red surveyed the endless rows of students, his ice-cold eyes in a glaze, and his mind far, far away. The masses of the student body fascinated Red as much as a toy holds the imagination of a child on

Christmas. The majority of the students at Blanding University would entertain Red for a while; but he knew that the enjoyment would never last for long. His mind was still tormented with morbid thoughts of revenge against Travis. The death of Travis would be true retribution for the death of Midget Moe, eye for an eye, and life for a life.

The aroma of the cookout rose from the grill in large puffs of black smoke, stinging Red's eyes. When the smoke finally began to clear, Red saw a vision that had haunted him since Midget Moe's funeral. Travis stood across the barbeque grill no more than ten feet away. A cold shiver ran through Red's entire body. The vision was like a tormenting nightmare, come back to devour reality greedily once again. Red's legs became stiff, and a sudden inability to catch his breath drove his heart pounding with joyful excitement when he saw Travis... or was it a sense of fear. *"No,"* Red dismissed the thought quickly. It was ridiculous for him to fear Travis. Red didn't truly fear Travis at all; he feared how he would react, what he might have to do.

Red studied Travis, not so much filled with fury as with amazement. Travis stood on the other end of the large BBQ grill unaware of Red's murderous stare. Travis laughed heartily as he bit into a large barbeque drumstick. Barbeque was smeared across his grin as he began to converse with a student standing next to him. He looked so peaceful standing there, so at rest with his life that Red was immediately envious. For months Red had been tortured by nightmares from Midget Moe's funeral, allowing his memories to fester in his sub-consciousness, invading the very sanctity of his dreams. Now, Travis seemed completely jubilant and content as he enjoyed his dinner. The scene was enough to sicken Red with hatred.

Red allowed the anticipation to build in his body, ebbing powerful signals of anger through his brain until he could no longer control himself. Focusing all of his anger in one pinnacle climax, Red paused. *"Now isn't the time to strike,"* Red thought to himself allowing the fury to slowly ebb away in his subconscious. There were far too many witnesses around and no way of making a getaway. Red knew that he could attack Travis now; it would be quite simple to physically assault Travis in front of the Pitt. With the aid of his friends he could perhaps even put Travis in the hospital. But what good would an old-fashioned fist beating accomplish? Nothing. Red made up in his mind that only true vengeance would ease his mind. Red realized that he would just have to wait one more day and true "street" justice would finally be accomplished.

Red suddenly realized that Larenzo was watching him.

"You ever get a cold chill whenever you see a certain person?" Red said silently staring at Travis. "It's the same feeling you get when you see a convicted felon eating his last meal. That's the feeling you get when you see a dead man walking."

"Absolutely," Larenzo nodded in the direction of Travis. "But, now is not the right time. Finals! Remember he has to take finals."

"I know," Red paused before he continued. "I'll wait."

That night, Red tossed and turned in his bed, struggling to force himself to sleep. His consciousness realized that the summer break was but three days away. Red knew that he wouldn't get much sleep that night or in the coming nights. The last days of school had almost arrived and Red knew that his chance to gain revenge for the death of his friend had finally come. He relaxed in his blankets and tried his best to allow himself to fall into a deep slumber. Eventually he did.

The twilight of the school semester had finally arrived at Blanding University signifying and end to cramming for tests overnight. The tranquility and peace of routinely rising to go to class was all at once replaced by the chaotic sprinting to buildings to take final examinations. All over the campus crowds of students rushed blindly behind one another on their way to class with number two pencils in their hands. In mere days the mirage that students called their home would be forgotten as they left to journey back to their parents' household, where they could spend there summer breaks peacefully.

From a stolen, parked, black Nissan, Red watched the rest of the student body with revulsion as they scurried around the campus on their way to finals. To Red they were puppets with their strings being pulled by society. How ridiculous they seemed caring about their grade point average and whether or not they returned all of the library books they borrowed throughout the school year. He hadn't felt that positive about school for a long time. In fact, he had never felt that way about school. For Red, those worries were for other students; they weren't for the likes of him. He had decided that he was well beyond the redemption that could be found at an institute for higher learning. For career criminals like Red, a college atmosphere was just somewhere he could lay low for a couple of years. Eventually, his past would always catch up with him. He could pretend to be a student, but his true colors would eventually show through.

The emotion that creates worry had ceased to function soon after his friend, Midget Moe, was buried. Only a deep embedded fury was left for Red to feed off of now. Red began to tremble as he watched them with anxious anticipation. Several students walked up the stairs to take their final exams. His anger had dwelt in him for so long that it began to bubble in his veins, throbbing, becoming as much a part of him as his heartbeat.

Red tapped his feet restlessly as he awaited Travis to walk down the street to hand in his work to Dr. Johnson, the chairman of the Mathematics Department. Red had waited months for the moment that he could take revenge on Travis for the brutal slaying of Midget Moe. Red tightened his grip on the steering wheel when he saw the first glimpse of Travis walking down the sidewalk towards the building. Travis trotted down the street as if he was another innocent student with a backpack full of books strapped onto his back. The bruises and scratches that he had acquired during the fight at the back-to-school party had all but healed, everything except a deep scar underneath his left ear, which would be with him for the rest of his natural life.

"There you are," Red whispered, and bit his bottom lip. There were tears of frustration in his eyes. The young man gripped his long dreadlocks in both hands and tied them behind his head in a ponytail with a rubber band. Red checked the .45 caliber pistol in his belt, removed it, and placed it on his lap wrapping it in a red bandanna. The gun shined, slightly blinding him when the morning sunshine hit the cold silver metal.

Red was frozen solid in his seat as he watched Travis happily enter the mathematics building and walk up the stairs to Dr. Johnson's office. He wanted to shoot Travis right then, but his legs were planted and his arms felt like lead. Red decided that it would be better to wait until after Travis left the building. There were simply too many witnesses to do anything right then, and that way there would be less bystanders and he'd also have a little more time to gain his nerve. It had been a long time since Red had committed a murder, and the idea of spending another night in jail was unacceptable. Red knew that if it ever came down to a life or death situation, he would never allow the police to take him alive again.

Red sat in his car for approximately fifteen minutes and silently stalked Travis as he emerged from the building happily walking down the staircase of the building with a slight pep in his step. It was obvious from the walk that he had passed his mathematics course with flying colors. Red's anger grew darker when he saw Travis' sparkling smile grow wider with happiness. *The nerve of that nigga smiling,* Red thought to himself as he watched Travis grinning from ear to ear. The smile infuriated Red, driving him to the very limits of sanity itself. "How could he smile after what he did to Moe?" Red whispered to himself.

Red hesitated for a moment placing his hands over his face. He thought that tears would fall, but in seconds the emotion of the moment had passed; when he raised his head Red's eyes were cold and dry as stone. Quietly opening the driver's side door to the vehicle, Red stepped out and rushed towards the smiling figure of Travis, with his gun held in his right hand. Travis never saw Red coming until he was almost upon him. Unable to truly defend himself against the impending assault, Travis shrieked in shock when he saw the weapon pointing at him.

The look of shock in Travis' eyes was enough to instill a sense of bloodlust in Red. He smiled at the look of fear, steadied his aim and slowly squeezed the trigger. The bullet exploded from the pistol, caving in Travis' chest like a cheap piece of roofing. Travis paused. He couldn't feel the excruciating pain pulsating from his open chest wound, but he knew it was there. He had seen enough hospital programs to realize that his body was in shock. Travis placed both of his hands on top of his chest, covering the gaping hole that was there. Gushes of warm blood poured through his fingers staining the pavement at his feet. Travis' bottom jaw trembled at the sight of the crimson blood on his hands.

"My God... You shot me," he said with disbelief in his voice. Travis felt a burning sensation rip through his chest and bile rose in his throat. He tenderly touched the wound and a subtle wave of hot pain rippled through his body. Mustering all of the resolve he could, Travis screamed out in pain, and rushed at Red with his hands outstretched as if too strangle the life from him. Travis' blood soaked hands grasped at Red's throat; Red had not so much as blinked or flinched as he pumped another slug into Travis' gut. When the second gunshot hit, Travis' lifeless body slumped to the ground at his feet. A squirt of warm blood fell, staining Red's sneakers. The only sound left was the ringing left in Red's ears from the smoking cannon in his palm.

Red ran off to his car before the body could stop twitching. An anxious energy washed over him. As the car pulled away from the curb, Red could feel his muscles tightening up and his heartbeat beginning to gallop. No matter how many crimes he was involved in, committing them never seemed to become easier. Once before he had committed this atrocious crime against nature and now he had again taken a life. This time the murder was done in broad daylight on the "secured" campus of a state-funded historical black university. Red was sure that someone heard the gunfire. It would just be a matter of time before the campus police were notified.

Red sped off in the vehicle. The tires of the black Nissan peeled off leaving only steaming tire tracks and the smell of burnt rubber in the air. Red smiled as he left the grounds of Blanding University. He was sure that no one witnessed the murder, and more than anything else, he was sure that Travis paid the final price. He was sure that Travis was dead. Red had gained the only thing that was important at that moment...revenge.

Within minutes, Red speedily pulled on to Highway I-95 north on his way to New Jersey. He knew that he would have to leave the state which he had come to call his new home. He never even had a chance to tell his friends goodbye. "It was best that way," Red reflected as he swerved in and out of traffic. Maybe one day he would be able to return to Blanding University when the heat eventually died down. As he drove away from South Carolina and the black university within it, he began to fantasize of the life he was leaving behind.

Alone in his car, with only the lonesome endless road to keep him company, Red daydreamed of the once free-spirited Kel, having to raise an infant in this morbid world with Crystal Kerry, how Bobby King loved the mother of his child intensely, yet couldn't give up the immense pleasure of other women, fighting against his own pimp lineage. Red's mind flashed of pleasant memories of Larenzo denying his obvious love of Joy, the painful suffering of Malik, struggling against the ever-present urge to use drugs, JC forever having to live with the knowledge that he would never play professional basketball because of a college injury, the frustration of John, banging on a dorm room door, as his girlfriend has sex with another man merely ten feet away. And of course, a vision of Midget Moe, lying peacefully in his coffin as if he were asleep, with his baby's mother and children crying as they lowered him in the ground.

They were gone now. That life was gone. His friends had all changed during that school year... everyone except for himself. School for Red was just an ingenious way to escape prosecution in the state of New Jersey. He never imagined that he would actually enjoy the college experience. Red had tried to live life by the rules of society but somehow he seemed to always be dragged back into the cyclone of pain, death, and crime. One day, if he was lucky enough he would be able to break these chains of despair, but Red knew that that day wouldn't be today. Today, he would have to be satisfied chasing after the shadows of his friends' best and worst memories. Today, Red was all alone on his new journey from the law.

So utterly alone...

"Just another school year at an Historical Black University," Red whispered to himself. "Yeah, I'll be back one day. Just wait; I'll be back."

About the Author

Ronald Baxter, the author of *Southern Comfort,* is a native of New Jersey/New York. He currently resides in Columbia, South Carolina. An Alumni of South Carolina State University (HBCU), Ronald works in telecommunications and is currently completing his second novel. Contact him at rondigga@hotmail.com

Printed in the United States
23230LVS00002B/202-246

9 781594 082146

FICTION

Welcome to Blanding University: Sex, drugs, violence, fraternities, parties, murder, and midterms. This is the world of Historical Black College & Universities in America. For Larenzo and his friends, life at the African American University consisted of more than just studying for test and handing in term papers, it consisted of surviving. For this group of college students, life away from their parents was more than just a learning experience; it became a rite of passage. The black experience of an HBCU in the Deep South was much different than anything their parents could have ever prepared them for. *Southern Comfort* is an intimate glance at the life of students attending a Black University in all of its joys and despairs.

U.S. $13.95

ISBN 1-59408-214-6

51395

9 781594 082146

CORK HILL PRESS
CORKHILLPRESS.COM